CLASSIC CASHES IN

Recent Titles by Amy Myers from Severn House

The Jack Colby, Car Detective, Series

CLASSIC IN THE BARN
CLASSIC CALLS THE SHOTS
CLASSIC IN THE CLOUDS
CLASSIC MISTAKE
CLASSIC IN THE PITS
CLASSIC CASHES IN

MURDER IN THE QUEEN'S BOUDOIR
MURDER WITH MAJESTY
THE WICKENHAM MURDERS
MURDER IN FRIDAY STREET
MURDER IN HELL'S CORNER
MURDER AND THE GOLDEN GOBLET
MURDER IN THE MIST
MURDER TAKES THE STAGE
MURDER ON THE OLD ROAD
MURDER IN ABBOT'S FOLLY

CLASSIC CASHES IN

A Case for Jack Colby, Car Detective

Amy Myers

This first world edition published 2014
in Great Britain and 2015 in the USA by
SEVERN HOUSE PUBLISHERS LTD of
19 Cedar Road, Sutton, Surrey, England, SM2 5DA.
Trade paperback edition first published
in Great Britain and the USA 2015 by
SEVERN HOUSE PUBLISHERS LTD.

British Library Cataloguing in Publication Data

Myers, Amy, 1938- author.
  Classic Cashes In. – (The Jack Colby, car detective
  series)
  1. Colby, Jack (Fictitious character)–Fiction. 2. Antique
  and classic cars–Fiction. 3. Packard automobile–
  Fiction. 4. Murder–Investigation–Fiction. 5. Detective
  and mystery stories.
  I. Title II. Series
  823.9'14-dc23

ISBN-13: 978-0-7278-8438-1 (cased)
ISBN-13: 978-1-84751-545-2 (trade paper)
ISBN-13: 978-1-78010-592-5 (e-book)

All Severn House titles are printed on acid-free paper.

Severn House Publishers support the Forest Stewardship Council™ [FSC™],
the leading international forest certification organisation. All our titles that
are printed on FSC certified paper carry the FSC logo.

Typeset by Palimpsest Book Production Ltd.,
Falkirk, Stirlingshire, Scotland.
Printed and bound in Great Britain by
TJ International, Padstow, Cornwall.

In memory of
Dot Lumley
Super-Agent, Super-Friend

AUTHOR'S NOTE

Jack Colby's sixth recorded case takes place in Kent, where he has his classic car restoration business at Frogs Hill, near Pluckley. It's from here that he also carries out his car detection work. As in his previous cases, some of the settings are fictitious, including Monksford, Frittenhurst, Staveley Park and Piper's Green, the nearest village to Frogs Hill.

My thanks for helping me with information go in particular to my friend Douglas Tyler, who graphically described to me his experiences as a bank clerk in Hull in the late 1940s, to my car buff husband James whose input on classic cars has been the backbone of the Jack Colby series, and to John Bath, chair of the Packard Club of Great Britain. Their help was invaluable, and the interpretation I have put on it is my own.

The team at Severn House has as always been a pleasure to work with, and my thanks are especially due to my editor Rachel Simpson Hutchens and cover designer Piers Tilbury. They've done Jack Colby proud.

ONE

Robberies in days of yore, a getaway car. . . .
'A *Packard*?' I repeated blankly. A fleeting memory of
The Ladykillers came to mind, which features a black
1930s' Packard in that role, while in the United States it was
famed as a magnificent family car. So how did a classic 1936
Packard tie up with the austere sixtyish well-dressed gentleman
currently entertaining me to tea in a superbly English country
house? 'You want a *Packard*?'

'Not *a* Packard, Mr Colby,' the dry voice explained. '*The*
Packard. Or if you prefer, a *particular* Packard. An eight-cylinder,
right-hand drive, One-Twenty saloon, registered in England
although not with the original registration number. Probably pale
butter yellow in colour, originally black.'

'May I ask why this particular car—'

'No, Mr Colby, you may not.'

I can do dry and stuffy too. 'In that case, I can't accept this
job. I need to know the context. I work on a freelance basis for
the Kent Police Car Crime Unit, and therefore any other job I
take has to bear that in mind.'

Philip Moxton stared at me thoughtfully. At least he wasn't
an eye contact evader, which was a good sign. 'I used to own
this *particular* Packard,' he said at last. 'I was obliged to sell it.
I want it back. Legally,' he added, super drily. 'I don't expect
you to don a mask and striped jumper to whisk it away from its
current owner, whoever he – or she – might be.'

I laughed. 'Put that way, I'm almost sorry I can't dress up in
fancy clothes. Have you any idea where this Packard might be?'

'Roughly, yes.'

Again, I was thrown, struggling for a clear idea of the possible
task ahead. 'Then why employ me to find it?'

'I want you to buy it for me.'

My face, as they say, must have been a study, and it was his
turn for mirth – although his was in the form of an unwilling
grimace. 'I shall pay for it. Never fear.'

'Whatever the cost?'

'Whatever the cost.'

'And if it's not for sale?' I was even more puzzled now.

'Its owner has recently died.'

Even more curious. 'Then—'

He cut me off impatiently. 'Because I wish it to be bought anonymously. Come, we are wasting time.'

Clearly this was not usual for the chair of the very exclusive Moxtons, the private banking arm of the huge conglomerate Fentons Bank, despite the fact that today he was 'relaxing' at his home, a Kentish stately mansion called Staveley House. Nor in fact was wasting time usual for me, Jack Colby, car detective. I was beginning to be sorry I'd come. It had been hard enough to find the place.

Staveley House was not far from Tenterden, in the west of Kent, but was the most private of private country houses I had ever seen. Hidden down a lane leading off a minor road, the entrance to its grounds was so well concealed that one needed more than satnav to find it. I'd been given directions, of course, but the gateway had seemed at first sight merely to be the vehicular entrance to a small Kentish stone cottage. It looked far more like a weather-beaten farmgate than the way to approach the no doubt sizeable home of a banking magnate.

Having opened the gate, I had driven in with caution. Evergreen trees and bushes shielded the entrance from undue interest from the casual passer-by and shrouded in mystery the path beyond it. Even as I closed the gate behind me I expected a furious farmer to leap out of the cottage to accuse me of chicken rustling – especially as one or two had been pecking incuriously at the roadside.

No one had leapt out, however, although, as I got back into my classic Gordon-Keeble again (have to impress new clients), it seemed to me that the cottage windows exuded an air of careful guardianship. Certainly it had been easy to imagine human eyes behind them watching my every move.

I had then driven along a track bordered on both sides with woodland, with leafy bushes pushing their way outwards over the path with all their late summer confidence. Then abruptly the woodland had ended and given way to a vista of seemingly endless parkland. I had driven well over half a mile before I reached a stark sign reading 'Car Park' and it had been clear my car would have to remain right there. I had left my Gordon-Keeble somewhat nervously as it is very precious to me. Reason had told me however that it was as safe there as in its barn-cum-garage at Frogs Hill where I live. Emotionally I didn't like abandoning it, but needs must when the mortgage has to be paid and a lucrative job might lie ahead.

I had duly walked along the drive somewhat uneasily wondering what was in store for me, until I was faced with a high wall of neatly trimmed yew hedge, with a gateway that at last gave me a sight of Staveley House. At first glance it had looked mock-Tudor, with its black beams, white plaster, red Kentish peg tiles and a rambling building with the odd gable or tower. A second look, when I took in the splendid chimneys, told me this was the real McCoy, sixteenth-century brick in places and probably much earlier in parts.

Philip Moxton had been there to greet me at the open central door, indicating that some kind of security system had warned him of my arrival. It probably consisted of cameras disguised as blackbirds in the trees. OK, perhaps that was a step too fanciful, but this chap certainly had security in mind when he bought this place.

Staveley House, I thought, was the kind of stately pile that should have a Rolls-Royce outside, with perhaps a Bentley or two for the kids. So why, I wondered, looking at Philip Moxton now, sipping a cup of tea from an antique bone china teacup, did he want a Packard, even if it was a *particular* Packard. It was true that Packards had been a status symbol in Britain in the nineteen twenties and thirties, but that didn't explain why a man only born, at a guess, in the early fifties would want one. A family car? Possibly, I supposed, in which case a Packard might evoke memories of his childhood long past if his parents had one hanging around. Even so, why should he ask me to buy it for him anonymously, and not tell me the owner's details?

There was one indisputable fact – that he wasn't going to tell me any more. That deceptively mild expression told me he had quelled and quashed far more vigorous questionings than mine. His expression also implied that I could take the job or leave it.

What did I have to lose provided the money transfers were sorted properly? I'd take the job – with a double check. 'Whatever the cost?' I repeated.

'Yes.'

'One problem then. If I turn up at the dealer's or owner's place with the cash I look like a dodgy character. If I give the seller a cheque that also could lead to a problem,' I explained delicately. I wasn't in the habit of having twenty or thirty thousand pounds hanging around the Frogs Hill Classic Restoration Company business account, let alone in my own private one.

'I'll arrange an express bank transfer.'

'Certainly, but I need to understand you better first.'

He flinched. 'This is not a social meeting, Mr Colby.'

'I agree. So we can talk frankly. I can buy the car in the name of Frogs Hill Classic Car Restoration Company, but even so arrangements have to be made. I will be buying it on behalf of a customer, who – I can legitimately say – wishes to remain anonymous. However, that will arouse curiosity in itself. Will you take that chance?'

'I shall have to do so. Naturally I realized that whether private seller or dealer, there would be an element of risk. Apart from the question of anonymity, I do not know you, except by reputation. That adds to the risk. Do you have more questions?'

The chair was clearly bringing the board meeting to an end by this flattening analysis. It was time to show that I wasn't to be flattened.

'Yes,' I said. '*Why?*'

To my surprise instead of cutting me off, he answered me. 'Because, Mr Colby, I must have that Packard before I die. And that may be very soon.'

That naturally shook me. 'I'm sorry to hear you're in ill-health.'

'I am in perfect health. There is, however, every possibility that I shall shortly be murdered.'

Top that for an exit line. I was so shaken I couldn't wait to get away, so after a brief exchange on details of procedure I left to rejoin my Gordon-Keeble with great relief. Oddly, I realized I'd rather taken to this man, and surely he couldn't be serious about his prediction? On the other hand, he didn't seem the jokey sort, and certainly Staveley House and its grounds seemed to be going overboard in their efforts not to be noticed. The windows of the room where Philip Moxton and I had been sipping tea looked out over the rear gardens which were a spectacular sight with late summer dahlias – but deserted. Did he live in this place alone, I wondered? Had he an army of servants hidden behind green baize doors? Hard to tell. As I drove up to the stone cottage at the entrance to the grounds, there was still no one to be seen. I opened the gate and drove through, but once again had that prickly feeling down my spine as though I was being watched. Human eyes? Or my imagination? It was pretty odd for the owner of Staveley to state he was facing the possibility of his own murder but yet have a gate that opened to the touch, an empty lodge and no overt security measures; which suggested there were many of these around, but that they were state of very high art.

I reached Frogs Hill with gratitude. My home lies a few miles from Pluckley on the Greensand Ridge, with the lowland of the Weald of Kent spread out before it. The nearest village is Piper's Green, but once there you would still have to work hard to track down Frogs Hill, which lies at the end of winding lanes that amble peacefully along the side of the ridge.

Driving through the gates, I began to relax as the familiar aroma of petrol, oil and grease that spelt home met my nostrils. It comes from the Pits, our name for the converted barn that houses the Frogs Hill Classic Car Restoration Company. Here, Len Vickers and Zoe Grant are installed, working away to their hearts' content on such exciting projects as a Jaguar 120 gearbox overhaul and a complete rebuild of a Sunbeam Alpine's running gear.

Len is sixty plus and curmudgeonly; Zoe is nearly forty years his junior and sharp witted. They ignore the differences between them – if they even notice them – and get on famously through their joint love, the innards of classic cars. Occasionally I'm allowed to help under their eagle-eyed supervision, but really they prefer me to keep to my own quarters in the farmhouse. I do pay their wages, however, so I can demand a modicum of their attention from time to time.

Now was one of those times. Except that I baulked at the last moment. It was clear as I got nearer the Pits that they were both engaged in anxious consultation over a gearbox main shaft and would have no time to spare for what they consider to be unimportant queries from the boss. I left them to it. It was Tuesday, and the Jaguar was already overdue to be restored to its owner in pristine condition.

'What bells do nineteen thirties Packards ring for you?' I asked casually the next morning.

'*Ladykillers*,' Len replied. He isn't a verbose man and he continued reassembling the Jaguar's gearbox.

'Right. The Ealing Studios film. One of the cars Alec Guinness and gang used in the getaway after the robbery.' The film had come out long before I was born, but it was one of my parents' favourites.

'Nifty in traffic,' Zoe contributed. 'Clutch and gear shift work like a dream.'

'I know a chap who wants one,' I explained. 'He's not planning any bank robberies so far as I know. Heard of any around?'

'Ask the Man Who Owns One,' Len replied in a rare display of wit. Even I knew the famous Packard advertising slogan.

'Or Harry Prince,' Zoe added, to wind me up.

'No way.' I refused to be wound. Harry Prince, local garage chain magnate, has a hand in a great many pies and he'd like Frogs Hill to be included. That's not going to happen. Harry isn't all bad, but discretion only applies to his own welfare and concerns. Over anyone else's he has none at all.

When Dave Jennings, who runs the Kent Police Car Crime Unit, offers me a job, I can bank on it that it's going to involve brain power – naturally enough because he has a great team which means I get the awkward ones. This job for Philip Moxton therefore sounded a bonus in that it should be reasonably straightforward. Which contrariwise made me suspicious that it wasn't going to be anything of the sort.

I was right. When I rang the Packard Club and various other motoring organizations the net result was that there was a rumour that one or two were available in Kent, but nothing more to back it up. That meant I either had to work my way through all the classic car dealers and magazines or use my contacts. I had had strict instructions from Philip Moxton to ring him as soon as I had a line on the car. I should tell him the price, he'd then give me the banking details and as soon as the cash was through I should pick the car up and deliver it to him.

I would have been amazed if I hadn't had fair warning that this was an unorthodox sale. 'Buy it sight unseen? What about a test drive?' I had queried.

'Not necessary.'

'Won't the seller think that strange?' I had asked mildly. A pause. Then: 'Find out the price. Tell me. Ring the seller. Go to see it, and buy it, whatever state it's in. If it's not currently registered or if they want to keep the plates, use your garage plates to bring it straight here. Don't stop for formalities.'

He really was eager. First find your Packard, I thought as I meditated on Zoe's 'kind' suggestion about Harry Prince. The classic car world is a close one which is good – usually – but on the outskirts of this tight-knit circle wolves prowl hopefully around, and Harry is one of them. So definitely not Harry for this job. Then, watching Len and Zoe at work, I had another idea.

Another prowling wolf, less ferocious although even more irritating than Harry, is Zoe's parasite – sorry, partner – Rob Lane. Rob has many infuriating qualities, but he's not a crook and brought up amidst the moneyed upper classes as he was, he knows that one does not split on a chum. I am *not* one of his chums, but I am his partner's boss, and therefore his meal ticket, so the same code – albeit warily – is applied to me.

'Is Rob around?' I asked Zoe.

'Working at Favvers.'

Working? Rob? I wisely didn't comment, but drove my Alfa straight over to his parents' gigantic farm near Faversham (Favvers for short). Rob was there, true enough, but working? He was sipping coffee and watching cricket on the office TV. That's my lad. Or rather Zoe's lad, luckily.

'Been to any good car shows recently, Rob?' I asked him cheerily.

'No.' Silence as he watched another few balls. Then he gave me a break. 'Why?'

'Looking for a 1936 Packard that's said to be up for sale round these parts. Confidential job.'

'Ah.' Rob looked wise.

'Thought you might know. Probably a private seller.'

My thinking went this way. Rob moved in the higher echelons of Kent society, thanks to his parents. When William the Conqueror invaded England in 1066 he was famously visited by a contingent from Kent intent on keeping its own economy intact, and I bet Rob's forebears were leading it.

Therefore, as Packards were in their day a status symbol and

as Rob and his father like classic cars, they might well know
who owned the Packard I was after. There couldn't be that many
in Kent.

'Who's after it?' he asked.

'Me, Or rather Frogs Hill. As I said, it's hush-hush, but we've
got a customer.'

'Fair enough, Jack. Commission?' Rob is sharp when it comes
to cash.

I swallowed. 'A sweetener for you.'

I hadn't checked expenses with Philip Moxton but my guess
was that this would prove no problem.

'Done. Leave it to me,' said Mr Rob Fixer grandly.

I gave him the details of the Packard I was after. 'I need a
price first,' I explained.

His eyes flickered. It's his way of trying to look intelligent
which in many ways he is, otherwise Zoe would not fancy him.
To me his sex appeal looked non-existent, but then how would
I know? Zoe can go into raptures over a Ford Edsel on occasion,
so there's no judging what she sees in him.

I wasn't certain I was following the right course in handing
Rob the job on a plate, but it was worth a go. Zoe and Len were
still engrossed in the Sunbeam Alpine overhaul when I returned
to Frogs Hill, so I faced up to my responsibilities as a businessman
and took the accounts – seriously behind – into the farmhouse
garden to work on. This took a fair time and I didn't finish until
the early evening.

If you're happy, a summer's evening can be blissful in late
summer; if you're not it's the saddest time of day as the sun
remembers it's nearly time to depart. It has one last burst with
the flower scents strong, birds saying goodbye to their latest
broods, and nature at the peak of its fulfilment – which is what
makes one sad if one isn't fulfilling anything. Frogs Hill is a
refuge, a place of healing, but it's incomplete without someone
with whom to share it. Ladies had come and gone at various
times in my life, kicking off years ago with my divorce after an
early ill-fated and brief marriage.

There's only one lady (apart from my daughter who lives in
Suffolk) with whom I had wanted to share Frogs Hill since that
time, and that is Louise, who had sailed into harbour only to
disappear on the dawn tide. Recently my hopes had been revived,

but having succumbed to the temptation to track her down I discovered that she was by then filming in Australia. The mobile number I had for her no longer worked. Emails remained unanswered. The sun was definitely sinking on that false hope. Only twenty-four hours after I had seen Rob the phone rang. He sounded highly pleased with himself – but then he always does, so I didn't get too hopeful.

'Found it,' he chortled. 'It's for sale – private, not a dealer.'

'Terrific, Rob.' For once I meant it.

'Told them it was for Frogs Hill, as you said, Jack. They asked who the customer was.'

As I'd guessed. 'And you said . . . ?'

'Not etiquette for you to reveal it.'

'Thanks.' I meant that too. 'Sheer genius on your part.'

'I know.'

Modesty is not his strong point. 'What's the price?'

'Thirty-five thousand.'

That sounded roughly in the right area although on the high side. 'Who's the seller?'

He gave me the address, which was near the village of Frittenhurst, not that far away. 'It belonged to Gavin Herrick, the actor. Died recently. Remember him?'

I did. He must have been a fair age because I remembered seeing him in TV and films years back and not that long ago I'd seen him in a cameo part. His suave style and figure carried him through despite his age.

'Gavin was a pal of my grandfather,' Rob added. 'Well over ninety when he died. Family wants to get rid of the car. I spoke to the son, Tom Herrick.' He paused. 'Had a bit of trouble though.'

There had to be a downside. 'In what way?'

'They were still very curious about this customer of yours. The son's wife – she's a cool one – said they didn't want to sell it to just anybody. The car had to have a good home.'

I'd met this attitude amongst classic car owners occasionally, but this one was unusual as it was coming not from the owner but from the next generation. Normally that means the inheritor is determined either never to sell it at all or to offload it on the first good offer.

'They're looking forward to meeting the customer,' Rob continued. 'Is that on?'

'Certainly. The customer is Jack Colby.'

'Over to you, Jack. But bear in mind my reputation is at stake. This sweetener is going to have to be good.'

His reputation? As a country lounge lizard? I managed to keep a serious note in my voice when I replied, 'Naturally, Rob. You deserve it.'

'I know I do.'

I thought this Packard story over carefully, wondering whether my imagination had been overworking. What it told me was that I was not getting the full story. Having come to the conclusion that it was on the right lines, I decided to ignore instructions and visit Philip Moxton unannounced. Caught off guard, he might be more forthcoming, and after all, surely not every casual visitor would be shot on sight.

I took the Alfa this time instead of the Gordon-Keeble. My daily driver would make it look less like a state visit on my part and more of a 'just passing by'. The gate was again unlocked, but I did notice that mysteriously it seemed to lock itself judging by the sharp click as I shut it. Odd. Those windows still glared at me but again no armed guard leapt out.

Someone else did though. A middle-aged man with a scruffy beard, working clothes and suspicious eyes. He was carrying a mug, and looked mightily surprised to see me. He didn't offer me a coffee, but he did study me, my car and then me again with great care.

'Morning,' I greeted him guardedly.

'Morning,' he growled, turning his attention to the coffee, although as I climbed into the Alfa I felt his eyes returning to me. No shotgun took out my tyres as I drove off, so either I must have passed muster or there was a booby trap ahead.

This time I saw a gardener or two in the park, but the car park was empty of human life. Only a line of cars suggested that staff or anyone else was around. Although there was no apparent booby trap, I still had the uncomfortable feeling that there was something wrong about this set-up. Nevertheless I reached the house in one piece and rang the bell.

I thought at first no one would answer it, but then the heavy door was dragged open.

It wasn't Philip Moxton on the other side.

It was a woman in carpet slippers with a pair of rose nippers in her hand. Offensive weapon? She was clad in smock and jeans, and looked about sixty or so. The housekeeper? No, she looked more like a gardener on the wrong side of the front door.

'Could I have a word with Mr Moxton?'

'Who?' she barked.

That took me by surprise. Maybe she was deaf. 'Philip Moxton,' I shouted.

'No need to yell. And no you can't.'

'Is he out?'

'I've never heard of him, whoever he is.'

She really could not have heard. I tried again. 'He owns Staveley House. He lives here. *Philip Moxton?*'

That did it. She glared at me. 'I own this house, thank you very much.'

Just my luck to run into the mad woman of Staveley House. 'Where is he then? In London?'

'Get out,' she boomed. 'I've never heard of this Moxton person.' And then she slammed the door in my face.

Rebuffed to say the least, I drove back to the gate where thankfully the bearded man was now sitting on the dilapidated bench sipping whatever was inside the mug. He was eyeing me rather triumphantly, I thought, while he played his role as village yokel. And role it was, I was sure of that.

'Can you tell me when Mr Moxton will be returning?' I had his mobile number to ring but I was feeling obstinate.

'Wrong house, sir. Never heard of him.'

'But I visited him here only two days ago.'

'Not here. I'd have seen you. These big houses all look alike, don't they?'

'This *is* Staveley House, isn't it?'

'That's right.'

'Then it belongs to Mr Moxton whether he's here or not.'

'No, sir, it doesn't and he don't live here.'

'Who was it answered the door to me? A lady about sixty, likes gardening.'

'That would be Miss Janes. She owns this place. Staveley House. It's hers.'

TWO

Now you see him, now you don't . . . Was this a joke? Optical illusion? Were there two Staveley Houses? Out of the question. Philip Moxton was a high-powered billionaire banking executive and not the kind of man to plan elaborate hoaxes. Nor would he employ eccentric house- or gate-keepers. I supposed this Miss Janes might be an eccentric relation but that didn't fit in with the gatekeeper's statement that she was the owner. True, Moxton claimed to be afraid of being murdered, but that wouldn't extend to repelling all legitimate callers. Tax avoidance measure? My take on Philip Moxton was that if he was worried about unexpected guests he'd have a secure gate and security system with guards, not one crusty old gent at an unlocked gate.

'How's the job looking?' Zoe asked me when I reached Frogs Hill. She'd actually left the Pits to question me.

'Very murky. The gentleman was not only not in but not known.'

Zoe frowned. 'Rob says he's an odd bloke.'

'Does he know Philip Moxton or just know of him?'

'Both. By repute and met him once. So go steady.'

'Yes, Mum.'

She glared at me and stalked back to the Pits. Which left me to ponder on my next step. One thing was clear. I wasn't going to put so much as a finger into this potential lions' den until I had investigated further.

I wandered round to the rear of the farmhouse to the barn-cum-garage in which my Lagonda and the Gordon-Keeble live. The Lagonda is a 1938 model redolent of the heady days before the Second World War removed them; although, even then, if one were lucky enough to get petrol, a Lagonda symbolized a kind of hope. The Gordon-Keeble was a sporting symbol of a different age, the 1960s – not of Carnaby Street and the Beatles but the years that held a firm assurance that Britain was heading somewhere good. Nothing that the succeeding decades have thrown at us has dented that image for me.

The Lagonda lifts my heart, the Gordon-Keeble is my faithful friend. They are comfortingly reliable. Any problem they present can be worked on and fixed. I wasn't so sure that Philip Moxton's job would fall under this category.

OK, I silently addressed them both. Where now? This job was already presenting the unexpected – never a good sign. I like challenges, but this one had all the hallmarks of being one that might escape out of my control. Brake failure! Time to grab the steering wheel, I told myself, so I took a deep breath and returned to my landline to begin.

Philip Moxton had given me his mobile number, which surely wouldn't be something that a banking magnate would normally hand out to a temporary employee. Experimentally I tried his landline first. Even if he was in London for the day, he'd be home by now.

At least the call was answered. 'Wrong number,' snapped the voice that had greeted me this afternoon – if greet was the right word for our encounter.

'Nevertheless would you tell Mr Moxton . . .' but I was speaking to a dialling tone.

I had half expected that reply, and it goaded me on. Now for the mobile number. I fully expected it to be on voicemail, but it wasn't. I was pleasantly surprised to hear Philip Moxton's voice, albeit with a mere 'Yes?'

'Jack Colby,' I replied.

Immediately the tone of voice changed. 'You have found it? You have a price?'

'I do. Thirty-five thousand.'

I decided I would get the business done first, rather than tackle the question of his vanishing act. There was such a silence at the end of the line that I hastened to say, 'It looks a reasonably good deal depending on the condition. You may be in luck.'

'May I?' he asked oddly. 'Is this a private seller or dealer?'

'Private. It's over the market price, but I can negotiate—'

'Private,' he repeated. 'And thirty-five thousand pounds. Thank you, Mr Colby. Accept the offer, provisional on speedy viewing to check it is the car I require, make the appointment, notify me, do what you need to in the way of formalities, put the Packard on your garage plates if you wish, but *buy* it, whatever the apparent drawbacks. Make a cash deposit of fifteen hundred pounds, express the rest of the money to the seller, pick the car up, notify me on this number and drive it straight to me. And –' he must have heard my intake of breath – 'you must naturally be concerned about your account. I shall transfer the entire amount of money to you now, plus a commission element which I trust will cover your fee.'

This time I recovered my breath, though to little avail. 'But—'

'The money will be in your Frogs Hill account at nine a.m. tomorrow, Friday, Mr Colby, if you'll send me the details. And, just one more matter, I believe it possible the seller will guess who this customer of yours is. Is there any way of avoiding that?'

'Only by inventing a fictional customer, which I dislike doing, or better by continuing to insist I cannot reveal it.'

'Which will provide them with the information they seek,' he murmured. 'I understand. However I am prepared to take the risk, despite its dangers.'

He began to bid me farewell, but it was my turn for 'just one more thing'. Two in fact. 'First,' I asked him, 'suppose this car isn't the one you owned?'

'I'm a wealthy man, Mr Colby. I will email you tonight the chassis and engine numbers of the Packard I require. It's unlikely that anyone would go to the length of falsifying the numbers in order to kid me this is the car I am after, so the information I am sending you should be sufficient. And your second question?'

Now for it. 'You say drive the car to you. Where would that be?'

'To Staveley House of course.' He sounded surprised.

'But today I was passing nearby and thought I'd call on you to give you the news in person. I was given short shrift by the lady who opened the door who claimed she had never heard of you.'

'A security matter, Mr Colby,' he replied dismissively, 'to avoid nuisance and other unwelcome callers. That is a necessary step in my position, both on the telephone and in person. Provided you call this mobile number there will be no problem.'

Put that way, it was reasonable enough, I supposed. I've never been a billionaire banking tyro so I wouldn't know. Nevertheless I still had a feeling that I was treading on quicksand. It had not escaped my notice that while being concerned about his own anonymity in the matter, he had not questioned me on the name of the seller. However, so far everything was perfectly legal, albeit unusual, so who was I to turn down what promised to be a generous payment for very little work?

It was indeed generous. Fifty per cent commission on thirty-five thousand was something to be welcomed – although I had to remember that Philip Moxton had probably not made his millions by being overgenerous without reason. The money had arrived as promised, but the owners could not see me on the Friday, a fact that Philip Moxton greeted with impatience. Saturday morning therefore found me and my £1,500 cash deposit driving over to Frittenhurst to meet this Packard. The village is not far from Headcorn and buried amid former hop gardens, now redundant and turned over to fruit or other crops. It still possesses a church although no longer a pub or even a shop. Oast House, the Herrick home, where once the hops had been dried, was in a prosperous area and looked as if its owner was reasonably prosperous too. It was nowhere near the size of Staveley House but converted oast houses aren't bought cheaply. They aren't large in themselves, however, and this one had a sizeable red-brick extension that blended in well with the oast itself. I could see this was in spectacular condition, built with Kentish ragstone and flint with its distinctive conical roof, cowl and the Kentish rampant horse figure on the vane.

I drove into the yard area where a tall hearty-looking man in his sixties came out to meet me and slightly behind him – both literally and with her welcome – came (presumably) his wife, Moira. I remembered now why the name Tom Herrick had rung a bell – of course, I'd seen his face on television many a time, not in leading parts, but as back-up in practically every crime series on TV. His father Gavin had been one up in the acting stakes.

No sign of the Packard yet, and after we had introduced ourselves, Moira asked me in for coffee, so perhaps it wasn't such a cool welcome as I had thought.

'He'll want to see the old heap first, Moira,' Tom joked. Not a very sensible way of talking about a car that he hoped to sell. He didn't seem anxious about the sale – indeed it was almost as though he thought the sale was a foregone conclusion.

A cool smile from his wife. 'Of course. Stupid of me.'

'I'll bring the lady out for you,' Tom said, walking over to the garage and opening it up.

And there she was. Straight out of *The Ladykillers,* save that as Philip had predicted this beauty was painted a buttery cream, not the original black. Even from the rear this looked authentic, however, with its glorious chrome bumpers and hubcaps, narrow wheels and the distinctive revolutionary spare tyre compartment tucked under the luggage boot.

'Looks great already,' I told Moira as he backed it out.

Tom pulled up in front of us and climbed out. 'Not a bad old lady, is she?' He patted the bonnet.

This grand old lady wasn't in the peak of condition but he was right. She might need repainting and some restoration but she oozed charisma in bucketfuls. Her solid, ancient, stylish lines were inviting me inside to relax in comfort. From the few rides I'd had in a Packard that applied to the driver too. Letting out that seemingly effortless clutch, one could go to the ends of the earth in her, a home from home. This was the 1935 model, the 120, that took the market by storm by being so good and so reasonably priced. That hadn't stopped it from being a status symbol as well.

'Want a spin?' Tom asked.

'Let's all go,' Moira said surprisingly. She didn't look like a car person. 'It would be a tribute to Gavin. My father-in-law died recently, which is why we're selling the car.'

So there seemed no mystery about that. Perhaps I had been imagining there was something odd about this deal – although it was true she seemed somewhat overearnest in her determination to convey this message.

'That would be great.' Philip Moxton had said a test drive wasn't necessary, but how could I turn down such an offer? 'It was Gavin's own car?' I asked.

'Very much so,' Tom told me. 'Had it for yonks, from a boy.'

That didn't seem to fit too well with what I'd been told by Philip. Odd. 'This particular Packard?' I asked. 'Or Packards generally?'

'Packards in general, I suppose. I don't know when my father first bought this one.'

Did I sense a slight hesitation in that reply? 'Is the original logbook still in it?'

'No, alas.' He grinned at me affably. 'An actor's life is not always a happy one financially speaking, and there was a period when my father had to let the car go. Fortunately he was able to buy it back again later, but the logbook had vanished. And the original number plates too.'

So that answered my question – or did it? 'It was the same car though?' Without waiting for his affirmation, I carried on, also *affably*. 'Mind if I check the chassis and engine numbers? Just a formality, but I don't want to be sued by my customer.'

'Sure. Go ahead.'

I did and made a careful note but I already knew they tallied.

The spin took us along lanes past fields and woods on either side. The fields are large and open in this part of Kent and I could almost imagine I was driving through the prairies of the USA. Perhaps the Packard thought it was too for its straight-eight engine purred happily along. She handled well, despite the steering being on the heavy side for modern taste. Nevertheless she obligingly negotiated the many sharp corners unfazed. The *Ladykillers* gang had chosen well. Next time I robbed a bank, this Packard would be my accomplice.

'What makes you a Packard enthusiast, Mr Colby?' Moira asked politely as we drew up at Oast House again.

'A paying customer,' I parried, 'although I do admire them. Who wouldn't? Thanks for the ride. I'm prepared to meet your price on it.'

'Are you indeed?' murmured Mrs Cool. Was there a slight note of sarcasm in her voice?

'Of course.' I tried to sound cool myself. 'It's just what my customer wants.'

A silence, then: 'So how about that coffee now, Moira?' Tom asked jovially. 'We can sort things out more comfortably in the house.'

As we walked inside the former oast house, there was an image flicking through my mind that I couldn't quite grasp. As we all sat down in their delightful circular living room (once the room where the fires to dry the hops were burning) I pinned this image down. It seemed as if I were in a scene from a thirties play, not by Noel Coward but . . . yes, J.B. Priestley. *Dangerous Corner,* one of those time-slip plays. Well into the plot, it takes an apparently insignificant point in the conversation, which results in the story being led in one direction. At that story's denouement, it reverts to the same 'insignificant' point and then explores what would have happened if the point hadn't occurred.

I wasn't in a time slip (I hoped) but I did have a feeling that this might be a dangerous corner with more outcomes than the one I had envisaged of simply taking the car to Philip Moxton and gratefully pocketing my commission. And yet on the face of it everything here seemed perfectly normal. Frogs Hill had bought cars before on behalf of clients even for one or two who chose to remain anonymous to the seller, so this deal was all straightforward, I told myself. Tom and Moira Herrick seemed hesitant about accepting the £1,500 cash deposit, but that too could be a natural response.

'Please take it,' I urged them. 'My client would not be happy if I didn't secure the sale. I'll send the rest of the money as soon as I get back.'

'Splendid,' Tom boomed. (Wasn't he straight out of a thirties play?) 'Let's say Tuesday then, this being a bank holiday weekend. We'll be around all day and have the old lady and all the paperwork waiting for you. All right with you, Moira?'

'Of course,' she murmured. 'Gavin would have wanted the car to go to an appreciative owner.'

'I'll ring you to check the money's come through. I'll send it by BACS.'

Delighted murmurs greeted this. As I rose to go (after the excellent coffee) a photo of Gavin Herrick caught my eye, amid the many photos of Tom and Moira at various stages of their marriage and of a glamorous young woman who was probably their daughter. The photo of Gavin had been taken on his wedding day with his bride.

'Dad with my mother, Nancy,' Tom confirmed.

'Is she still living?' I asked politely.

Tom shook his head and Moira answered for him. 'She died young, but that –' she indicated a picture of Tom and a woman with a young child – 'is Tom with his sister, Gwen. She's two years younger than Tom.'

Just a normal family and the usual photographs. And yet not so normal, I reflected, with Gavin Herrick as part of it. He had been a great actor and Tom too was on the stage. Was there an element of role-playing here that I wasn't picking up?

We talked for a few minutes more and parted on good terms. As I drove off, however, I briefly looked back. Standing by the Packard were Moira and Tom clasped in each other's arms. In joy? Relief at the sale? Or just sad to see it go? Which of these, I wondered – or none of them?

'I do not like this delay. You're sure there will be no trickery?' Philip asked sharply when I rang him (on his mobile of course) to tell him the news that I couldn't pick the car up immediately.

His response puzzled me. 'I can't see why there should be.'

'No undue interest in the identity of your customer?'

I remembered Moira's comment about the appreciative owner, but there had been nothing to indicate that his anonymity had been a serious issue. 'No,' I replied.

A silence. 'Pick the car up on Tuesday as early as you can then. Have you left it to them to confirm the arrival of the money?'

'No. I'll be ringing them. I like to keep control in such situations.'

'Excellent. You should have had a career in banking, Mr Colby.'

'I'll stick to cars,' I joked. 'They're less risky. Despite dangerous corners,' I added without thinking.

A pause. 'We all have dangerous corners in our lives, Mr Colby. They are unavoidable. What matters is how we take them.'

I wondered how he had tackled his and what they were. I hadn't forgotten his calm certainty that someone was out to murder him. My so far brief scanning of the web had revealed that Philip Moxton was the son of Donald and Elsie Moxton, that he was born in 1951 in Kent, and that he was currently chair of Moxton Private Banking. He was divorced, with one son, Barnabas, born 1981. I had toyed with the idea that the gorgon who guarded Staveley House was his ex-wife, but somehow that didn't fit.

'You'll drive the Packard to me straightaway?' he continued.

'To Staveley House?' I asked innocently.

'Of course. That is my home.' A pause. 'I await your call, Mr Colby. On *Tuesday*.'

I logged into my account on the Tuesday morning on tenterhooks. The money had arrived on Friday and it had now left, so the game was under way. All I had to do was ring the Herricks to check that it had arrived safely. I felt as nervous as though it had been my own car at stake, not one for a client, as I rang the Herricks' number. All was well, they told me, and I could pick up the car when I liked. I suggested right now. It's not often I earn £17,500 in commission (less a sweetener for Rob) for very little work, and I wanted to draw a line under this one.

I was full of the joys of summer as Zoe and I set off for Frittenhurst. She had leapt at the chance of coming with me to drive my Alfa back while I collected the glorious Packard. Philip Moxton had told me to take a taxi and he'd pay on delivery, but Zoe would have none of that.

'I'm that taxi. I want to be in on this deal,' she had declared. 'Anyway, Rob wants to know how it works out.'

Oh well. If *Rob* wanted her to come with me, I had no option. Not that I wanted one. Zoe is a great companion. Her red hair – no longer in the spikes she favoured a year or two back – brown eyes and lively face gave her a style all her own. One which she doesn't change for Rob, so perhaps there's more to Rob than I give him credit for.

'If you're going to get a custard pie in your face,' she informed me as she fastened her seat belt, 'I want to chuck one back.'

'Have you brought one?' I asked. I wouldn't put it past her.

'No, but I've got a stale doughnut.'

'That'll do.'

'Sure there's nothing weird about this deal?' she asked belatedly, as the Oast House cowl hove into sight and we turned into the driveway.

'No, I'm not sure.'

'Good,' she said happily. 'I bet Len five quid there was something fishy about it. He said no. Maybe American car geeks are always weird. I told him this Moxton man wasn't American but he stuck to his point. So I pointed out that all British ones are too. He denied it. Apparently Frogs Hill had a Studebaker Champion in once and he didn't take to the owner.'

It was a damp dull morning, but even so I could see as we drove up that the Packard looked great. I even heard Zoe catch her breath as we saw it waiting for us. It looked splendid sitting by itself in the large yard, exuding all the confidence and style of a bygone age.

'Phew. Is this a film set?' she breathed. 'Does Marlene Dietrich step out of this beast?'

'I doubt it, but it's for real.' It looked so stagey sitting there that I could hardly believe it myself, but here were the Herricks coming out to greet us so it was for real.

Moira was actually smiling. 'We've polished her up specially for you.'

'Doesn't she look grand?' Tom contributed.

I agreed. I almost had a lump in my throat, as I concluded the formalities with Tom. He wanted to keep the plates so I fixed my Frogs Hill plates on, a few more words passed between us, and then I climbed into the Packard.

Zoe immediately bounded up to me, clearly thinking she was getting the rough end of the deal by taking the Alfa back. 'Where are you taking it?' she hissed.

'Straight to her new owner as ordered.'

'I'll follow in the Alfa. Then I can run you back to Frogs Hill.'

'The new owner –' no names as the Herricks were waiting to see us off – 'says he'll get a taxi for me.'

'I told you – I *am* that taxi.' Zoe would brook no argument. She would be trailing me all the way to Staveley House. No problem. After all, I was driving this magnificent creature.

The gate was actually already open at Staveley House when I swept up with the Alfa tailing me. The lodge keeper – or hit man? – was watching impassively today as though he had nothing else to do in his job than wave me on. I couldn't resist stopping the Packard though. I wound down the window and shouted:

'Here to see the owner of Staveley House, Mr Philip Moxton.'

Not a quiver on his face. 'OK to drive on.' He didn't even query Zoe's arrival. Our earlier encounter might never have happened.

No car park for me this time. It was straight to the house, where I could see Philip Moxton waiting outside. There was someone with him, a man of medium height and exquisite tailoring. He was perhaps in his early fifties, but Philip made no effort to include him in this joyful arrival scene. Zoe was still on my tail but she did have the courtesy to park modestly some way away in order not to mar this wonderful moment.

The look on Philip's face when he saw the Packard was a delight. He loved this car, that was for sure. He must do, because as I pulled up he *ran* over to caress the Goddess of Speed ornament on its bonnet. Perhaps he didn't believe it was real either. The other man stayed where he was, either out of tact or lack of interest.

'You've checked the engine and chassis numbers?' Philip demanded.

'I have.' (I'd already told him that on the phone.) 'They tally.'

'But no logbook.'

I'd told him that too. 'Only for the last twenty years.' I handed over the paperwork.

He nodded slowly. 'Yes, I understand. I'll register it immediately.'

'Do you want a drive in it while my plates are still on it? You'll have to wait until it's registered otherwise.'

He smiled. 'Thank you, Mr Colby. I can wait.'

I was staggered. He could *wait*? After all this rush to buy it? No doubt that he loved it though. His eyes were devouring it, and I could have sworn there were tears in them. And yet he could *wait* before driving it?

Curious people, these bank managers.

And that was that – at least for a few days. I remembered his fear of being murdered, which made it all the odder that he didn't want to rush to drive it. There was nothing I could do about that, however, and nothing more that he wanted of me. I therefore dismissed the job from my mind, rejoicing that at least the mortgage was no problem for a month or two.

And then later that week, everything shifted gear. On Friday evening I was wondering whether to give Helen a ring. She was an ex-girlfriend whom I still met every so often. It seemed a waste of a fine evening to do nothing. Len and Zoe had left for the day and I didn't fancy TV or working in the garden. I was about to ring her when the doorbell rang.

Frogs Hill is out in the wilds which means that unexpected visitors are rare and so a touch of caution is advisable. I peered through the curtains to see a car parked outside. It was a Vauxhall and I didn't recognize it. It was so battered that no respectable armed gangster would look twice at it, however, so I reckoned it was safe to open the door.

I groaned. I was wrong. It wasn't safe at all.

'That's not much of a welcome, Jack.'

It was Pen Roxton, nose quivering. Whatever she wanted, it wasn't going to be anything to help me. She's the sharpest journalist I know, and the quivering nose meant she was after a story.

THREE

I was so appalled that I automatically stood barring the doorway. In fact, this is much the best course of action where Pen is concerned. She must be in her mid-forties, she's sharp-faced, sharp-witted and sharp-edged. I hadn't seen her for some time, not since a memorable occasion when our paths had crossed and she had to retreat defeated. Now like the Terminator she was back, and from the look on her face with a mission just as portentous.

'I'll come in,' she told me. (That's Pen for you.) 'Won't keep you long.'

'Good.' Not that I believed her.

She marched past me as I stood aside, still somewhat dazed. She made straight for the farmhouse kitchen, appraised her surroundings and announced that coffee would be welcome. 'I never drink alcohol on a job,' she informed me virtuously, taking a seat at the table.

I surrendered, made the coffee, produced some passable biscuits and sat down with her, wondering what the 'job' was and how I came into it. I hoped she would take the point that as I had not made any coffee for myself, I must have other plans.

She didn't. She didn't waste time though. 'About this Packard,' she said.

Whoops. On guard, I warned myself. 'Which Packard?' Not a brilliant comeback of mine, and it didn't stall her for a moment.

'The one you were driving on the Headcorn road.'

'Well spotted. I was delivering it to a customer. Why do you ask?'

'It was a mid-1930s model, wasn't it?' Pen is reasonably good on classic cars. Or thinks she is.

'It was.'

'Any story there?'

'Not that I know of.' I was doing better now. 'It's not my
favourite classic but the one you saw me in was a magnificent
example, so I can understand its appeal.' Why, I wondered, had
she picked on this particular car? She must have seen me in
dozens of different cars over the years. Moreover it would have
been hard to see me at the wheel of the Packard, given its relatively small windows. That made me wonder whether Rob had
been chatting.

'The editor's missus heard there was one for sale. Was it that
one?'

'No idea. Did she want to buy it?' Pen works for the *Kentish
Graphic*, a weekly newspaper that veers between the uprightly
moral and the sensational, seldom stopping in between. Pen veers
accordingly, though she favours the sensational.

'No. Someone she knew was selling it. She got the impression
the car had a history. Want to comment?' Her iPad was ready
and waiting.

'That's news to me.'

'Don't fence with me, Jack,' she said amiably.

'Okay. Scouts honour, Pen, I've no idea. I bought it for a
customer and delivered it.' (I was never a boy scout but it was
true anyway.)

'*You* bought it?' The nose quivered. 'Why?'

'I sometimes do – or rather the company does.'

She sighed. 'It's been a quiet month, Jack. Take pity on me.
Thought there might be something there. The missus thought it
was a bit of a family heirloom. Ah well, win some lose some.
I'll call it lost. Thanks for the coffee.'

This was unusually gracious for Pen. She even gave me a
smile – which caused me to bear in mind that she *never* calls
a story lost. Not before it *is* lost anyway, and then that makes a
story in itself. This renders her a good journalist and a pesky
nuisance as well. Nevertheless, I felt almost cordial towards her
as I waved her off in her dilapidated Vauxhall.

She leaned out of the window with a passing: 'Haven't robbed
any good banks recently, have you, Jack?'

Surely just a casual remark because a 1930s Packard was the
getaway car in *The Ladykillers*? Nevertheless it meant that
the Packard remained in the forefront of my mind, instead of

beating a retreat with honours. It stayed there uncomfortably lodged. Like the Buick, a Packard signalled affluence. It then occurred to me that bank robbers – if successful in their trade – were indeed affluent, so Pen's remark might just have had some significance.

In vain I told myself that other matters needed my attention. I knew Dave Jennings had several jobs in hand that might or might not make their way to me and in the Pits we were especially busy, as classic cars owners revved up for the autumn season before their beloved cars became semi-grounded for the winter. The Packard was a distraction that I couldn't budge, however, like a particularly annoying pop-up on a computer. Every button I pressed was in vain. The Packard was illegally parked in a corner of my mind, gloating at its power. I mentally kicked it, ignored it or tried to reason with it, but it stayed there grinning at me with those stylish headlights.

This went on for a week or so until at last I decided to acknowledge its presence, when I read in the local paper that the grounds of Staveley House would be open this Sunday, for one day only. From which I gathered that this was a rare event indeed, and certainly it seemed out of keeping with my experience of the place.

The idea of dropping in there tantalized me. How did this tally with Philip Moxton's eccentricities? Would he be there? Would Miss Janes be the owner of the house this weekend? What about his fear of being murdered? I couldn't believe that he would be present if that had been a serious concern. But suppose he was there? I could ask him how the Packard was running. He might be driving it in the grounds, even if not on the public roads. The last time I checked with the DVLA, the Swansea licensing organization, it hadn't yet been registered.

I thought about taking Liz Potter with me, a friend and former lover, but she turned me down. She had a garden centre to run, and her husband Colin, who sometimes obliges her by helping out, was away. I knew Zoe would be tied up with Rob. Helen was also busy. Life was looking bleak on the female companionship front, until my daughter, Cara, paid me a surprise visit. This is also a rare event, since she's usually busy helping her partner Harry on his Suffolk farm. The visit therefore might be ominous because she was in trouble but it might also be handy.

'What's wrong?' I asked anxiously, when I found her on the doorstep. I hadn't heard her car draw in.

She laughed. 'Don't be so pessimistic. Can I come in before I tell you? Thought I'd stay overnight. Not inconveniencing your love life, am I?'

'Far from it. There isn't any.' It had taken an upturn some time ago when Louise, my lost love, had left me a note to let me know she had passed by. That was encouraging since no one can just 'pass by' Frogs Hill. It's so buried in the lanes that a definite plan has to be made. Her high-profile theatre and film career makes it doubly hard to make contact, but the discovery that she was on the other side of the world had been the clinching point that I was history. Typical for my love life. My long ex-wife, the Spanish werewolf Eva, who is Cara's mother, is a lot nearer than Australia unfortunately, but hopefully permanently living in Spain. Long may that continue to be the case.

'It's good news,' Cara told me once settled inside. 'At least I hope you'll think so.'

'Tell me. I need good news.'

'Harry and I are going to be wed – next year we thought.'

I was stunned. I'd never thought they'd get round to it. As a result, I blurted out the first thing I thought of. 'Are you pregnant?'

She was furious. 'Father!' she said – to infuriate me. She was outraged not at the question, I realized, but at the suggestion that the decision to marry had been in any way forced. 'No, I'm not.'

That cleared up, we settled down happily to discuss the whys and wherefores of her news. It was only after she went to bed that I realized that as father of the bride I had certain obligations in the financial department. This posed a problem as the Frogs Hill finances are definitely up and down with the jaws of Harry Prince ever open to catch it in down mode. On the other hand, by next year I could be rich, even though the commission money from the Packard deal wasn't going to last that long.

That of course brought the Packard back into my mind . . . but this time I was able to soothe it by telling it I'd be paying it a visit on the morrow.

The gateway to Staveley House stood open and there was even a man selling tickets, although not the lodge keeper (alias hit man). As there had also been advertising signs and directions along the lane, there was an air of normality about Staveley today that made me wonder whether I had imagined the whole charade I'd been treated to on earlier occasions. As we drove through the park, signs directed us not only to the car park I'd used before, but to a much larger overflow park, also nearly full. I'd brought the Lagonda today, so as we drove in we were the cynosure of all eyes.

There outside Staveley House stood the Packard, parked centrally and alone in the large forecourt. It had occurred to me that Philip Moxton in his enthusiasm might have had it repainted its original black, but to my relief he hadn't. Black can make any car look gloomy and even sinister in some circumstances but thankfully this Packard was still beaming a sunshiny welcome to its comfortable bosom. I saw by the plates that it was now reregistered. Standing by it were two guards, ostensibly to answer questions, I supposed, although more likely they were there to protect it. I would have thought that today the chances of its being nicked were nil, however.

'Is that it?' Cara breathed, gazing at the buttery creamy lady before us. I'd told her the story as far as was seemly with client confidentiality. 'That is some car.'

'So the brothers James Ward and William Doud Packard must have thought when they proudly whipped the covers off their very first Model A way back in 1899, and this 120 series was a real triumph, the all-round family car.'

'Thanks for the lecture,' Cara said drily. 'Even we country bumpkins can appreciate quality.'

Coming from Cara that was some tribute, but I overcame the temptation to stop right there and lecture her some more on the wonders of the Packard. Instead we sedately walked round the house to the rear gardens which I had glimpsed before through the windows of Staveley House. Now they were spectacular with autumn colours and could be admired at their best.

Correction: *should*, not could. Most of my mind was still concentrating on the Packard. Why did Philip Moxton have it on display so prominently? He did not strike me as a man who flaunted his possessions, indeed the opposite, so why the show? Was he making a statement of some sort? If so, what was it? The car wasn't especially valuable in financial terms, and however much it meant to him personally its mere display on his forecourt wasn't sending any other meaningful message to the world – as far as I could see, at least. Perhaps I was missing something.

'Does it mean anything to you?' I asked Cara absently.

I earned a scowl. 'Farmhand I may be, but I can still appreciate gardens.'

'Sorry. I meant the Packard.'

She considered this. 'Yes, it looks Walt Disneyish standing there.'

I saw what she meant. It looked as if it might take off any moment like Herbie. And perhaps, I thought for no particular reason, that might not be a bad idea.

As we walked along one shady path through the trees, I could see Philip way in front of us, but he was in earnest discussion with two other people, so I didn't rush up to say hello. It was a warm humid day for early September and the afternoon began to take on an unreal aspect, with visitors appearing and disappearing silently along paths and around corners, so I was happy enough to agree with Cara's suggestion that we sit down and admire the scenery. A paved barbecue area had been turned into a temporary café serving cream teas, and as Cara claims she has a degree in judging these we promptly made for it and ordered two. She did well with this one. The scones were warm and fresh, the jam tasted home-made and the cream could have come straight from the churn.

My feeling of unreality persisted, as we fell into a lazy hypnotic silence, which I eventually broke. 'Ever heard that true-life story about the Petit Trianon gardens at Versailles and a sunny afternoon?' I asked my daughter out of the blue.

'I don't think so.'

'Two lady Oxford academics on holiday in the early twentieth century strolled round them and headed for the picturesque mock village constructed at Marie Antoinette's whim in the eighteenth century. There was a fashion in France then for olde English gardens and rural cottages. The ladies found themselves looking right at Marie Antoinette herself enjoying a picnic with her ladies on the olde village green.'

'A pretty legend,' Cara commented. 'It must have been a dozy day like this one, so they imagined it or mistook a pageant or some other fancy dress show for the real thing.'

'No, there was much more to it than that. The layout of paths and rockeries in the Petit Trianon gardens have changed a lot since the eighteenth century, and even by the time the two ladies visited them they were very different to the ones that Marie Antoinette would have known. The gardens and village that they described, however, proved to be exactly as Marie Antoinette would have known them.'

'They'd read a book about them,' Cara said uncertainly.

'There was no such book or plans available that they could have accessed. Nor did they make the whole thing up – they left discussing it for too long for that to be the case. Neither of them realized for some weeks that the other one had seen the same things; they'd each thought they were hallucinating.'

'You've been living near Pluckley too long. That's full of ghosts, isn't it?'

'O ye of little imagination.'

'O me of much common sense.'

'There are more things in heaven and earth—' I began to quote.

'But not here in Kent,' Cara said firmly. 'What's your point anyway?'

'This –' I waved a hand round the idyllic scene before us – 'families, fernery, flowers, Mother Nature beaming and a beautiful old house. They don't seem real.'

'These scones and cream are,' she said firmly.

She was right, I supposed. I was just carried away by the perfect September day, the classic cars, the classic mansion, the classic garden of perfection, classic Sunday afternoon guests, and a classic cream tea. What was wrong with all that?

I couldn't answer myself, that was the problem. There was nothing I could see that was amiss and yet my antennae twitched. Was it the gardens? Surely not. It must be seeing the Packard again. My whole connection with it felt unreal. Was this another staged performance? Was that dangerous corner approaching?

No sign of it yet. I could now see Philip Moxton clearly, however. He was sitting on the paved terrace taking tea with – yes, the formidable Miss Janes, the enigmatic lodge keeper, and a couple of other people. One of them looked like the man I'd seen with Philip when I delivered the Packard. They didn't look as though this was a closed group, however, so now could be the time to approach Philip to satisfy myself there was nothing more to the Packard story than a straight sell-buy deal.

My plans were forestalled for, as Cara and I rose to leave our table, three other people arrived to take our place. Two of them I knew and hardly expected to see here.

'Hi!' I said meaningfully. Maybe this greeting was the insignificant item of conversation that provided the dangerous corner in the Priestley play, but if so, I might never know. What I did know was that it was mighty strange to see the Packard's former owners, Tom and Moira Herrick, here.

Moira blushed red when she recognized me, and seemed bereft of words. Not so Tom, who rushed to explain their presence with great cheer.

'Couldn't resist. Had to have a peek at the old girl.'

Moira found her voice. 'Gavin would have been along here like a shot,' she told me enthusiastically.

The third of the party, the girl I'd seen in the photograph in the Oast House, was in her mid-to-late twenties, both taller and slimmer than Cara and gracefully elegant in tight jeans and smock. She raised an eyebrow and looked interested. From her likeness to Moira (save that she wasn't favouring the cool iceberg image) she was indeed their daughter.

'So you knew where the Packard's new home would be?' I asked.

'Oh *no*.' Moira had herself well in hand now. 'We love gardens and when we saw the Packard there we could hardly believe our eyes. What a surprise.'

'It must have been.' I laughed sympathetically. 'That's us car lovers for you. Bonded to our cars for ever.'

'You're right,' Moira agreed. 'Each one has its own aura, doesn't it? It seems to call to you.' She glanced at her husband, but he didn't seem to be listening. He was more interested in staring at the group on the terrace.

'My Fiesta doesn't,' the girl put in and was belatedly introduced by Moira after I had introduced Cara to them.

'Our daughter Emma,' she said. 'Jack Colby, darling. He handled the sale of the Packard.'

'So *you're* Jack Colby,' Emma replied, somewhat enigmatically.

I was somewhat puzzled because I hadn't thought I had made

that much impression on her parents. I agreed that I was indeed Jack Colby, and she gave me a lightning appraisal which seemed to have more to do with me personally than as a car buyer. It wasn't pursued, either because Cara was with me or because I had imagined it. I reminded myself that I was Cara's father and therefore it was highly unlikely that Emma had any interest in me other than as an acquaintance of her parents. Good grief, I thought. Was this an early onset of old age, imagining young women fancied me?

'Do you know Philip Moxton?' I asked.

'Of him,' Moira replied. The subject was instantly dropped as Tom, still intent on the terrace group, broke in with:

'Timothy Mild's with him, Moira.'

'Who's he?' Emma asked.

A slight hesitation. 'The CEO of Moxtons Private Banking. Lives at Smarden. Wonder what he's doing here.'

'Perhaps he likes gardens,' Emma said flippantly.

'More likely discussing whether Moxtons goes global or not. Only rumours, of course,' Tom added hastily. 'Anyway, about that Packard, Jack. I thought I'd better mention to Philip that the spare tyre has a pinprick hole in it.'

'Philip' I noticed. Very chummy for someone who didn't know the buyer. Curiouser and curiouser.

'Let's go over and have a word with him, Moira,' Tom said firmly.

I was not wanted on the voyage, that was clear, and Emma began to chat with Cara about the theatre. It turned out that Emma was in the business, as were her parents, although Emma was on the production side. Cara is (or was) a keen amateur actor and even though she had moved from her London job to the farm in Suffolk she was still active on the amateur stage. Usually professionals and amateurs don't hit it off whatever the line, but this pair seemed to be doing just that, so I didn't intrude. Now that Tom and Moira were talking avidly to Philip and the woman – to whom they hardly seemed strangers – there was no point in my trying to nab Philip's attention, even though Timothy Mild and the lodge keeper had now left the party. So when Emma was summoned by Tom to join them Cara and I headed for the car park.

On the way, however, I took a probably illicit detour to where

I had guessed Philip Moxton garaged his cars, the old stable complex. I was curious to see what car Philip drove apart from the Packard.

'Why?' Cara asked when I told her this.

'The Packard can't be his daily driver, so what is it?'

'Why's it so interesting?'

I found it hard to answer her because I wasn't sure myself. 'You can tell a lot about someone by their choice of cars. He might have a Rolls or two tucked away.'

He might, but if so they were not only tucked but locked away when we reached the stables. In the courtyard stood a classic Rover P4 in the peak of condition, but this too hardly seemed a daily driver to take him to the railway station and back. Whatever that was must be behind those doors, which looked firmly padlocked. Usually it's the classic locked away and the daily driver left out in the rain.

But then Philip Moxton was not a usual man. I strolled over to the garage to try to get a glimpse through a crack, but I was foiled.

'What be you doing here?'

The lodge keeper had loomed up behind us, having either followed us or spotted us through the arch leading to the gardens. He did not look pleased. Far from it. That beard was quivering with rage.

'Sorry,' I said. 'We took a wrong turning.'

'What a lovely Rover,' Cara said enthusiastically, and the look on our non-friend's face that had said I would be shot at dawn softened a little. Cara has that effect on people.

'She's a beauty,' he replied. 'Runs like a dream.'

'Packard running well?' I asked cheerily.

The softer look promptly vanished. 'Ask the boss,' he snarled.

At least he was talking to me. 'When I see Miss Janes, I will. I didn't realize she was the owner of the Packard,' I said brightly. 'Mr Moxton must be one of the gardeners.'

I've never seen a face purple so quickly. 'He's not a bloody gardener. He keeps to the house. The gardens be mine – and Miss Moxton's,' he added.

Miss Moxton's, eh? I was getting somewhere. For Miss Janes read Miss Moxton. The telephone receptionist must be Philip's sister. 'Ah yes, you did mention that Miss Janes . . . owned the house. I see she's here today.'

He seemed not to hear me. 'These gardens –' he announced to the world in general – 'they're a work of art, they are. The house – that's just a load of old stones and bricks, but these gardens they're living, changing all the time. That's what we need here at Staveley. Take what nature gives and give something back to it. See? That's gardens for you.'

I thought about putting in an argument for the house too, but one look at this man made me agree that I did indeed see his point. He was obviously not just the lodge keeper but gardener too.

Cara valiantly took up the baton again. 'The best of gardens, like this one, live in people's memories, like the Petit Trianon in Paris.' She ignored my gurgle of surprise. 'Yours is a masterpiece, Mr . . . er . . .'

'Carson. John Carson. No one gets in the way of these gardens,' he informed us. '*No one*. See?'

I hastily saw. I was younger than him, taller than him, heavier than him, but there was something about his skinny pent-up frame that made me think twice about defying this edict.

Cara departed next day, with plans for the wedding approved so far as they went. Cautiously I agreed they didn't sound too expensive; wedding in the local church where Harry was a stalwart and the reception on the farm 'with good farm fare', she said vaguely, so provided this didn't mean my feeding five hundred or so it sounded manageable. Besides, I remembered I planned to be rich by next year. Something to look forward to.

I needed it. No jobs were offered to me, the phone line was silent both on my personal and professional life. The days ticked by until finally Len and Zoe took pity on me. They actually came up with the idea that I could help them in the Pits. They are seldom enthusiastic about this, but on this occasion we all thought it a good idea. Especially for this restoration job. It would keep my hand in. It was a blue Riley 1.5 litre and they graciously let me look after the retuning.

At last the Packard began to recede from my mind. After all, what was there to mull over? Philip Moxton had said he feared to be murdered but there was nothing I could do about that and it couldn't be anything to do with the Packard. Or could it? I wondered. The Herricks clearly knew Philip Moxton. Is that why he didn't want his name revealed as the purchaser of that car? Were they the ones he suspected of wanting to murder him? If so, why have an open day when anyone could turn up, including the very people he suspected? Or was the plan to flush the potential murderer into the open? No, Philip Moxton didn't seem the type to play games of that sort.

I tried yet again to push the Packard out of my mind, but its buttery yellow grandeur still refused to budge. It was still on my mind on Monday morning when the owner of the Riley called in.

'How's it going?' he asked.

'Not sure I would like it painted black.'

'Painted *black*?' He looked aghast and I quickly came to my senses.

'Not the Riley. Sorry. Had something on my mind. A Packard at Staveley House.'

He grunted. 'That's where John Carson's the gardener, isn't it?'

'Right. And he plays watchdog at the gates to make sure no one runs off with his petunias.'

'You want to be careful of him.'

'I got that impression too.'

'Rumours.' He tapped the side of his nose – why do people do that? Lips I could understand.

'About what?' I asked cautiously.

'Moves with a doubtful lot.'

I didn't like the sound of this. 'How doubtful?'

'Very. He's Richie's father. Heard of him?'

That rang an unpleasant bell, especially as this was Friday the 13th. 'The one who fences a slick operation to the continent?' And when he nodded, I added, 'But his father's not that sort. He's a gardener after all.'

'There isn't a different sort,' he said simply. 'Watch it.'

I'd no need to watch anything, I reminded myself. The Packard job was over, and so was my responsibility to Staveley House and its weird occupants. As if to confirm this, three days later on Monday morning Dave Jennings rang me at last.

'Ever heard of the Car Crime Unit?' he joked. He'd been out of touch for so long I was tempted to say no, but self-preservation made me hold it back.

'Got a job for you,' he said.

'Firm?' I added hopefully as pound signs flashed up before me.

'Yes. Missing Volkswagen Golf.'

'That's not my field,' I said, puzzled. 'I do classics. What year?'

'Four years since it drove into this world.'

'Love the idea of a job, but why me?' His team is perfectly capable of tracking down modern Volkswagens. It's only classics where specialist knowledge is sometimes needed that bring me into the picture.

'This is a special,' Dave said seriously. 'Brandon wants you in.'

Brandon? DCI Brandon of the Kent Police and I have an uneasy working relationship when from time to time murder makes its entry on stage. 'Tell me the worst,' I said.

'Murder case in Monksford.'

The two sat somewhat oddly together. Monksford is a sizeable village buried south west of Ashford not far from Shadowhurst. Its centre is pleasantly olde worlde, but the new housing estates all round it have enclosed it so completely that it seems in a time warp.

'A dodgy one?' I asked Dave.

'Not at first sight. House ransacked, car nicked, owner shot. By name Geoffrey Green.'

'What does the second sight tell you?'

'Couple of odd things. Brandon will explain when you get there. Which will be, like, *now,*' Dave added, giving me the address.

'*Now?*' Why the urgency?

'Forget whatever else you were planning to do today. *Now.*'

'In that case, let's get back to the root question,' I said patiently. 'I'm a car detective. Why me in particular?'

A pause. 'You really want to know?'

'Yes.'

'Your card was found in Geoffrey Green's pocket.'

FOUR

What could be so urgent about this case that it demanded my instant presence? It's true crime scenes move fast, but even so a card in the pocket would seem to merit a follow-up visit by the police rather than a summons to the actual scene. But if the great Brandon had requested my presence, far be it from me to deprive him of it. It was rare for a DCI to take personal charge of a crime scene so who was I to object? The question was whether he wanted my help or whether I was a suspect? I don't give out that many Frogs Hill cards but enough that the odds were against the latter, whoever this victim was and whatever the motive behind his death. Theft seemed the most likely, but that wouldn't have caught Brandon's personal attention. Anyway, I told myself uneasily, it was far too soon to prejudge the issue.

I patted my trusty steed (otherwise known as my Alfa) on her bonnet, and told her we were setting off for a date with the noble DCI Brandon, who I'd been told would be waiting for me at the murder scene.

'Won't you be there?' I had asked Dave.

'Thanks,' he'd said, 'but I'll give this one a miss. Unless,' he had added, 'this case is bigger than both of you. I doubt that though.'

'Then why the summons to me?' I'd asked. I'm not particularly modest but I am aware that my services cost money, which automatically puts a case into the 'special' category.

But answer had come there none.

I wasn't that bothered by the fact that my card was in Geoffrey Green's pocket, but I did wonder whether it was the Frogs Hill Restoration business card or my private one. I'd asked Dave, but he had no idea. It might be an interesting point. If it was the business card, why would the owner of a fairly modern Volkswagen Golf be interested in classic car restoration? Perhaps he had wanted to buy one? That didn't seem to fit either. So it remained a question to be dealt with at some point.

The drive to Monksford was not a long one, once I had skirted Ashford. It's a peaceful place where murder does not leap instantly to mind. Miss Marple might have plenty to do in such villages but in real life it's less frequently encountered. I grew increasingly puzzled as I turned off the minor road to the centre of Monksford and then into the estate where the murder had taken place. There was such a sharp divide between the farmland and the edge of the estate that it looked as if development had come in relatively recently, perhaps ten years previously.

As I drove round the corner into Spinners Drive, I saw a long row of similar, though not identical houses. Number 28 was hard to miss, not because the numbers were obligingly large on the doors but because of Brandon's array of cars and vans which directed me straight to it. It was a small detached house in the midst of a row of semis as was the style along the entire road on both sides of it, and the gap between the detached houses and the neighbours' garages was very narrow.

What do these observations have to do with my summons to Brandon? Nothing, save that it made the question of what my card was doing in the victim's pocket even more mysterious, since it would be unlikely that the victim would have had a rare Rolls-Royce or its ilk tucked away somewhere.

Brandon wasn't exactly waiting with arms akimbo for me, but I could see him in the small front garden bordered by crime-scene tape. This encircled not only Number 28 but Numbers 26 and 24 as well, perhaps because the gardens were open-plan.

Once I'd navigated my way past the log-in at the crime scene access point and quickly donned scene shoes, Brandon proved his usual imperturbable self. Not that imperturbability denotes a laid-back approach to his work. It's one of his most useful tools. It discomposes his witness or suspect, who then can't wait to let loose a torrent of information in the mistaken hope of convincing his listener of its truth.

'Thanks for coming, Jack,' he said. 'Want a look at him?'

Brandon's a hunting dog by nature. The slightest whiff of a scent and he's off, but he doesn't like wasting time on false leads. I followed him into the house somewhat reluctantly, but I knew better than to let him see that. I didn't know Geoffrey Green and I didn't want my first and only acquaintance with him to be his murdered body, but one doesn't say no to Brandon.

'Your card,' he began, leading the way into the first room, a living room and, to my relief, with no sign of its late owner. I had time to steel myself.

'For the restoration business, I imagine, but I'm pretty sure I haven't met him.'

'It's your personal card.'

That surprised me, but I still hadn't heard of Geoffrey Green. Cards get around.

'Green was late middle age,' Brandon continued. 'Travelled a lot – London mostly, several days a week and sometimes weekends according to the neighbours. Variable times. Thought to have had a flat in London. Other than that, the neighbours don't know a thing about him. Kept himself to himself. No one heard anything for sure last night, although someone thought they heard a car about eight o'clock; Green invariably put the car straight into the garage, though.'

'So no one would have seen it in the drive.'

'Quite. No opportunist theft. Ready to look at him?'

'Sure,' I said bravely. 'Was it a straight break-in or someone he knew? Presumably the former as the car was nicked. How did he die?'

'You'll see. Knife probably. We'll know more shortly.' Brandon glanced at me, perhaps reading my expression correctly. 'Died during the night between nine and two approximately. Downstairs so more likely to be before midnight. Neighbours said Green was often coming and going and they were never sure whether he was here or not.'

'Could he have come back and disturbed an intruder?'

'Perhaps, but unlikely,' Brandon replied. 'There was an amateur attempt at window breaking at the rear. So it could have been someone he knew.'

Brandon has the knack of making me feel instantly guilty. 'Not me,' I said firmly. 'I've no idea why he had my card.'

'You wouldn't have left it in his pocket if you'd knifed him.'

'Thanks.' A compliment from Brandon? Treasure it. 'What about this Golf that's missing?'

'Garage self-locked behind the departed vehicle. No keys found so far.'

This was routine stuff, and it was time to get to the point. 'Why was it so important to have me here now?'

The piercing eyes gleamed at me. 'It seems an odd scene. That coupled with your card was the reason.'

I had to face it. I was going to have to view the body even though Brandon still showed no sign of wanting to escort me there.

'The body was discovered at eight thirty this morning,' Brandon continued, 'when the cleaner arrived. She wasn't expecting Green to be here, so it was a double shock. She's been taken home. He's in there.' Hardly to my surprise, he indicated the double doors leading through to the rear room, but he still didn't move.

'What is it that strikes you as odd?' I asked.

He hesitated – unusual for Brandon. 'The whole thing is too neat.'

'The case or the scene?' I asked.

'Everything,' he said obliquely.

I'd already noted that the room we were standing in was spartan. There was nothing personal in it. Even the bookcase was impersonal in its book collection – Dickens, Christie, guide books and so on. The TV, gas fire, armchairs, sofa, table – all were immaculate but told me nothing about their user.

'So apart from looking at the poor bloke what's for me to do?' I asked him warily.

'Your field mainly. The Volkswagen.'

'OK. That's straightforward. What else?' I was sure there must be something because otherwise Dave's team would be on the case and not me.

Brandon surprised me. 'For once, Jack, I don't know. Maybe your views on whether the car theft was the motivation for the murder or another attempt to make us think theft was the motive.'

'OK. I'll let you know my gut feeling when I'm further in. I'd better take a look at him, I suppose.' I braced myself.

Without another word, Brandon took me there, not through the double doors which were now being checked by the forensic team, but into the hallway and through to the dining room where sheeting covered what was obviously the victim. It couldn't cover the carpets and walls where blood spatters were all too clear, however, and I had to steady myself for what was to come. I've seen dead men before, quite often, but cars are my line, not corpses, so I had a tight grip on myself as Brandon went over to lift the sheet.

'It's worth seeing if he rings any bells with you,' he said. 'The face is OK, the knife or whatever it was took him in the chest. Several times.'

I wondered why he needed any bells rung as he already knew who Geoffrey Green was, but I didn't ask him. I was flattered in one way that he'd called me in, wary in another, even though all I had to do for the moment was to tell him whether or not I knew Geoffrey Green.

As the sheet exposed the face, my stomach lurched. I *did* know Geoffrey Green.

But I knew him as Philip Moxton.

I've often wondered how Victorian ladies so predictably fainted on the spot after a shock. Tight corsets couldn't always have been to blame. Now I knew the answer. I hadn't fainted, but Brandon was concerned enough at my white face to take me back to the incident van outside and sit me down. I'm not sure 'concerned' is the right word, as what interested him was my reaction. The hunting dog had the scent in his nostrils and it wasn't a false one.

Tea's better than coffee as a restorative and forget about brandy. I'd never tasted a cuppa as good as the one I was handed in a paper cup. After I'd blurted out who Geoffrey Green really was to Brandon, I fed disjointed scraps of information to him, while I wrestled with my own emotions. I'd come to like Philip Moxton on the brief visits I'd paid to him. What was worse was that he had told me he was afraid he'd be murdered and I hadn't taken him seriously. For all I knew of the world of billionaires they all might have that at the back of their minds or security wouldn't be such an issue. If he'd been that scared, he'd have drawn in the Met or hired body-guards, wouldn't he?

'You're sure that's who it is?' From looking rather pleased that his prediction that this case was an odd one was correct, Brandon now looked very bleak. 'Not just a lookalike? Any doubts at all?'

'None. I gave him that card you found some weeks ago, when I did a job for him.'

'What job?' he asked, instantly alert. I saw his team closing in around us like a pack of wolves, hungry for information.

'He wanted me to find a Packard classic for him. One that he used to own.'

Brandon seemed inclined to dismiss this but I wasn't sure he'd be right to do so. 'It could be relevant,' I told him.

'Why?'

I summed up what I knew and told him about my visits to Staveley House, but somehow that didn't quite convey my own feelings about it. I ended up with a lame 'The car was very important to him.'

'A car doesn't get you murdered,' he commented, but I could see Brandon was already reconsidering this statement, perhaps in view of a couple of cases where a car had played a very big part in the case.

'Not usually,' he amended. 'We'll search the house again to see if anything ties in with Philip Moxton. We've already identified the victim as Geoffrey Green so assuming you're right, do you have any clues on why an active billionaire should be living a double life as a semi-recluse?'

'He was afraid someone was out to murder him.'

Brandon isn't one to faint with shock either, and I'd never seen him look so thrown off course from his usual imperturbability. 'Rightly?' he asked.

'It's possible. Moxtons Bank is going global, so it's rumoured – could have been something to do with that.'

'*If* this is Moxton. The cleaner says this man's Green, the neighbours say it's Green and he's been here for some years, so that would seem to do away with a sudden desire to escape business worries. Is Philip Moxton married?'

'Divorced with a son, according to a biog I read, but it was coy on details. There's a woman living at Staveley House, but she didn't strike me as a second wife, an ex-wife or a lover.'

'Whether she is or not, the neighbours say the only woman they ever saw here was the cleaner, and very occasionally someone from the village. You're sure about this identification?' he pressed me again.

'Try the landline at his official home, Staveley House.' I gave him the contact details. 'Ask for Philip Moxton. Don't say who you are. You'll get a strange reaction.'

Brandon glared at me. He dislikes acting on suggestions immediately. He likes to digest them first, but today he needed to know quickly because if I was right even I could see a whole raft of problems lying ahead for him. He punched in the number. It took a time, but it was answered.

'Never heard of him,' screeched that inimitable voice loud and clear.

'I understand Mr Moxton owns Staveley—'

'*I* own Staveley House.'

Brandon rang off. I'd expected him to follow this up by announcing his official status, but he didn't. Instead he said, 'I *could* still think you're barking up the wrong tree with Philip Moxton, Jack, and that was just a screaming woman at the end of the line who's never heard of him.'

'True,' I agreed. 'So here's the number for you to try Philip Moxton's mobile if you can find it.'

A startled look. 'Inside,' Brandon barked, not only to me but the nearest and dearest in his team. If it was Moxton's body there would be a fair chance that his mobile would be in Number 28, I reasoned, as we all trooped in in our scene shoes. Brandon keyed in the number on his mobile while we all held our breath. Especially me. Luck was on my side, because Philip hadn't switched the mobile off. We all heard it ringing in a drawer in the living room.

One of the forensic team fished it out and answered it just to double check. 'OK,' Brandon said briefly. It was promptly bagged to be checked for calls and DNA. 'A billionaire banker,' he commented. 'A double life was his idea of security. Pity it didn't work.'

He looked unusually dejected and I almost felt sorry for him. 'You could try the bank, Moxtons,' I suggested. 'Ask for his PA, just to triple check.'

'We will. I'll tackle that maniac woman at Staveley House later.'

He indicated he still wanted me around, so I returned to the incident van to wait, but it didn't take long before he joined me. 'Moxton is not in the office today. He's at home. Wouldn't give home address, until I forced the issue. You were right. Staveley House of which he is the owner. I did get that much, but I've no doubt that alarm bells are ringing amongst the banking powers that be. And others.'

I knew Brandon would be in a tight spot. When the news

broke, he would have every tabloid in the UK chasing after him
and if this story about going global was true half of the world
banking press too. Nor would he and the Kent Police be handling
this by themselves. If there was any sign that organized crime
might be involved in Moxton's murder then the National Crime
Agency would be on the case, even if it wasn't the Met. And
perhaps those secret operatives my father used to refer to as 'the
men in hats', would be on the scene as well. All Brandon could
be certain about at present was that one person – Jack Colby –
claimed it was Philip Moxton, although only one or two items
of evidence suggested he may be right.

'We'll put a press blackout on it for present. This is the murder
of a man found dead in Monksford.' A pause. 'You said Moxton
was expecting to be murdered, Jack? Afraid?'

'More accepting the situation, I think, if that's possible. He
was matter of fact about it.'

'Did he happen to mention whether he expected the murder
to be of Philip Moxton – or of Geoffrey Green?'

I'd been released after that punchline. It's not often that I get
floored in one by Brandon, and I couldn't hold it against him,
as my revelation had undoubtedly floored him. Killed as Moxton
or Green? The former was more likely but the possibility of the
other couldn't be excluded.

'Don't go anywhere for the next week or two, Jack,' Brandon
had formally instructed me.

My first thought had been that I was indeed a suspect again,
but again he surprised me. 'I could need your help.'

'For the Volkswagen Golf theft or the Packard job?'

'The cars,' Brandon said, 'seem to be the least of my problems,
but I'll talk it over with Dave Jennings.'

'I'll get on to the Volkswagen if he okays it. It seems unlikely
as a motivation for planned murder. It wouldn't fetch too much
for the thief as a stolen car – maybe four thousand – but it would
depend on how much four thousand meant to the thief.'

Silence from Brandon. Then: 'I'll bear that in mind.'

For some reason I had felt reluctant to bring the Packard into
it, perhaps out of a perverse affection for it, but I had to disgorge
my growing suspicion. 'What about the Packard? Surely it's more
than coincidence that that odd story was followed so quickly by

Moxton's murder? There's something weird about the seller knowing the buyer and probably vice versa, but wanting to pretend they didn't.'

Brandon had done me the courtesy of thinking this through. 'If this Moxton identification is confirmed, I'll call you in officially, on the off chance it may have something to do with the murder though I can't see how. Until then ask as many car questions as you wish, but not in my way and not on my time. I'll clear that with Dave.'

Point taken. 'Does that apply to Monksford village and those people who occasionally called on Green?'

He eyed me keenly. 'Don't build your hopes on that. They were probably only reclaiming catalogues put through the door. As for the village, the news will have spread by now that Geoffrey Green is dead and we'll be making our own enquiries there. If you want to stop off there to admire the scenery or chat about cars, I can't stop you, but *keep me in the loop.*'

I got the message. 'And don't put in a bill.'

The centre of Monksford is pleasant without overdoing the picturesque. It has developed over the years with a Victorian gable or two imposing itself on the red-brick cottages from earlier centuries, which makes it a comfortable sort of village. Perhaps that was why Philip Moxton had chosen to live here. It was large enough to be anonymous without being forbidding. The road wound its way through the centre rather than dissecting it, with the result that each turn brought a new perspective to it. Its independent shops had largely vanished, but I could see a butcher's shop which looked well patronized, a baker's and an all-purpose shop with a post office facility advertised outside. The Norman church was set back from the road, but was close enough to be an integral part of the village; it was reached by a pathway and with a largish house at the far end that might be or once have been the vicarage.

Right by the road was the George and Dragon pub, which looked interesting so I went in for a drink. Conversation immediately stopped while I was silently assessed – but I seemed to pass muster.

'Morning. Police, are you?' asked one regular – judging by the proprietary elbow on the bar.

'No, but there's been a bit of an incident on the estate.'

'Oh yeah?'

It was obvious they all knew from their lack of follow-up. 'I've just come from there. I was asked to call in.' (There was nothing confidential about that. Half the residents of Spinners Drive had been watching at their doors or windows.)

I was the centre of attention. 'Why's that then?'

'I hunt down stolen cars for them and a Volkswagen was stolen.' True enough but the ensuing silence told me that pursuing stolen cars was not a popular trade round here.

'Who was this Green fellow?' someone else asked.

I didn't have to answer this because a new arrival was only too happy to take over. 'My missus cleans for him. One of those chaps who lives here but don't mix. Londoner. Reckons he's one of us because he lives in the country. Real shock it was for my missus to find him like that. Not fair. Blood everywhere.'

He gave the impression that Geoffrey Green himself was to blame for mischoosing his place and time of death, much as I sympathized with his wife for having been the one to find him.

'Are you a neighbour of his?' I asked.

'Other side of the village, but I knew the bloke. Did odd jobs for him. Nothing much,' he added hastily, perhaps in case this turned him into a suspect. And perhaps it did – I wondered whether he liked Volkswagen Golfs.

I chatted over my drink for five minutes and then departed because I wasn't going to get any further here. As I came out of the pub, I realized that the establishment I'd taken to be a baker's shop was in fact a cake shop, incorporating a café that served light lunches. My kind of place for information, I thought, even though I wasn't hungry. Lunch would take time to reach me and while I was waiting I might gather more local gossip here than in the pub.

There were only three people running it, a young girl selling the cakes, a waitress and a somewhat older woman in the kitchen who, from the glimpses I had of her as she emerged every now and then, looked middle aged. If it wasn't my imagination, however, her mind seemed elsewhere, and serving lunch seemed to be an ordeal for her. The waitress brought the menu to me and I chose fish pie. I was in luck because several new customers arrived, which meant my meal was delivered by the woman in the kitchen. Now I could see her properly she looked in her mid-to-late forties, an attractive brunette without being overtly sexy.

I gambled. 'You must have known Geoffrey Green well,' I said to her.

She instantly stopped her retreat to the kitchen and stared at me suspiciously. 'Are you from the police or press?'

'No. Classic cars are my line. Stolen ones. Hunting them down, that is,' I added. 'Don't want you to get the wrong impression.'

She didn't laugh. She looked worried in fact. 'So you do work *for* the police then?'

'Sometimes. That's for the Car Crime Unit though.' I didn't want to provide any more information, so I turned my attention to the fish pie. Luckily she wasn't deterred.

'So who's had a classic car pinched round here?' she asked sharply.

'No one. You've obviously heard about Geoffrey Green's death. His car was stolen. Not a classic but the police thought I might be able to help. Did you know him well?'

'He was a nice man and came in sometimes for lunch.'

'I met him a few times myself. I thought he worked in London though?'

'Did he?' She was definitely stonewalling. 'He didn't come in very often so I wouldn't know.'

The fish pie was very good, but I sensed her eye on me after she returned to the kitchen. I was right because when I paid the bill she told me her name was Wendy and asked me for my phone number. She'd call me, because her brother liked cars (she said).

When I drove back through the estate to see what was happening at Number 28, it was obvious the crime scene was still in progress. The incident vans were still there, although there wasn't much sign of action save for one PC guarding the scene.

'Is DCI Brandon here?' I asked him, after parking the car.

Luckily he recognized me so he told me the DCI had been summoned back to HQ and that after the body had been taken away all work on the case had been suspended. This didn't look good. It confirmed that Geoffrey Green was indeed Philip Moxton but also indicated that there would be more fingers in this pie than those of the Kent Police.

It looked to me as though the kettle was coming to boiling point and this was confirmed when I spoke to Brandon on my mobile.

'We're waiting for the Met,' he told me. 'Everything's on hold meanwhile. Even Downing Street is involved so we're in for a summit. Hold any horses you have, Jack.' A pause. 'Or keep them at a quiet trot.'

FIVE

Against the odds, Wendy did ring me, and surprisingly early in the morning for social calls – nine o'clock sharp. I asked if she'd talked to the police but she didn't stop to answer. Tuesday was her day off, she told me, so could she get the hell out of Monksford and come to Frogs Hill please? I was only too happy to agree.

She had seemed a pleasant woman – attractive too – but I didn't flatter myself I was her target, except perhaps as a bolt-hole and substitute confessional. Otherwise I could see no reason for her picking on a stranger to visit if, as seemed probable, her relationship with Geoffrey Green had been a personal one.

Only ten minutes later I had a call from DCI Brandon. Didn't anyone love me for myself, not just as an ally when the going got tough? I braced myself, although what he had to say was hardly a surprise.

'You were right, Jack. It's Philip Moxton.'

'That's bad,' I said sincerely. Having it confirmed by Brandon himself somehow made it worse. I'd met Philip, liked him, worked for him and now I was going to be caught up in finding his murderer, whether Brandon remembered I was on his payroll or not. If he didn't – well, I wasn't going to let Philip down if I could contribute anything to the case.

'Too right. I'm having to work with the Met now, only it seems it's rather more than that.'

As I'd thought. Really bad. 'Where are you based?'

'The Met has moved in on us at Charing.'

Charing Police HQ is overcrowded as it is, and it's hardly fit for its own purpose, let alone the Met's, so Brandon indeed had my sympathy.

'You're back on my payroll – temporarily,' he added.

'Understood,' I replied, mentally reviewing my bank balance.

'Did you glean anything from the village?'

'I've one lead. You probably have it too. Wendy Parks who runs the café. She's decided to spend her day off with me. *Her* idea.'

'Yes, she's on our witness list. Grass doesn't grow under your feet. I suppose that's no bad thing for a classic car buff like you.'

The first joke I'd ever heard Brandon crack. We were really getting matey now. Then the joking finished.

'I've given you a clean slate so that the Met shouldn't need to grill you to cinders. You're just a car expert employed by me. And another thing, Geoffrey Green's murder has already crept into the press, but we don't want any mention of Moxton yet or that it might be linked to his bank. You said there were rumours around that it was going global – too right. They're in the midst of negotiating a European merger. Moxton was against it, Timothy Mild, the CEO, was pushing it.'

'Interesting. He lives locally.'

'Met him?' Brandon shot at me.

'No. Seen him, yes. He was twice at Staveley House with Philip Moxton when I was there. I gather it's big, this merger?'

'Very and you told me Moxton was scared of being murdered.'

Just as I finished talking to Brandon, Wendy drove into the forecourt in an ageing Audi, and her arrival was an uncomfortable nudge that I needed to get on with Geoffrey Green's missing Volkswagen. What, I wondered, did Brandon expect of me on this front, now I was officially his 'car expert'?

'Found you first time.' Wendy grinned. 'Admittedly, satnav helped, but your instructions were pretty good.'

She looked with interest at the Pits, which today – unusually – looked the epitome of an efficient busy garage. Even Len seemed as if he was actually in a hurry, rather than his usual tortoise-like approach. In his book of fables the hare never wins. Today he and Zoe were both in the Pits doing a double act on the Riley, Len busy replacing the drive shaft and Zoe working on the exhausts.

'Am I intruding?' Wendy asked me uncertainly. 'You all look so busy here.'

'You're doing us all a favour,' I assured her. 'They like nothing better than keeping me away from the sharp end of operations. Let's go into the farmhouse and I'll do the honours with coffee.'

Once I'd produced my best instant and she'd been duly polite about it, we ground to a halt. I was leaving the running to her, but she seemed reluctant to open up. Perhaps she was regretting having come.

'What's this about, Wendy?' I asked at last and she flushed.

'It doesn't seem so easy to tell you now.'

'Then let's go for a walk and you can pick your moment.'

She jumped at this idea, fished out some trainers from her car boot and off we set. The footpath I chose leads eventually to Piper's Green, our nearest village, but it passes some good views on the countryside on the way – and they provide an escape route for the tongue-tied. The Greensand Way ridge must have heard a lot of confidential confessions over the years.

At last she managed to blurt it out. 'I knew Geoffrey, but I can't decide how much I need to tell the police – if anything. I don't want to tell them everything because it doesn't seem right, but I have to do so because this . . . this *thing* happened to him. Why? Did he really just try to fight off a thief? We don't get many robberies in Monksford so it seems weird. I know I'll have to talk to someone, but the police are formidable and family and friends can only offer sympathy. I need a bit more than that. Is it OK just to talk to you?'

Steady, I thought. 'Yes, but you'll have to tell the police everything in the end, and sooner is better than later. You can't judge what might be material to Geoffrey's murder, but they can. Officially I'm only following up the Golf theft.'

I couldn't scare her by telling her that every detective in the Met and secret services would shortly be tearing her every word to minute shreds and reconstructing them, correctly or incorrectly. 'In any case,' I continued, 'because I do work for the police, anything you tell me that might have the slightest bearing on Geoffrey Green has to be reported to them. Accepted?'

She pulled her face. 'I'm not sure.'

I gritted my teeth. Upset or not, this was one obstinate woman. 'I'll make it easier. Will what you tell me make you a suspect in Green's murder?'

That shook her rigid, and her expression grew even more mulish. 'Of course not.'

Time for more pressure. 'Someone in Monksford is going to know about your friendship with him, so if you haven't spoken to the police, that's black mark number one. They know about you.'

'You're making it sound as though I'm guilty until proved innocent.'

I'd lost her, so somehow I had to retreat to get through to her. I'd have to go back to that dangerous corner of my working for Brandon and try again. 'Look, Wendy, you need to grieve for Geoffrey. When anyone dies there's a heck of a lot of paper-work for the family to do. In Geoffrey's case, think of talking to the police in that light. It's necessary information to be filled in for them if his murderer is to be found. Only after that can you collapse and mourn properly. I don't know how close you were –' her blank face told me little – 'but we all have to go through it sometime or other.'

'I suppose you're right.' She'd obviously had enough of this view of the Weald – or of me – because she turned round and marched onwards, a sturdy defiant figure betraying nothing.

I was getting fed up with this, especially as it was she who had wanted to see me. I couldn't yet tell her about Green's double life as Philip Moxton, so I had one last try with the cards in my hand. 'Were you the only person in the village that Geoffrey was close to?'

To my relief, this seemed to work. 'There was an old man he used to visit occasionally. Sam West at Fairview House.'

'Any particular reason they were friendly?'

'I don't think they were close. Sam used to work in banking and accountancy and they both liked chess so that was probably the draw. Geoffrey was a financial adviser. And as for me, don't get the wrong impression, Jack. Geoffrey and I were companions, not lovers. He was divorced way back, and I was widowed five years ago. He came into the café every so often and once in a while I'd invite him down to my beach hut on the coast, or he'd come over to my house.'

Gently does it. Go steady. 'Did you visit his home?'

'Very occasionally. He wasn't retired and he travelled a lot on business, so he sometimes had to leave the café at short notice.'

'To go to London?' Or to Staveley House? I wondered.

'He never told me. He was often gone for days.'

'If he was in the financial world, what did you two have in common? Cars?'

'*Cars?*' She managed a laugh. 'He wasn't interested in cars and nor am I.'

'Not even old ones?' Like Packards, I wondered. Perhaps I'd been wrong and this wasn't Philip Moxton we were talking about. It was certainly getting interesting. Even if he was leading a double life, Philip wouldn't – surely couldn't – suppress an interest in classic cars if he had one. But if he had not given any indication to Wendy that he was a car buff, how on earth did the Packard fit into the story?

'I don't think so,' she replied. 'We both liked music. Oh – and yes – I forgot to tell you we went to Bayreuth for the Ring Cycle together. We went on a coach tour there.'

'Lucky you.' So surely this acquaintanceship must have been stronger than she'd indicated.

Wendy had a slight Wagnerian air about her in her determined sturdiness as she strode along the path. I could just see her as Brunhild, stirring up the Valkyrie sisterhood with a nice Nordic horned helmet. Not that this lady looked quite as tough as Brunhild but she might *think* she was. I wondered why, however, if the relationship was as she described, she had hesitated so much over talking about it.

'How long had Geoffrey lived in the village?' I prompted her.

'I think he came about seven years ago. My husband was alive then, so I only got to know Geoffrey after I opened the café four years ago.'

I had to push the issue. 'Forgive me for asking this, but though you might not have wanted more than companionship, did he?'

Wendy was ready for that. 'No. The reason he came to my home on occasion was only because it was more private. He wasn't a social mixer, and didn't like the idea that his neighbours might keep track of his visitors and stir up gossip that we were a regular item. My home is a barn conversion on a farm on the outskirts of Monksford. We used to own the farm but when my husband died I sold it together with the farmhouse and kept the conversion for myself.'

'Would you call Geoffrey a recluse?' I couldn't get to grips with Philip Moxton. What had made him tick? Women? Work? Fear? Isolation?

'Of course not,' she said surprised. 'He travelled a lot, he got tired and he liked relaxing.'

'Did he have children?' Had Philip Moxton ever mentioned his son Barnabas to her? He hadn't to me.

'He never spoke of any, nor about his former wife. I don't have children, so it didn't occur to me to ask. We just accepted each other.'

There was a note of pride in her voice, but to me it struck an unreal note. Curiosity is a natural human failing or talent, according to how one looks at it. On the other hand a lack of curiosity might have been one of things that had attracted Philip to Wendy. She seemed self-sufficient and the last thing he would want was someone curiously asking questions about his past life.

Wendy noticed my lack of comment. 'Are you implying Geoffrey might have been leading a double life with a wife and eight kids tucked away?'

'No,' I was able to say truthfully if misleadingly. Not unless eight kids belonged to that dreadful woman at Staveley House and she was not Miss but Mrs Moxton. Wendy's question made me push harder though.

'If you knew him only as a companion why are you hesitant about telling the police?'

She was ahead of me on the narrow path, and talking was difficult. There was no reply to my question and the Piper's Green pub was in sight. She was making it plain that the subject was now closed.

Nevertheless I had a text from her later that day to say she'd follow my advice about volunteering information to the police. She was going to be highly annoyed with me when the truth about Philip Moxton came out and she realized that I had been holding back on her, but I was more interested as to whether she was or would be on Brandon's suspect list as well as being a witness. She had seemed straightforward enough, despite her obstinacy, but I couldn't rule out the possibility – even likelihood – that she had been economical with the truth as to what her relationship had been with Geoffrey Green. Had she harboured thoughts of marrying him (with or without the knowledge of who he was) and then been rejected? Was there some other woman around? Did money come into the picture? The will for example? That raised a question in itself: did Geoffrey Green have a will of his own or was it Philip Moxton's?

None of my theories about Wendy or the Moxton case quite fitted. As theories go, I was in for a rough ride on a bumpy road. It proved even bumpier than I had expected. 'That dreadful woman' rang from Staveley House the following morning on the Frogs Hill office line and I nearly dropped the receiver as the familiar voice barked at me.

'Are you Jack Colby?'

Without waiting for anything more than a bleat of 'yes' from me, she swept on. 'I want you over here now.' The head teacher had spoken.

'But I can't—'

'You can. Staveley House,' she had the courtesy to add, in case I thought she'd moved to Moscow.

'For what reason?'

The news that Green was Philip Moxton was surely going to break at any moment, as the story of Green's murder had received great attention in the nationals. I found it hard to believe Miss Janes-cum-Moxton didn't know about the Green identity although it was possible Philip had kept the details from her and merely told her he had another residence for security purposes.

Reply came there none from the lady, the self-styled owner of Staveley House – as indeed she might now be. The last thing I wanted was to rush over to Staveley House again. I reminded myself that I was on Brandon's payroll and I had wanted to be involved for Philip's sake. Now I was, although technically I was in it only so far as determining whether the Packard and Golf had played any part in Geoffrey Green's murder and if so what. True, I felt I owed Philip Moxton for not having reacted to his declaration of fearing to be murdered, but dealing with his dotty sister was surely not part of my penitence.

Rebelliously I drove over to Staveley House once more. It was unlikely that Miss Moxton would be on her own with just John Carson and any other staff around. There'd be some police presence at least. There was indeed. A huge sign on the roadway announced the gateway's presence and two uniformed PCs guarded it. I could see no sign of Carson.

'Jack Colby,' I said, leaning out of the window. 'Appointment with Miss Moxton or Miss Janes.'

One PC stepped forward. He regarded me impassively. 'Who are they?'

Here we go again. 'One person and she lives at Staveley House.'

'You're not on my list. What's your business?'

I resisted temptation and showed him my police ID. 'Ring the house and tell whoever answers that I'm here. Police business.'

He did, with a distinct and grumpy expression that conveyed 'why didn't you say so in the first place?' and then barked out, 'And the name's Miss Joan Moxton for future reference.'

'It changes from time to time,' I informed him affably.

I left the Alfa in the car park there and walked up to the house with some foreboding. There had been several cars there, and one of them, a Bentley, hardly looked like the latest police issue so I wondered what awaited me. Downing Street?

Only one car was parked in the forecourt of Staveley House, the Packard, and a fine sight it was. I doubted whether it had been moved since I came to visit the gardens with Cara. It looked lonelier than ever.

The door flew open almost immediately I pressed the bell, and there stood Joan Moxton, alias Miss Janes, in corduroy trousers, smock, that greying black hair and fierce expression. I could see no offensive weapon in her hand, but I kept my distance just in case.

'You took your time,' she informed me.

'I have a fair way to drive,' I said mildly, 'and a business to run.'

'So I'm told.'

She didn't welcome me in. She didn't even invite me in. All she said was: 'Take that away.'

She waved a hand indicating I should turn around. I did so and saw the only object to which she could be referring as 'that'.

'The Packard?' I was astounded. 'What's gone wrong with it?'

'Nothing. I just want it gone. Out of here. For good. Here are the keys – and all the registration documents.' She thrust a large envelope into my bewildered possession together with the car keys.

I struggled with reason. 'You want to sell it?'

'No, just get rid of it. Keep it for all I care.'

I cleared my throat. An excellent if self-conscious method of gathering one's wits and preparing for battle.

'Are you the Packard's legal owner, Miss Moxton?'

'How would I know? Just take it.'

'Then how do I know?'

This confused her. 'My brother's dead. That means I can have the car and give it to whom I please. You. Take it.'

I stood my ground. 'But I have to be sure who does own it now that your brother has died. It's early days and there's probate to consider.'

'Oh very well,' she said impatiently. 'Come in and talk to him.'

For a moment I thought she meant her brother, but even Joan wasn't that confused. When I followed her into Staveley House for my second – and I hoped last visit – she led me to the room where I had talked with Philip. At the table sat two middle-aged men, both looking so staid and uncomfortable that they looked out of place in this madhouse. I knew one, by sight anyway. It was Timothy Mild, who as CEO of Moxtons had been Philip's bosom friend, or perhaps enemy – or both. He looked at me with a companionable 'we're in this together' nod, as we formally introduced ourselves. Joan had shown no sign of doing so.

'Tell this man what you told me,' she ordered the other man, who had so many papers in front of him he was obviously a solicitor, accountant or executor. He was studying them with such intensity that his embarrassment was obvious.

'Something about the Packard standing outside?' I prompted him. 'Miss Moxton seems to want me to take it away, but I'd like to know more about the legal situation of ownership before I consider doing so.'

As Joan still refrained from introducing me, Timothy did the job for him. 'Jack Colby, James. The police mentioned him to us. James Hall is Philip's solicitor and executor, Jack.'

James rather reluctantly rose to his feet. 'Could I . . . er . . .'

I helped him out. 'See my police ID. Certainly.'

He examined it for so long I feared he was going to accuse

me of faking it, but perhaps he was merely still embarrassed. Anyway, I was duly accepted into the magic circle, if three can be a circle. 'I was called in by the police over Geoffrey Green's death,' I began experimentally.

No one looked puzzled, so that situation was clear.

'The very idea that my brother was murdered because he was Philip Moxton is quite ridiculous,' Joan boomed in. 'Clearly some village lout killed him.'

'You knew he had this alias?'

'Of course. I'm not a fool. Philip had this absurd notion that he would be murdered so now he is dead everyone assumes he was killed because of who he was. It was clearly someone who wanted to steal his Golf. This ridiculous arrangement of two names was entirely his idea. His residence was here, but if anyone called whose name or face I did not know, I had to deny all knowledge of him. If it was someone I did know, I should telephone him and he would make an appointment to be here. I would point out, however, that it was as Geoffrey Green that he was killed. Nevertheless, I agreed to his plan. I had no choice. It seemed reasonable enough.'

Put that way, it did. 'Is Philip Moxton's dual life as Green now established without doubt?' I asked James Hall.

'Yes. Miss Moxton has identified him. There is bank documentation too.'

So that was one problem out of the way. Now for the next. 'What is the legal position over the Packard?' I asked. 'Did Geoffrey Green as well as Philip Moxton leave a will?'

Timothy Mild hooted with laughter. 'That would muddy the waters nicely.'

James Hall paled at such levity. 'I have been in touch with a solicitor who occasionally acted for Geoffrey Green. He has not mentioned one. However, you may be assured that I have given Miss Moxton my permission for you to take the car away now. It was bequeathed to her in Mr Moxton's will and the car was registered in his name, so you need have no fear in taking the Packard.'

Joan looked grimly satisfied. I wasn't sure that I was, however.

'That might not be enough if I sell the car on her behalf.' It occurred to me that I was talking as though I was actively wanting to take it, which was a sobering thought. It was an attractive beast and my instinctive love of classic cars made me think it deserved a better home than with Miss Moxton. Perhaps I should give it back to the previous owners, despite the fact that they too seemed anxious to be rid of it. Or perhaps she should. I doubted whether she would though. She might even send it for scrap.

The thought of that warm buttery princess standing out there on the forecourt, lonely and unloved, made me realize that I couldn't risk that. The word sell however had enraged Joan Moxton.

'Do as you like with the damned car,' she yelled at me. 'But I told you not to sell it. To *no one*.'

'I couldn't guarantee to keep it. I might have to give it away, perhaps to a museum.'

A silence, which Joan at last broke. 'If you must, but *not* to the Herricks.'

Now we were getting somewhere. James Hall and Timothy Mild seemed to be paying attention to anything but what was going on between Joan and myself.

'You do know the Herricks then? Of course you do,' I quickly added. 'They were here at the Staveley Gardens Open Day.'

A withering glance. 'I know them. I don't like them.'

'How about your nephew, Barnabas? Mr Moxton had a son, I believe.'

Timothy speedily rejoined the discussion. 'Barnabas is about to become a very rich man. I doubt if he needs an old Packard.'

James Hall replied speedily too. 'As the car was specifically willed to Miss Moxton, I think you may be assured that Barnabas will not be contesting the issue.'

'Wouldn't he like the opportunity of having it now that Miss Moxton has declared she doesn't want to take the gift up?'

James Hall hesitated. 'That is up to you, Mr Colby.'

Timothy wasn't going to leave it at that. 'I think you'd find he's not interested, Jack.' He seemed rather amused.

No one seemed inclined to expand on this, which left me with one problem. 'If I take it, I'd have to return tomorrow for the Packard. I've driven my Alfa here.'

'Oh really, Mr Colby,' Joan said impatiently. 'One objection after the other. You can return for the Alfa. I want the Packard gone *now* and that's all there is to it.'

This woman really was single-minded, but I wasn't going to

give way. She'd make the decision for me, however. I couldn't leave the car in her hands. It would be at the scrap merchants within hours.

'Tomorrow, Miss Moxton,' I repeated. 'I'll take the car at your request, but I have a business to run.'

At this point Timothy intervened. 'You take the Packard now, Jack. I'll drive your Alfa back to your home. I can get a taxi over to mine.'

'That's good of you,' I said gratefully, 'but—'

'Not that good.' He laughed. 'My car's at home, not here. James gave me a lift but I live near Smarden and I gather you're near Piper's Green.'

'I'll run you back to Smarden afterwards.'

It was a done deal, and we walked out to the cars together as I handed over the Alfa keys. 'This murder must have hit you hard,' I said. 'You must have worked closely with Philip Moxton.'

He considered this. 'Yes, and we got on reasonably well, but he was chair and I'm CEO. Not an easy relationship.'

A man with my bank balance could hardly chat about the higher echelons of banking today, and he seemed anxious to avoid that subject after we arrived at Frogs Hill and had a quick coffee together. That meant I was searching for common ground. Despite his aura of hail fellow well met and general air of affability, there was a sense of power about Timothy that made me think I wouldn't want to work with him. He didn't seem to be a classic car enthusiast and in order to get back to the subject of Philip, I had to force the issue.

'I met Philip on one or two occasions. He must be a huge loss to the bank.'

He shot a glance at me. 'The founder – or in this case the founder's son – is always a big loss. There are often compensations – in business terms, I mean.'

'As in this case?'

He smiled. 'Perhaps. We shall see. The bank is on the brink of an exciting future.'

'This rumoured merger?'

I expected him to slither past this but he grasped the nettle. 'Just so. Philip was a traditionalist so he was often up against the modernists.'

'Such as yourself.'

'Indeed, Jack. Such as myself.'

He was frank enough about his differences with Philip then, but he would be used to putting as many cards on the table as possible in difficult situations. It didn't alter the fact that he would have had plenty of reason to want Philip out of the way.

Indeed, there seemed to be plenty of motives for people to want him removed. The arrival of a large fortune for the son and perhaps for the sister too could be motive enough. And then there was the Packard to consider. Could something that had arrived so close to his death and which was clearly of great importance to him be a contributory factor? If so I was now holding the baby and a very large baby it was. What on earth were Len and Zoe going to say? It's one thing admiring such a car from afar. To have it on one's doorstep for ever is another matter. It was like a puppy that was outgrowing the excitement of its arrival. But I was morally obliged not to sell it. What then? Put it in the next Women's Institute raffle?

Meanwhile Dave Jennings had asked me to call at Charing HQ. He'd called this morning and it was now past lunchtime, so he wasn't too happy, when I arrived. 'About that Golf, Jack.'

Not the Packard. We were back to the Volkswagen. 'Do you and Brandon really want me to go all out on that?' I asked. 'Your team's far better equipped than I am.'

'This case is different, worse luck. I've got my lot working the usual routes, but Brandon wants you nosing around on it too. You know why, don't you? He's up against it with the Met and is clutching on to you in the hope these cars will provide a line he can call his own.'

'Fair enough. But you could tackle that, so why me? Not,' I added hastily, 'that I don't want the job.'

'You met Moxton over that Packard and, hey presto, Moxton is found dead. On the off chance you're right about the cars being linked to the murder, he gets the credit, so that's why he wants you on board and not sailing off to the Pacific for a seaside holiday.'

'Very flattering.'

'Not really,' Dave said seriously. 'He's covering his back and hoping for a winner. Have you any leads on the Golf yet?'

'No. I've put the word out to my best channel though.'

'Could be an amateur job. Keep on trying the usual suspects

if only for the look of the thing though. And get in with the Monksford locals. Brandon thinks you have charm in this respect. I don't see it myself.'

'I do my best,' I murmured modestly.

'Sniff, Jack, *sniff.*' Dave dropped the banter. 'For all our sakes. Brandon could be lost over this – and if he's lost, we're all gonners. Ta, ta, Jack.'

I returned late from a briefing by Dave's team over the Volkswagen and it was nearly dark by the time I reached Frogs Hill. I had something to eat and then went upstairs to blessed bed. And the doorbell rang! Last time it had rung this late in the evening . . .

It rang again. The security lights were blazing and I could not only see the Packard but another familiar car parked at its side. An old Vauxhall. Wearily I made my way downstairs and opened the door.

'Goodnight, Pen,' I greeted her. 'Good to have seen you again.' I tried to close the door. It was a good try, but it failed.

A foot encased in an inelegant trainer was put in the doorway. 'Just passing, Jack. I did ask you whether you'd robbed any banks recently. I see you've taken my advice and brought the loot home. What a car, eh? You've been holding out on me, Jack. It's payback time.'

SIX

'**N**o comment,' I answered briefly, ignoring the foot. 'Oh?' said Pen. 'That sounds interesting. Here for a restoration job, is it? I don't think so.'

'No comment.'

Once in a while Pen takes the hint and goes away. Tonight she didn't. She stood there beaming, glasses slipping down the quivering nose and foot remaining firmly positioned.

'A *real* story then.' She said it with relish, and it wasn't a question.

This was a battle of wits, I realized. I had either to invite her in or tell her to get lost – and either choice would give her the whip hand, in which case I would be ceding the issue. I couldn't risk that. She'd become the world's most persistent stalker.

'Police case,' I told her, not budging an inch.

She looked highly satisfied. 'So it *is* Philip Moxton.'

'What is?' I asked guardedly.

'That murder victim over in Monksford.'

'Police case.'

'Great,' she said with even more relish. 'The Met and the rest will be moving in. Best news I've heard in weeks. His Packard was it?'

'What was?' I'd been taken off guard so I hurriedly repeated, 'Police case.' This at last got through to her.

'Understood,' she said seriously. The good thing about Pen is that up to a point you can trust her. The bad thing is that you don't know what that point is. As now.

'I heard a whisper . . .' she began reflectively.

'And no doubt turned it into a clarion call of truth,' I finished for her.

'As if,' she snorted. 'I'm getting cold out here, Jack.'

'Sorry, Pen. I'm knackered. And I can't go any further anyway.'

'You haven't gone anywhere yet,' she pointed out sourly. 'Is it true that a Packard just like this one was involved in a bank robbery once way back?'

'*The Ladykillers*,' I said promptly.

'Not a movie. For real.'

'Quite possible. All those thirties robberies in the USA.'

'No, here in the UK.'

'*Here?*'

She had caught me off guard and she recognized victory. 'Just wondered. Goodnight, Jack. Sweet dreams.'

'What?' Len grunted, 'is this doing here?'

The Packard was still standing outside the Pits. I hadn't known where to put it for one thing, so I'd brazened it out. To me it gleamed of gold, it spoke of ages past, it conjured up fond memories of Alec Guinness, of old Hollywood films. True it looked out of place in rural Kent, but so what?

'It's back,' I told him nonchalantly.

'What's wrong with it? Was it the wrong car after all?' Zoe asked.

'Right car.'

I'd heard on the radio this morning that the truth was out. The murder victim in Monksford was now believed to be Philip Moxton. That should take the wind out of Pen's sails, I thought, somewhat relieved. Pen likes an exclusive on whatever line she follows up. Whichever she chose, she'd have plenty of company.

Len and Zoe had heard the news too. 'But what's it doing here, not where that poor chap was murdered?' Zoe demanded.

'He wasn't so poor. And his murderer doesn't have to have been someone who had it in for Philip Moxton. It could have been a spur of the moment attack on Geoffrey Green either for cash or his car.'

This was ignored. 'So they got him after all,' Zoe reflected. 'Didn't you tell us Moxton was scared of being murdered?' She gave a scathing look at the Packard. 'How long's it going to stay here?' she demanded.

'I don't know.'

My turn to receive the scathing look, then Zoe voted with her feet and returned to the Pits. Which left Len and me to sort out the Packard.

We regarded it together, as I broke the news. 'It's mine,' I told him.

His head turned to me in disbelief. 'You *are* going to sell it, aren't you?'

'Not yet.'

Len looked at me suspiciously, then turned back to the Packard.

'Beast of a car,' he finally growled.

'Magnificent beast though.'

I felt defensive. There it sat, over seventy years old. It had seen life, but what life? I wondered. Did Pen's hint that this car had been involved in a UK bank robbery have any foundation? It was a right-hand drive, so it could have been here since it left the Packard company in 1936, according to Philip. Nevertheless why did Pen think it might be *this* car involved? Its registration number was comparatively modern. The chassis and engine numbers would be a giveaway, but they would have been beyond Pen's powers to check. Besides she'd shown no sign of wanting to get closer to the Packard. My conclusion was that either she was on a fishing expedition or that she knew something about the car that her boss had seen for sale and that it must be this one.

'Ever heard of a *real* bank robbery in this country using a thirties Packard?' I asked Len hopefully. 'Not just *The Ladykillers?*' 'I wasn't around in the thirties,' he growled. 'Or the forties.' 'I've always imagined you were born with a monkey wrench as a rattle and that oil rag of yours in your hand.'

Len gave a sniff, which could be taken either way and he too marched back to the Pits, where he didn't have to take insults from the boss. On the other hand, now that Len and Zoe had both washed their hands of me and the Packard, I didn't have to explain more fully how the car got here. That tricky tale could be postponed. I couldn't see them taking kindly to the Packard becoming a fixture. Nice guest, but forget permanent lodger.

Meanwhile I decided to remove the Packard to the safety of the rear barn, hoping the Gordon-Keeble and Lagonda wouldn't be too snooty at the arrival of a shiny yellow Packard older than either of them.

Once out of sight, I managed to put it temporarily out of my mind so that I could concentrate on the Volkswagen. It was almost a relief.

Dave's team had covered the ports and other obvious channels, but I had a feeling that the Golf was a lot nearer to home. All due respect but the stolen goods market in Volkswagens is not a high-powered one. I therefore pondered my next step, if, as I suspected, it was shut up in someone's garage or barn until the fuss had died down. The hitch in that theory is that family and neighbours have to be in on the secret otherwise the arrival of an unknown car might occasion comment, even excitement. 'Looking after it for a friend' can also lead to complications. In any case, the key question for me was where to start. It was an unusual theft, because an opportunist thief would have to be desperate to break in and leave a trail of evidence behind. It still seemed to me that DCI Brandon and Dave Jennings were better equipped than I was to follow this trail, so they must really be keen on my uncovering a link between either one, or both, of these cars and the murder.

My only hope was that the thief, amateur or professional, would want to rid himself of the Golf sooner or later and therefore my route had to be through the professional gateway. I'd told Dave that I had set my best contact on it and that was true. This is my chum Brian, a professional spider who creeps unseen into all the webs around him. My speciality, and his, is classic car theft, however, so I was less sure of my ground with him over a modern car. As the pace was speeding up, I decided to call him to see how it was going. As usual he picked up, asked my name and put the phone down. He does that every time. He can speak, but he likes to know to whom he's speaking, so he prefers to call you back. Which he'll do if he knows your number. Being a professional, he believes in order, if not law, so he rang back immediately.

'Give me a break, Jack,' he pleaded. 'You told me it was a hot job, but I didn't bloody realize it was this hot. No one will touch it now.' He sounded almost aggrieved that I'd had to trouble him – despite the fact that win or lose he rakes in a tidy sum of money for being a nark. 'Forget me,' he continued. 'Try the Volkswagen chap round your way.'

'He does just Volkswagens?'

'*Naturellement*, old sport. A specialist, you might say. Pinches anything from a Ghia to a Golf. Richie Carson.'

My heartbeat became a thump. I'd been missing a trick. 'John Carson's son.'

'Wouldn't know. Nasty piece of work is Richie.'

This was the second time I'd had this warning and that meant he was really bad news. I wondered whether Richie and John worked hand in glove with each other.

'Any weevils around?'

Weevil is the word Brian likes to use because it delicately avoids the term nark or grass or snitch. None of the latter go down well with interested third parties who might have joined us unheard.

'Not known. You're on your own with this lot. Good luck.'

'Thanks.' I put down the phone and wondered if there was anyone from whom I could call in favours. I was going to need them. Most of those who really owed me wouldn't come into contact with the likes of Carson, although there was one who was worth trying. A lad who owed me for turning a blind eye when his mates were jumped on by Dave's men. Highly irregular but I wasn't sure he was guilty and while I was 'looking the other way' he scarpered. But he *was* guilty after all. It taught me a lesson but it didn't seem to have taught him one.

He was keen enough to repay the favour, and he knew exactly how to get hold of Richie Carson. It had surprisingly quick results, because Mr Richie rang back himself mid-afternoon. One might almost think my contact was working for him . . . Richie was amazingly keen to drop in at Frogs Hill but the mere thought of Len's face if Richie's reputation had spread to him made me suggest a pub. 'Don't want to bring you all this way,' I said tactfully.

'Too public, Jack me lad. Coffee shops are better.' He named one in Ashford.

'How do I recognize you?'

'You will.'

I did. When I reached the meeting place, he was already there, sitting at the rear, smartly dressed in sober blazer and dark trousers. No tie, but then he wouldn't want to look conspicuous, he told me. He had to be joking, of course. We stood out a mile in this conglomeration of suntanned youngsters and mums with pushchairs. But he was right in one way. No one took the slightest interest in us. I think I'd have known Richie despite his dress code. I have a feeling for the Richies of this world. They are with you and they aren't. They don't fit. They're like Kipling's cat. They walk alone. He was of medium height, medium build and at first sight inoffensive. So, no doubt, was Napoleon.

'You work for the cops, Jack.' It was a statement, not a question.

'I do. The Car Crime Unit. Freelance on the classic car side.'

Cards were on the table and this didn't seem to bother him. 'Just like to know where I am. What do you want with me? And whatever it is, remember it's a favour.'

'Noted. It's just one Golf I'm interested in. All I need to know is whether it's been through your hands or if it's currently in them. If that's the case we'll need to have it back and know where it came from. No questions asked. It's a murder case.'

'What murder case might that be?' He was taking a lot of interest in his coffee.

Dangerous corner coming up, and I took it at full speed. 'The Moxton case. He owned the garden where your father works.'

He nodded. 'Yeah. Killed at Monksford.'

It seemed as if I had passed the corner, with a straight road ahead – I hoped.

'Your father's the gardener at Staveley House, right?'

A long pause. 'Dad's OK, Jack. You just remember that. And ill winds and all that too. The gardens go to Moxton's sister, so that's my dad happy. Him and those gardens – don't think of nothing else, does Dad. You remember that, Jack, and we'll get on just fine. One track mind and let the rest of the world go by. So this car then. The Golf. The car that bloke went to and fro in from Staveley to Monksford. No reason I shouldn't turn it back to you if it comes in, but you'd be advised to keep the details to yourself. If it's already gone, I'll tell you now. Deal?'

'Deal, except that if it's material to the murder I can't guarantee the small print.'

He thought this through. 'Fair enough,' he said obligingly. 'Keep me in the loop, though. Deal?'

I wasn't going to get any further, so I gave him the registration and other information. 'Deal on both counts.'

He promptly consulted his iPad. 'Not listed.'

'Could it have been through your hands on false plates?'

'Nope.'

I decided not to enquire just how he could be sure of that. There's such a thing as professional secrets.

'If you haven't seen it, is it possible it could have gone through other channels?'

He looked at me pityingly. 'It could, my friend. But it wouldn't. Might start out that way, but word would reach me. It ain't come. OK?'

I had to stick with that. 'OK.'

'And one more thing,' Richie added. 'No dealing with my dad over this, eh? Dad and me don't follow the same trades. Not even on the same page. He calls me every now and then and that's the lot. Understand?'

I did. The soft voice didn't fool me at all. The message came over loud and clear.

'You're no gardener, I take it.'

Richie chuckled. 'Gardens don't move. Cars do. He only wants one thing out of life does Dad. That garden of his at Staveley. He thinks it's his, anyway. Met him, have you?'

'I have. I don't think we'll become bosom friends.'

'Not advisable. Might get on his wrong side. Or mine,' he added amicably. 'Remember that too. We're only human, Dad and me. There's only so much we'll take.'

Could I trust him? (Well, within limits anyway.) Trust and car crime are uneasy bedfellows, but I reasoned that in this case he had nothing to gain by lying.

I'd done all I could on the Golf, short of personally checking every barn and garage in the country, so I turned back to the Packard. It had a story that might or might not have relevance to Moxton's murder, but if it did, the key to it must surely lie with Tom and Moira Herrick. They proved elusive both by telephone and email so I risked turning up on the off chance on Friday morning, hoping they didn't have the same intricate procedure for repelling invaders as Philip Moxton had used. Moira opened the door, and her face promptly dropped out of gear. She stared at me blankly, completely thrown. I couldn't blame her. She was clad in jeans and smock and looked as though Packards were the last thing on her mind.

'Tom's out,' she managed to say, her usual calm nowhere to be seen.

'I was in the neighbourhood and wanted a brief word about the Packard, so I thought I'd try my luck.' I endeavoured to sound disarming and not like a police bloodhound.

'Oh.' Her face moved back into gear, as miraculously Tom appeared behind her. He was doing a good impression of being heartily glad to see me.

'Come in, come in,' he cried.

So in I went, despite the stormy look that Moira was offering him – and me. Perhaps I was wrong about that, however. It was more glazed than stony as she led me into what Tom announced as his study.

Coffee was offered, a stroll round the garden, a chat, a chair – it appeared nothing was too much trouble, as Tom fussed around me.

I let them lead the conversation, but the word desultory would sum it up best, until I broke in at a time of my choosing.

'I thought I'd pop in to tell you that I own the Packard now, at least temporarily.'

The look on their faces was a joy to behold. 'Joan's sold it to you?' Moira asked incredulously.

'Moira!' Tom intervened sharply, but it was too late and they both knew it. Their relationship with the Moxtons was far closer than they'd claimed.

Moira burst into tears and fled the room. I felt somewhat guilty, although it seemed an extreme reaction for such a poised woman.

Tom attempted a comeback. 'We saw the car at that open day at Staveley. Got to know the Moxtons there. Terrible news about the murder.'

'Yes,' I agreed. 'And that's the reason you're going to tell me how you knew them, and how the Packard comes into it.'

He looked defeated, his fingers drumming on the arm of the chair. I could afford to wait while he thought up a story. He seemed genuine enough, but he was an actor after all and could be acting now. I ostentatiously looked round the room to give him time to dream up an explanation. There was a portrait of his father on the wall; Gavin Herrick had been a young man then, but had that same look of amusement that he could communicate so well on stage and screen. There was also one of his wife by the same artist judging by the style. It had a lightness of touch that conveyed a sparkling, lively woman, who had matured from the eager young bride in the wedding photo.

'Is your mother still alive?' I asked, as a run-up to nailing him on the Packard.

'No, she died when I was fourteen.'

The interlude seemed to do the trick. 'You say *you* own the Packard now?' Tom said brightly.

'Yes. Cleared by Philip Moxton's solicitor.'

'Why did you buy it?' His tone changed to belligerence, which was interesting.

'I didn't. His sister Joan gave it to me.'

'She did *what*?' Tom managed – acting or not – to look both furious and nervous at the same time.

'I'm far from eager to keep it. In fact,' I lied, 'the reason I came to see you today was to ask if you'd like it back. No charge. Expenses only.'

Tom gazed at me, then began to laugh hysterically, which brought Moira running back into the room. 'He wants to hand it back to us, Moira. Joan *gave* it to him.'

Moira went very pale, but she was back in full control. 'You must think this very strange, Jack.'

'I do.' I noted the friendly use of 'Jack'. So they must think it was time for the truth – or part of it.

Tom gave her a kind of nod and she continued, 'We realized right away it must have been Philip Moxton who commissioned you to find and buy the car. Only he would have . . .'

'Wanted it to be an anonymous sale,' Tom amplified for her when she hesitated.

'Why?'

'It was a sort of –' his turn to hesitate, then he added lightly – 'game.'

'Who were the players?' I asked. This had all the hallmarks of another fantasy being spun for me.

'Tom's father Gavin,' Moira said bitterly. 'And Philip.'

Tom broke in again. 'It goes back further than Philip. His father Donald. He and Gavin were old mates.'

If Donald was anything like Philip in character, I couldn't see the image of 'old mates' being applicable, but I murmured something appropriate. 'So what was the game?'

They seemed at a loss for words, so I asked again.

'It was to do with the Packard,' Tom managed to say. 'Whoever owned it was top dog.'

So far not much fun in this so-called game. 'Then why didn't one refuse to sell it to the other?' I asked reasonably enough. 'Or not sell it at all if this anonymous lark was the regular pattern?'

'It wasn't quite like that,' Tom muttered. 'Both Gavin and Donald went through hard times, lost track of each other and had to sell the car, but somehow or other the other one always got it back. That was the game. That's what we called it . . .' His voice trailed off, perhaps seeing my incredulous expression.

'So why did you sell it to me if you knew Philip Moxton to be the anonymous purchaser and if you didn't want him to have it?'

I wasn't buying this rigmarole. At the back of my mind I remembered Philip's obsession with security and his conviction that he was going to be murdered. Had I been the bait, and taken this couple right to him? Even if that was the case, however, Philip had agreed to take the risk.

Tom's answer was speedy, too speedy perhaps. 'Because,' he

told me, 'we and our daughter Emma thought enough was more than enough after the recent death of my father. We knew Philip would then be looking for the car. Donald Moxton died twenty or so years ago. It would be no use our giving the car to Philip – he had to obtain it for himself to play the game. We wanted him to have it and for that to be the end of it. Even my father agreed that before he died.'

Getting better, but I still was not convinced by this weird tale. The coincidence of the timing was too great between the Packard sale and Philip Moxton's murder. They were both looking too bright-eyed and on edge for this to be a complete confession. More, perhaps, a try-on, or, if I were charitable, a partial truth.

I wasn't here to be charitable. 'And now?'

'Philip is dead,' Tom said flatly. 'We don't know how and can't see how the Packard could have been involved. That's why Joan gave the car to you. She has decided as we did that enough is enough. The game is over.'

Moira looked much brighter. 'So you see that's all there is to it,' she informed me. 'No way do we want the car back.'

Tom picked up somewhat more graciously. 'Good of you to think of it though, Jack. Thanks.'

First the shock-horror of the car being handed over to me, now apparently all was well that ended well. If this was their farewell note, it failed. 'What about Philip's son, Barnabas?' I asked. 'Doesn't he have a say in this? Do you know him?'

A pause. 'We've met,' Tom replied.

'Wouldn't he want the Packard?'

I fully intended to find this out direct from the horse's mouth, but I was interested to hear the Herricks' answer.

The pause was even longer this time. 'I can't answer for Barney,' Tom said.

Throw the dice one more time. 'One last question then. How can you be so sure this game of yours had nothing to do with Philip Moxton's murder?'

Tom was eager to reply. 'The Packard is not worth much by Moxton standards, so I hardly think it could have influenced his death. After all, his sister has given it to you, which surely suggests it's unimportant. Just a family matter.'

He sat back with what seemed a huge sigh of relief and from

the cool smile that played around Moira's lips she shared it. Why?

I duly reported back on this so-called game to Brandon and Dave, but neither grew excited and I could see why. An old game, even if it was more feud than game, could hardly have led to a relentless tracking down of Moxton's whereabouts in Monksford.

Both Brandon and Dave had told me to carry on the Packard line though, as well as the Golf. 'The son's a weird fish,' Brandon told me, when I said I'd like to check the Packard out with him. 'Not close to his father.'

'Did the son mention anything about a game between the two families?'

'No. Might do if questioned though. Want to meet him? Every reason to as you own it now.'

'True.' I'd been going to hunt down Barnabas anyway, but it was nice to have official blessing. 'What about the divorced wife?' I didn't want her descending on me for damages if I got rid of the Packard.

'Off the radar. Lives in France. There's one woman you might think about though. Wendy Parks.'

My antennae shot up. 'What's she got to do with the Packard?'

'Nothing so far as I know. But Geoffrey Green rang her at seven thirty on the evening he was killed.'

'And she didn't mention it to you?'

'She said she didn't take the call. She was out that evening. No message left.'

I hadn't heard from her since our meeting, apart from her text, so this was news to me. Another question mark where Wendy was concerned. I was about to end the call when it occurred to me to ask: 'What's so weird about Moxton's son?'

'You'll see.'

I saw.

Barnabas Moxton lived in Rye. Twenty-four Lowther Street didn't sound like the palatial mansion where the son of Philip Moxton might be living. I made my way through the cobbled streets of the old town which is dramatically perched on top of a hill. Once a port, Rye is now a mile or so from the sea and below it stretches marshland, a paradise for wild life.

Number 24 proved to be one of a terrace of old cottages in a side lane off one of the main streets of the town, but it wasn't merely a dwelling house. The ground floor was a small arts and crafts shop, with a window stuffed full of paintings, pots, and odds and ends. Some looked excellent quality and some were aimed at tourists alone. At first I assumed Barnabas was living over someone else's shop, but finding no side entrance I went in to enquire. Barnabas answered charmingly to his name.

Weird? He was about thirty, blond, healthy-looking, and standing in his emporium packed with vases, cups, plates, mugs, books and pictures he looked rather like a Greek god who has unexpectedly found himself imprisoned in a cave. I explained who I was and why I was there, but after a careful glance at me he seemed more interested in some books he was rearranging on a table.

'Are you the potter, Mr Moxton?' I enquired, taken aback.

He blinked. 'Everyone calls me Barney. And yes, I am the potter only I'm not very good at it, so I sell other people's stuff too.'

This was disconcerting, because I could see his point when he waved a tentative hand towards a row of plates and vases. 'What about the paintings?' I asked.

'I'm not too good at that either.'

'What *are* you good at?' I asked, amused.

'Birds.'

I blinked. Anyone less likely to be an automatic switch-on for women once they had got past the initial Greek god image, I have yet to meet. Luckily I didn't comment because he continued, 'I'm a twitcher. Birdwatcher. I go birdwatching when I can and I paint them a bit too. The marshes are a superb sanctuary – I think there was even a redshank there the other day though that's unlikely since they're not normally seen in this part of England.'

Belatedly it dawned on me that most of the books, paintings and pots had a common theme. They pictured birds from fowls to falcons.

'If I paint Rye on them, they sell,' he told me ingenuously. 'So I do all right. After all, they are authentic.'

'But your father—'

'I know what you're thinking. That my father supports me, so it doesn't matter if I don't make a living. But he doesn't – didn't – and

I do,' he told me defiantly, then switched subjects. 'You said it's the car you've come about.'

I had, but I was still bemused by Barney Moxton. 'Doesn't your wife or partner object to the birdwatching? Or does she share it?' This was a fishing expedition on my part, but that's why I was here.

'Partner. And I'm not sure if she objects. I've sort of mislaid her.'

I gazed at him wondering if he was for real. He grinned.

'I'm not as daft as I sometimes sound,' he assured me. 'She comes and goes. She likes towns and I like the country. We're not actually married. That would be difficult as a lot of my bird-watching is at night.'

'I can understand that.' An odd way to run a relationship, I thought, but who was I to talk? Louise had come – and gone – in my life. At least Barney's lady came back.

'I'm very sorry about your father,' I told him.

'So am I,' he said seriously. 'I loved him very much. It's just that we didn't get on. Will the police find out who killed him?'

'I'm sure they will. Do you have any idea who might have done it?'

'No, not yet. I have been thinking about it. I don't think Aunt Joan would have killed him, would she? I'd hate to think that.'

'It could have been someone who knew him as Geoffrey Green. Did you know about that alias he used?'

'No. Did you?'

'I didn't, but I've seen where he lived as Geoffrey Green and could see how he must have enjoyed that.'

'Good.' He nodded slowly. 'That's nice to know, because I don't think he enjoyed Staveley very much, not like Aunt Joan does. He's left the gardens to her and the right to live in the house. Did you know that?'

'No.'

'He's left me nearly everything else. It's a responsibility, you know. But I think I'll still do it.'

'Do what?' I asked, but a tourist had come in and Barney's attention was now on selling her a pot and explaining that the bird painted on it was a greenfinch, not a goldfinch. I switched back to the car. 'Your father bought a classic 1936 Packard through me before his death,' I said when we were alone again.

'He bequeathed it to your aunt and she's given it to me outright. The solicitor okayed it. Is it OK with you?'

'Oh yes. I heard about it.' Barney didn't seem very interested in it, but I felt I should make doubly sure.

'I'm happy to give it to you,' I offered.

'I already have a car,' he said simply.

'Not a Packard, I imagine – not that it would be an ideal choice for someone living in Rye.'

'My father wouldn't have liked to hear you refer to *a* Packard. It was always *the* Packard. Like Sherlock Holmes, you know.'

I was bemused.

'Irene Adler was always *the* woman,' he explained. 'Just one word can make a difference. But I don't want *the* Packard, thank you.'

I tried a random shot. '*The* Packard? Because of the game?'

An instant shutter fell over his face. It had obviously rung a bell with him so there might be something to be gained in pursuing this line, despite its being an unlikely one. 'The game your father apparently played with the Herrick family, beginning with Gavin and your grandfather Donald?'

'That's over,' he said. The loquacious Barney had vanished and his lips were tightly closed. What did that tell me? I'm no psychologist but I do my best with what senses I've been given. They were telling me to go forward.

'Not for me it isn't,' I told him. 'I'm concerned because a journalist I know implied that the car had something to do with a bank robbery. Was it stolen in one?'

'No.' He was fidgeting with a couple of mugs on display.

I pressed on. 'It couldn't have been in a recent robbery. A Packard would stand out a mile.'

'The game really is over,' he said almost piteously.

I felt a brute for pushing further, but I was driving without a map and since I had to work with Brandon's satnav for this journey as well as my own, that meant accelerating into unknown territory.

'Not,' I repeated, 'for me.'

I'd no idea what reaction I might get, but I certainly couldn't have foreseen this one.

A heavy sigh. 'Then you'll have to come to the barbecue.'

SEVEN

When I left Barney I was only slightly less perplexed than when he had first delivered his invitation to the barbecue. What was this barbecue all about? He hadn't made this clear, save that it was taking place on Saturday evening and that of all people the *Herricks* were officially hosting it. Nevertheless it was some sort of joint event with him and probably one or two others. This left me up a gumtree, as the saying goes. A sticky situation up or down. Apparently Barney knew the Herricks well enough not only to be invited to the barbecue but to share it with them *and* invite me as well. Plus a companion if I wished. He didn't mind a bit, even when I experimentally suggested Wendy Parks.

Strange. Even stranger, however, seemed the inappropriateness of his sharing a barbecue so relatively soon after Philip's death with a family that had at the very least a long-standing rivalry with the Moxtons. Nevertheless Barney had assured me that it was in no way celebratory of anything. I wasn't to think that at all.

'I liked your father,' I had said to Barney, completely bewildered.

He had flushed. 'It's a gathering to show that the game really is over. My father would have approved.'

This didn't sound 'in no way celebratory' to me. 'Who won?' I asked.

'No one. That's the point,' he told me earnestly.

'Should I arrive in the Packard then?' I had meant it sarcastically, but he took it seriously.

'That's a brilliant idea.'

Some game, I thought, but nevertheless it was an opportunity to be seized. Curiosity proverbially killed the cat, but I reckoned I would still have six lives left even if I was the one who ended up barbecued.

I spent the next few days glued to my computer, following up Pen's bank robbery hint. I had no success though, and concluded that Pen was as much in the dark as I was. She had merely been casting out flies to catch unwary fishes. I also devoted myself to the history of Moxtons as an independent private bank. A story of good planning, it seemed to me. Donald Moxton had acquired his first bank in 1948. It was then called Randolphs and run by an Alfred Randolph. Donald had changed its name and expanded his burgeoning empire over the south-east of England by buying similar small private banks. In 1960 he made his bid for higher stakes, by acquiring one in west London and turning Moxtons into an unlimited liability company. He was on his way up. His next acquisition in 1970 was a triumph, firstly because it gave Donald a highly desirable seat at the London Clearing House, making him one of the big boys, and secondly because a few years later he put his son Philip, then aged 25, in charge of it.

So there they were, father and son, planning for the next step. That came in 1981 when Moxtons was taken under the wing of the giant Fentons conglomerate. Donald did splendidly out of his sale of shares and continued to run Moxtons Private Banking under Fentons' aegis. When Donald retired in 1987, Philip naturally took over the chair and his future was paved with gold.

Despite my further explorations on the web, there was no mention of a bank robbery, although that could be explained by the fact that no bank would boast about such an event and that the robbery, if any, was probably well before the Internet provided mass circulation. I wasn't therefore any the wiser about that or about Philip Moxton himself, save that he must be a very rich man indeed if he had inherited Donald's remaining shares and fortune.

I was marginally further forward on the 'old mates', Gavin and Donald, although still at sea on when their friendship – if that is what it was – had begun. I could discover only one element in common between the two men. Both of them had come from the largish village of Biddenford, near Woodchurch. Both were roughly the same age, Donald born in 1922 and Gavin a year later, and both were at school there – but it was not the same school. Donald attended the local grammar school from age eleven but Gavin was at private schools from the age of five onwards. Unlikely then to have been close chums from school-days. It was possible their parents were friends, but that too was unlikely. Donald's father was the village greengrocer, living above the shop, Gavin's was a solicitor in Hawkhurst, living in Biddenford in what was clearly a substantial detached Victorian house. In those days at least their families would not have been moving in the same social circles.

The Second World War might have provided a firmer meeting ground, as at eighteen, they would have been at conscription age in September 1939 and would undoubtedly have been called up in due course, subject to medical fitness. I had no luck in establishing a link there either. Donald had gone into the Army, Gavin to the Air Force. It was possible their paths could have briefly collided but that was unlikely to have established an enduring friendship. As for post-war careers, Donald went straight into banking and Gavin into an acting career. No clues there either.

Back to the sunny yellow monster outside: the Packard. It was then I realized that I had been so stunned at the Packard's arrival that I hadn't checked what came with it. I'd checked the essential paperwork of course, which included the car's very recent history, but I'd taken Tom at his word when he told me the original logbook was missing. It might have given me some clues as to how this 'game' had developed, so could I be sure Tom wasn't being economical with the truth? It was at least worth a look in case something of interest remained in the car. I rushed out to the Packard and opened the glove compartment. Empty – well, except for a half-used roll of Polo mints, an old map of Kent, and a small packet of tissues. No logbooks, no papers of any kind.

Was that by accident or design? I wondered. I could ask Joan Moxton for any paperwork she might have and if no luck there I'd tackle the Herricks on Saturday. But somehow I knew I wasn't going to strike lucky there either. If the original logbook was being deliberately withheld by either party, would that suggest it could tell me more than they wished me to know? Such as? I pondered this. If nothing else I'd like to find out who first owned the car, which might help track it onwards from the day it left the Packard factory.

The barbecue could be a way forward. That would be good, because I was at present on a hiding to nowhere with the Packard and suspected DCI Brandon might be getting sniffy on the subject. Dave was certainly sniffy on the Golf. With that in mind, I took action and rang both Wendy Parks and Geoffrey Green's other contact in Monksford, Sam West, to arrange a date for Thursday. They might not be able to take me forward on the Golf but it would do no harm to have a clearer light on Philip's life as Geoffrey Green. I therefore set off on Thursday morning in grand style with my Gordon-Keeble to Monksford, heading first for the café.

Wendy's face brightened as she saw me, not I suspected for my personal charms, but because I might know how the police case was going. There were hardly any customers for morning coffee so she was able to leave the kitchens and join me – which she was eager to do.

'I've had my police grilling,' she told me wryly. 'Duly roasted on all sides and left raw within.'

'Brandon's not usually as hard as that.'

'Perhaps, but it turns out that Geoffrey tried to ring me that evening on my landline. He knew I never bother much with my mobile. I wasn't in and I never check all callers unless they've left a message, which he didn't. I hate thinking that if I'd been in I might have been able to help or prevent what happened in some way.'

'He'd have dialled nine nine nine if it was an emergency,' I pointed out gently.

'Yes, but I seem to have been the only person in Monksford who could claim to have known Geoffrey. Even his cleaner didn't really *know* him because he was usually gone when she arrived and Sam West only met him very occasionally. Same with the neighbours. I'm afraid therefore that yours truly has been marked down as number one suspect. I suppose their theory goes that Geoffrey rejected my advances or that I knew he was Philip Moxton and that he had left me something in his will.'

Whoops! Caution on approaching this one. I cocked an interested eye at her.

She looked embarrassed. 'It appears he has, so that little something puts me firmly on the list.'

'Geoffrey Green's will or Moxton's?' I asked. It looked fairly certain that the nightmare of two wills had been avoided but it would be interesting to know how much she was now in the picture.

She stared at me aghast. 'I don't know. Wouldn't it be invalid if it was one made by a man who didn't legally exist?'

'Who's the solicitor?'

'Hall & Parsons. James Hall is dealing with it.'

That confirmed that point then. I wondered how much the 'something' left to Wendy was but she didn't volunteer the information, hardly surprisingly. 'I'm sure he must have left legacies to quite a few people,' I reassured her, 'so I doubt if you'll be singled out by the police for that reason. Don't worry. Unless of course you're in the habit of carrying a kitchen knife around with you.'

A poor joke, but she managed a laugh of sorts. 'Not on Thursdays, so you're safe.'

'Seriously, Wendy, if you'd killed Geoffrey, there'd be DNA left somewhere.'

'I told you I had visited him there before.'

'Did you smash a window and climb in on that occasion? Do you have a Golf tucked away at home?'

She tried to smile. 'Are you officially investigating the case yet?'

'No. I'm still on the two cars,' I told her. 'The Volkswagen and the Packard.'

'What Packard?'

No harm in telling her, especially as I planned to drive her in it on Saturday if she wanted to come to the barbecue. Wendy listened politely but asked no questions, so I played a wild card.

'Did Geoffrey ever mention a game to you?'

'What game? The so-termed beautiful one?'

'No. I don't see Philip Moxton as a football fan. This game must have been a family thing anyway. Are you curious about the other side of Geoffrey's life?'

'Yes, I feel I've been short-changed,' she confessed.

'There's a barbecue over at Frittenhurst on Saturday evening. It's at the home of Tom and Moira Herrick, who previously owned the Packard. At least one member of Philip's family will be there. His son Barney. I've full permission to bring someone with me so why not you? Would you find it rough going?'

She thought for a moment. 'Thanks, Jack. Yes, I'd like to. Should I bring a dish?'

'I'm told it's a hog roast and a large scale party, so no need.'

'Isn't it odd,' she asked somewhat diffidently, 'that the family are attending parties so soon?'

'That's what's interests me.' That, and the Packard – which
brought me back to the Volkswagen. 'Wendy, that Golf of
Geoffrey's – you wouldn't have any idea where it could be?'

She couldn't be putting on that look of amazement. 'No idea.
I presume it's been flogged to someone else. You're not thinking
it might still be in his murderer's garage?'

'It's unlikely, but you might keep a look out for it. Which was
Geoffrey's regular garage for MOTs and so on?'

'He used the local one, just as I do.'

Could that have a link to Richie Carson? I wondered. Dave's
team would have covered that. My hopes would lie with Carson
himself.

Sam West's home, he had warned me on the phone, was hard
to find. Indeed it was. The lane wound its way round so many
corners and took so long to negotiate that I thought I'd reached
the south coast – until it stopped abruptly and turned itself into
a bridle path and then open farmland. The Gordon-Keeble isn't
used to this kind of mucking around in tight spots and I shuddered for it as I backed into a hedge to turn round and drive back
up the lane. Fingers crossed that the hedge wasn't concealing a
nice deep ditch. The fingers worked and this time I did find Five
Acres, a seventies' bungalow overlooking farmland and Sam's
peaceful retirement retreat.

Sam looked in his mid-to-late sixties, courteous, grey-haired,
fit and clearly active. He was busy mowing the extensive lawn
when I arrived which explained why he hadn't seen or heard me
pass.

'The only thing I regret about moving here,' he told me. 'It
was my late wife's dream to have a garden this size, but she died
a year or two after we bought this house. Now, shall we have
coffee? I've laid it ready.'

He led me into a pleasant conservatory and bustled about as
though I were an honoured guest. 'I'm not sure how you think
I can help you, Mr Colby,' he said anxiously. 'I've told the police
the little I know about Geoffrey Green.'

What he meant was: '*Why are you bothering me?*' but I decided
to ignore that interpretation. 'It's the Volkswagen I'm particularly
interested in. Would you mind running your evidence through
again for me in case it has any bearing on it? I'm from the car
unit of the police, which is a different department.'

Luckily, being old school, he took the point straightaway. 'Ah, how I remember that problem.'

'You were in the police?' I asked.

'No. Accountant. I suppose in the light of this extraordinary news I now see why Geoffrey liked to talk once in a while. It took him away from the banking world and yet we both dealt with figures. He was a busy man, so we never got to know each other well and I was amazed to hear his true identity. He told me he was a financial consultant and a day trader on the stock-market. I day-trade too, so that and a love of chess is what we had in common, even though I see now that our careers hardly matched.'

'You had no idea he wasn't who he purported to be?'

He hesitated. 'No, I've been thinking about that. I thought when I first met him that Geoffrey had somewhat the same manner and look as someone I'd briefly worked for early in my career. That was Donald Moxton, so I was quite right. I forgot it until this terrible thing happened. He must have thought he'd found refuge here but banking is a tough business nowadays and there are no hiding places.'

'Did you tell him he had the same mannerisms as Donald Moxton?'

'No, and now I'm glad I didn't. The Geoffrey I knew might have been even more alarmed. I might have mentioned it to Timothy Mild though, who worked with Philip Moxton. He lives not that far away and we play golf together at his local club.'

'I've met him at Staveley House. Did he visit you here – could he have known about the Geoffrey Green masquerade?'

Sam looked startled. 'I don't know. He hasn't been here to see me, but I've no idea if he knows the village otherwise. I doubt if Geoffrey would have taken him into his confidence over the dual identity because their working relationship was troubled to say the least.'

'Timothy seems to get on well with Philip's sister Joan.'

'That may be politic.' Sam hesitated. 'No harm in telling you, I suppose. It's common gossip in the City and had even reached me before Timothy told me about it. Philip was absolutely opposed to this merger with EU. He inherited his father's instinct-ive desire that the banking profession should remain solely UK-based. In Donald's time no such move would have been

considered and even offshore accounts had barely raised their
heads. Donald's motto was: "Plough a straight furrow, and keep
to the same field," and Timothy said Philip followed firmly in
his footsteps.'

I laughed. 'Very British.'

'It worked for a long while,' Sam continued, 'but times have
changed and are still changing. They have to and Timothy knows
the merger is the right thing for Moxtons. But he said that Philip
remained adamant and the whole deal was about to collapse.'

I wondered whether DCI Brandon knew about this, remem-
bering his earlier offhand remark. Philip's death would be highly
convenient for Timothy's career. It added up, though it wasn't a
line I felt comfortable with, as I'd taken a liking to him during
our chat after the arrival of the Packard.

'Was Donald Moxton a popular boss?'

He grimaced. 'Hierarchy was strict in the sixties and the
establishment still ruled. Spit and polish and the right school
were all that mattered, although Donald Moxton wasn't from the
right school. The rumour was that he was a bull in a china shop,
who scooped up all the pieces he smashed, put them together
again and made a fortune.'

'Interesting but ruthless.'

'Indeed. Of course there were other rumours,' Sam said.

'About what?'

'How Donald Moxton got the money to buy his first bank.'

'The usual channels – partners, loans and backers?'

He regarded me pityingly. 'Not in the austerity days of the
late 1940s.' A polite cough. 'You said you were from the car
unit, Mr Colby. This hardly seems relevant.'

'In fact it is. As well as the missing Golf, there's a Packard
in the story, which Philip Moxton bought through me shortly
before he died. Did Geoffrey Green ever mention Packards to
you?'

Sam shook his head. 'I don't think Geoffrey was very interested
in cars, so that surprises me. As for the Golf though, how can I
help on that?'

'It hasn't so far surfaced, and it's just possible it's still in the
murderer's barn or garage. Would you know it if you saw it?'

'I doubt it. He drove it here once or twice, but I don't have
instinctive recall on cars. Cream, wasn't it? I'll keep my eyes

open. You're welcome to have a look round here if you wish. But it could have been abandoned anywhere.'

No, I thought, it would have been spotted by now. So where was it?

I'd envisaged a smallish gathering in the Herricks' large rear garden. How wrong could I be? Large signs pointed to Court Orchard, which was down a track along the side of the Herricks' home and gardens. In the days when this was hop-picking country, hop-pickers would have been swarming down here from London and from all over the south of England to harvest the hops. The oast house, now a beautiful relic, would have been working full tilt, the inimitable smell of hops would be in the air day and night.

Now there were cars everywhere, parked along the road, and also filling a field on the far side of the track. The Packard was special, so there was no way I was going to park it on the road. It was the field that Wendy and I bumped our way over in great style. I could see her gritting her teeth and preferred not to dwell on what the Packard was making of this rough treatment. Now that we are so used to power-assisted steering, it felt heavy and I could almost feel its aggrieved reactions.

For all its laid-back appearance, the barbecue was guarded by a ferocious security force of three when we finally parked and arrived at the entrance.

'This,' Wendy observed, 'is not the world that Geoffrey Green moved in. He'd have hated it.'

'It was Philip Moxton's world though,' I said. 'Maybe that's why he treasured Monksford. He didn't have to worry about security.'

'Maybe he should have done,' Wendy said sadly. 'But believe me, Jack, this kind of mob wasn't his style.'

I could see her point, even from the little I had known of Philip Moxton. There was a mass of people here, a marquee, a band, a bar, a hog roast and burger barbecue and much, much more. I'd imagined a family gathering of people, maybe a dozen or fifteen. No way. There must be eighty or so here already and behind us there were still cars arriving in droves. Immediately we entered, Barney came up to us, and I introduced Wendy to him. 'I'm from your father's Geoffrey Green life,' she blithely told him.

'Good,' he said with great satisfaction. 'That links the circle, doesn't it?'

Wendy looked taken aback at such an easy ride. She'd been nervous on the way over as to how her presence would be greeted. 'I'm not going to be a freak sideshow, am I, Jack?' she'd asked me. 'A sort of second wife tucked away. I wasn't. We were friends, that's all.'

'I don't know how they'll react,' I'd told her honestly. 'But it will be interesting to find out, won't it?'

A grin. 'Yes.'

Barney's reaction was, as usual, unexpected. 'Where's the Packard?' he asked immediately.

I told him and he was horrified. 'Don't leave it there. You must bring it in. I'll have the gates opened for it. It must be centre stage.'

I tried to be tactful. 'What about the Herricks? It isn't their favourite subject.'

He looked at me. 'Jack, bring it in please.'

A gentleman of force when he wanted to be, I thought.

And so the Packard made a star entry through the gates. No one fainted or objected as it reached its position (allotted by Barney) which was indeed in the middle of the field near the central hog roast and bar. Immediately it became the cynosure of all eyes, though what lay behind some of those eyes was difficult to tell. Not everyone seemed pleased to see it.

Somewhat to my surprise considering her diffidence, Wendy went off on her own without waiting for me to make introductions. I watched her making the rounds of the guests with no sign of reticence, but then lost sight of her as my attention was abruptly torn away from her. I was standing by the Packard and Moira had swept up to me, a commanding figure in silk shirt, designer jeans and boots. She pointed at it in horror.

'What's that thing doing here?'

'Barney thought it a good idea.' Had I been set up? If so, it was my own fault for suggesting it to him even if I hadn't meant it. 'It seems an appropriate contribution to the game that this barbecue ends,' I added. I couldn't be in any deeper water than I already was.

'Barney's *contribution* is paying for all this,' Moira said crossly. 'I suppose it had better stay here.'

'Provided I don't find it barbecued.' I was growing tired of being a punchball.

'It won't be.' Moira calmed down. 'The game really is over.' A pause. '*Philip's* game, anyway.'

It wasn't difficult to pick up Moira's innuendo. 'You mean his life as Geoffrey Green.'

'Yes. With your little friend whom you kindly brought. Quite a surprise for us all.'

'*Us?*' I queried. 'You mean the Herricks and Moxtons? But that's over, as you said.'

She flushed. 'Yes, of course.' Then she apparently caught sight of someone she just must talk to, and was gone. It didn't take a lot of working out that the link between the two families went beyond a mere exchange of a car over the years. Did 'my friend' Wendy affect that? Were they ganging up against her? Why should the Herricks care about Wendy's part in Geoffrey Green's life?

When Emma Herrick suddenly materialized at my side and announced herself as the Herricks' ambassador, it was clear that Moira had dispatched her daughter to keep an eye on me. Obviously by bringing Wendy I had thrown down a gauntlet and Emma had the task of picking it up and disposing of it. That was no problem. Emma was easy to chat to, as well as looking gorgeous in a slinky silk dress.

'Mum says I should do the honours and introduce you to people.'

I smiled at her. 'Is the word people synonymous with game-players?'

It didn't throw her. 'Partly,' she said happily. 'Although your friend isn't one.'

'Wendy was a friend of Geoffrey Green's. They did things together.'

'I bet,' Emma commented mildly.

'She says not.'

'Maybe she's right. But it's a heck of a lot of money to leave except to a *very* dear friend.'

This was a mental thump between the shoulder blades. 'A heck of a lot?' Wendy had said a little something.

'A cool million or two.' She laughed at my astounded expression. 'Barney won't miss it, but even so it makes you think. Joan is hopping mad.'

'Whoa!' I said. 'This is all very matey.' Just how far did the Herricks' relationship with the Moxtons go?

'Not mine. My parents' friend. They were all at university together.'

Sometimes one has to drag a story out in bits and pieces and this was well worth following up.

'Who,' I asked gently, 'do you mean by *all*?'

Emma took a sip or two of champagne, while she considered this. 'I suppose I should tell you if you want to understand the game, though goodness knows why you should. The Packard's only a car after all.'

'*Only* a car? But it certainly seems to symbolize something. Tell me what, Emma.'

'That's why I'm here. OK. Tom, Philip, Joan and Gwen were all at Oxford at the same time although in different years.'

'Gwen?' I queried. 'Tom's sister?' There had been a far closer network between the families than I had guessed.

'Ah,' Emma said reflectively. 'Yes, she is. Tell me what you *do* know about the Herricks and Moxtons,' she invited me, and I duly did so. I had nothing to lose and possibly a lot to gain.

'Well,' she commented, 'so far as I can tell, they haven't misled you over the game. You're just missing a major piece or two of the jigsaw.'

I groaned. 'Such as?'

'For a start you're a player short, so let me introduce you to Gwen.'

She took me over to a jolly-looking woman of about sixty, currently chatting to Tom. He took one look at me and he too decided there was someone he needed to talk to urgently on the far side of the field.

Emma grinned, reading my thoughts correctly. 'Gwen, this is Jack Colby. Jack, this is my aunt, Dad's sister. Gwen, the game's up, the gloves are off.'

Gwen's eyes glinted. 'Sure about this, Emma?'

'Quite sure. We've told the police most of it anyway, and Jack works for them over the Packard issue.'

'That dinosaur is still an issue?' Gwen said. I couldn't tell whether she was neutral in this battle of wits or a powerful participant. 'Well, Jack,' she continued, 'you won't have seen me on stage or screen like Tom or my father Gavin or Emma here. I'm the one without the talent.'

'Only in that way,' Emma said firmly. 'You've inherited your mother's gifts.'

'Perhaps. My mother, Nancy, was a very special person, Jack. So is my son, Barney.'

With this casual – or not so casual – statement a lot of jigsaw pieces snapped into place and knocked me mentally sideways.

'You're Philip's former wife,' I managed to croak.

Of course. The fact that she lived abroad didn't mean she couldn't be a player in the game. She wasn't off the radar, as I'd been told. She was here, very much with her own cards to play. 'You're Gwen Moxton.'

'The missing link, Jack,' Emma said. 'The marriage was so much in the past we tend to forget about it.'

'I'm very much an ex,' Gwen airily confirmed. 'So Herrick please, not Moxton.'

They seemed very anxious to imply that this was an irrelevant factor in this case. 'I was told you live in France, Gwen.'

'I do some of the time. I have a small house there, but mostly I live here. I brought Barney up here but Philip thought I lived mostly in France. I'm not stinking rich, incidentally. When we divorced, Philip wasn't in the financial position he reached thereafter, so I'm not living on the proceeds down on the Riviera.' A pause. 'You understand why I'm telling you this?'

I made a stab at it. 'The game,' I said. 'It was really about you and not the Packard.'

I noted the quick glance she gave Emma.

'No, the game was strictly between my father and Donald, and then Philip. Gavin never liked Philip and this ridiculous rivalry over the Packard made it worse. My father owned it at one point, and in revenge Philip married me. When we divorced my father demanded the Packard back.'

I was reeling. Cars are important, but not *that* important. 'Didn't you have a say in whom you married?' I asked.

'Of course, but I have a rebellious nature. When my father made his objections clear, I persuaded myself that Philip was all the things Gavin wasn't. Stable, serious, academic and reliable. I adored my father; he was impulsive, rich one minute, poor the next, and he never minded which. He forbade me to marry Philip, which made me all the keener.'

This was crazy. 'But surely Philip wouldn't have married you just for the game?'

'I hope not and I don't think he did. I adored him at first and he liked that. He was just incapable of demonstrating any feelings.'

'If he had any,' Emma put in.

'I think he did,' Gwen said reflectively. 'Perhaps he did for that friend of yours, Jack. Moira is convinced Wendy knew Geoffrey Green was Philip Moxton. Maybe I'll have a chat with her. We might have a lot in common.'

'She tells me she was just a friend.' I was beginning to wonder about this.

'Does she? Although Philip was incapable of showing emotions, he was very enthusiastic about sex.'

Half of me wished I'd never brought Wendy, but the other half gave me a pat on the back. Bring all the players together and all sorts of interesting situations can occur.

'Do you have feelings about the Packard, Gwen?' I asked. 'You wouldn't like it back, would you? Barney turned it down.'

She shuddered. 'No, I would not. It might look a comfortable old beast to you but to us it symbolizes a whole lot of problems. Wherever we went the game hung round our necks like an albatross. I'm told Joan gave it to you and I'm not surprised. It was always there in the background. Don't let the other side get ahead in the game. Philip, Tom, Joan and I all thought we'd thrown off the shackles of the game at university and then we believed it so again when you bought the car on Philip's behalf. That was our final throw. We sold the car so that Philip could believe he had won. With Philip gone, Joan gave it away and now *you* bring it back here *with* Barney's encouragement. Thanks a bunch.'

She looked so woebegone that I hastily said, 'You won't see it again, I promise.'

'Old Packards never die,' she said savagely.

'They just rob banks,' I said idly. It was just a casual remark but there was a speedy reaction.

'What do you mean by that?' she asked sharply.

Sometimes one hits a bullseye without planning it. 'A journalist

I know said this might be the Packard that had once been involved in a bank robbery.'

'Are you implying my father or Philip robbed one?' She looked very grim.

'It seems unlikely. But there might be a story in the car's past history. The logbook's missing, and that might have given me a hint. Would you have it?'

'No. None of us has.' Then belatedly: 'Sorry. And there isn't such a story.'

I wasn't convinced on either score, not the logbook nor that this was the *full* story. But I wasn't surprised now that Barney had suggested I came here.

The Packard was certainly a draw. I maintained my guard at its side, having done my duty by the hog roast and stood like a guest of honour at a party and let people come to me. This time it was Joan Moxton, looking determined to be friendly – which was clearly a struggle, especially as John Carson was with her, just as grumpy but definitely smarter dressed. I wasn't surprised to see him. This man had too much of a proprietorial air over Staveley not to play a larger part in her life than advising and working on the gardens. How much of a part did he play in his son's career? I wondered. Was he, as with Joan, a sort of Rasputin or Machiavelli controlling the puppet strings?

'So you've brought that old monstrosity here,' Joan remarked, doing her best to keep up the jovial angle. 'Can't find anywhere else to dump it, eh?'

'I didn't realize how popular it was. People just can't get enough of looking at it,' I said. 'Pity the logbook is missing – it would be nice to tell them more about its history. Would you have it at home?'

That stopped the joviality. She glared at me. 'No.'

Time to bring Carson into the act. 'Did you ever see it around?' I asked him.

'Nothing to do with me.'

'Pity. I'll have to get the information from other channels.' I hoped this would produce a climbdown but Joan stared me out. 'Do as you like,' she said.

'But not round our way,' Carson added.

'Do you have barbecues at Staveley?' I asked to keep the

conversation afloat. They so much wanted it to end that it was tempting to keep on going.

'I don't give my life to those gardens to have them set on fire with barbecues and the like,' Carson informed me. 'We've got plans for those gardens and they don't include nothing like hog roasts. See?'

'John and I see eye to eye over Staveley.' Joan came to life again now that we were on a subject she was comfortable with. 'We shall be making the gardens truly glorious once more, now that Philip's gone. He wouldn't let us touch them, even though we're going to revert to the pleasure gardens they were in the eighteenth century. He wouldn't have it. Staveley had to stay the same as when our father designed the grounds. Now we can get to work. Give it a year or two and you'll see the results.'

She rambled on but I was aware that Carson's eye was still upon me. When there was a lull in the flow of garden talk, he broke it with, 'Got a message for you.'

Careful here. 'Who from?'

'My crazy son. He says to tell you the requested package got posted on by mistake! Don't know what he's talking about.' He glared at me as if defying me to say he was lying.

I did know. Richie was playing his own game with the Volkswagen Golf. No turning it over to the police as arranged. It could be out of the country by now. 'Tell him I'll be in touch, Mr Carson.'

'If I see him I might.'

It was clear why Richie hadn't rung me himself. Either something had genuinely gone awry or he'd changed his mind. I'd thought he would keep to the bargain, but he hadn't. That must mean his own interests had superseded mine. At least he'd let me know, which must mean something – even though his father was currently eyeing me up for possible composting material. Richie had been anxious to assure me that 'Dad' was OK. In what respect though hadn't been clear. Was it over the Volkswagen and therefore Geoffrey Green's death or over Staveley and Philip Moxton's? Either way, did Richie protest too much?

Looking around, it seemed that Philip's death had benefited quite a few people here, not only John Carson. There were Timothy Mild, CEO of Moxtons, and Joan, for a start, not to mention Barney. He was a mystery. Had it changed the lives of Tom or Moira or Gwen? I couldn't see how, save that Barney had inherited a huge fortune and had two families, the Moxtons and the Herricks. And then, I remembered, there was Wendy Parks, Geoffrey's friend who had inherited a great deal of money – and money, it should never be forgotten, is the root of all evil, including murder.

I watched Joan and John Carson walk away, and ridiculous though it sounds I almost envied them at that moment. Likeable or not, they had sorted themselves out in life. They had a mission, they had each other. Could I claim as much? I had Frogs Hill, I had my daughter Cara, I had Len and Zoe, but was I lacking the spark that brought the engine to life? When I walked off into the sunset as that pair was doing, what could I claim? I had everything, but nothing. Not like that couple ahead of me, nor the many others milling around.

Nonsense, I told myself briskly. It was time to treat myself to some late strawberries and cream and to check Wendy was OK. I could see no immediate sign of her, so I helped myself to the fruit, ate it with great enjoyment, and then set off to circulate. Now that it was nearly dark, the evening was taking on an air of mystery and since it was late September a chilly one at that. Cardigans, sweaters, even jackets were appearing, and impromptu dancing was taking place near the band. Not everyone was dancing though. Many couples were still strolling around, though I could see no sign of Wendy.

I did see Barney though. He and a partner were wandering off towards the trees at the edge of the field through which a path led to the Herricks' garden. Since the woman was in red I thought it might be Wendy and I would join them. But her back was to me and a few more paces told me this wasn't her, even though there was something familiar about her. Perhaps she was the come-and-go lady in his life. They were laughing, his arm was round her and she turned slightly towards him.

My head began to swim and my eyes to play tricks. For a moment I had thought it was Louise, my lost lover.

Then she turned round to point at the band, tucked her hand under Barney's arm, and they strolled on.

It *was* Louise.

Jealousy is a red mist, they say. It must be she who was Barney's come-and-go girlfriend, and Barney had just inherited a billionaire's estate.

Then something made her look back and Louise saw me staring at her.

EIGHT

Ever felt frozen in time? The dangerous corner was upon me and I couldn't even grip the steering wheel. What to do next? Should I rush up to her, greet her like a casual acquaintance from yesteryear? Demand that Barney hand her over immediately? Or should I give myself time to think? Would she come over to me? Had she even recognized me? Did she care? Was I history?

The question was answered for me. Louise turned away and she moved on with Barney.

Wendy appeared at that very moment and must have realized that something was wrong because she stopped whatever she had begun to say and looked over to where my glazed eyes were still focused.

'Do you know her?' she asked curiously. 'That's Louise Shaw, isn't it? The actor?'

'Yes,' I managed to say. 'And, yes I know her – knew her.' Mistake. Wendy was instantly on the alert.

'Girlfriend?' she queried.

'Ages ago.'

'Ah.' She looked worldly-wise. 'She thinks you're with me. Tied up. Harnessed.' And as I must still have been looking out for the count, she added politely, 'You look unavailable, Jack.'

Unavailable? *Me?* How wrong could she be? 'So does she,' I said defensively. Then I wondered how I could possibly know that.

I didn't!

Instantly I was on the move running after her with no notion of what I was going to say when I reached her. Louise and Barney seemed to be heading for the Herrick family group. Dangerous. I didn't want to come face to face with her there. I had to detach her from Barney before they got there.

In dreams you can't run. Your mind manages it, but not your legs. Mine felt like that now. I wanted to be the giant in the story my mother told me as a child; he had boots that covered seven leagues with each stride. But I wasn't that giant. I was the clown who managed to trip over his own big feet and sprawl on the ground right behind Louise.

The commotion made her turn round – and then double up with laughter as I scrambled to my feet. 'We met like this once before,' I managed to say.[1]

Her face softened. 'Yes.' She was still giggling. Barney looked rather bewildered, but caught the general drift of the situation and ambled away. The scowl I directed at him might have had something to do with it.

I was alone with Louise.

And then, in my confusion, instead of saying something sensible such as 'I love you', I took the belligerent route. 'Are you two a couple?'

She looked startled, not unnaturally. Louise normally has a calm serene face but that changed.

'No. Are you and Wendy Parks a couple?'

'No.'

As a result of this terse exchange, we both mentally regrouped – at least I did, and she seemed to as well. 'Likely to be?' I ventured.

'No.'

'Nor me.' A pause before I produced my next gem of love talk. 'I thought you were in Australia. How was the film?'

'Penal servitude. Released early and made a dash for the homeland.' She looked as uncertain as I felt about what the next step should be.

My next step was towards her. She moved back. 'Later, Jack. Too much going on here.' She said it gently, and not – I thought – as a put-off. My hopes cautiously rose.

She was right. People were buzzing here, there and everywhere, the burgers and hog roast were in full flow and dancers were ready for the next session as the band regrouped.

'At Frogs Hill?' I suggested. Stupid, stupid, *stupid.* Speeding along far too fast.

She hesitated, but at least she didn't stalk away from me. 'Not quite yet. Anyway, don't you have to take Wendy home?'

I groaned. 'Yes.' I'd forgotten about that.

[1] See *Classic Calls the Shots*

'See me before you leave?' As olive branches go, this at least looked fruitful. I graciously agreed I would.

Questions, hundreds of them, battered and bustled their way through my head like fireworks in a darkened sky. Amongst them was how come Louise was here at the Herricks' party – or was it Barney's party? Who was her contact? Did it matter? I wrestled with this and even wondered if she had known Geoffrey Green. That would account for her knowing who Wendy was. Then I realized the contact could be Tom Herrick, since he and Louise were both in the theatre world.

Who cared? The merry-go-round whirling in my head came to a stop. This was a frabjous day, callooh, callay and nothing mattered now I knew she wasn't hooked up to Barney.

I watched her as she joined the Herricks' group, and then still dazed I strolled back to the Packard, while I gathered my social wits for further partying. Not a bad old beast, I thought fondly patting its buttery coloured bonnet like an idiot. I was fond of everyone and everything; it was a stupendous evening and a glorious car. Perhaps I would even keep it. There was room for it at Frogs Hill and surely I could pacify Len and Zoe. Why not? The world was a wonderful place and its possibilities opened up as an infinite path of glory lying ahead of me.

But then the shadow arrived in the form of mine host, Tom Herrick, who stood plumb in the middle of my glorious path forward. He was not happy. 'You do know what you've brought here, Jack?'

'The Packard? I asked, genuinely surprised. Symbol or not, it was only a car and didn't deserve all this venom.

'No. You've brought trouble. Wendy Parks.'

I braced myself. After all, I'd brought Wendy here partly to see what the reactions were. 'Barney was all in favour of my bringing a companion.' If I was the patsy in this game of theirs, I was at least going to turn it to my advantage.

'A companion's one thing,' Tom growled. 'Wendy Parks is another. You know that.'

I wasn't standing for this. 'Hang on,' I said firmly. 'I'm an outsider. I was invited, and I brought Wendy as agreed with Barney. I'm not part of any game. Over and out.'

'This isn't about the game,' Tom said grimly. 'It's about legacies.'

Ah. Now I was on track. 'That's not your concern either,' I pointed out rather obviously. 'It's Barney's, Joan's and maybe Gwen's. Not yours.'

'A bequest of several million to Wendy Parks should send up question marks in anyone's mind, especially the police's.'

'*Several* million?' I echoed stupidly. The last I had heard it was one or two. This was going up and up. Then I pulled myself together. 'I still don't see it's any of my business or yours.'

Tom remained on the attack. 'Barney's my nephew.'

'I know that *now*,' I emphasized coolly. 'But unless Philip's will and the Packard relate to Geoffrey Green's murder, my focus is on Monksford and his stolen Volkswagen. I can't yet see that the Packard has anything to do with that. Nor your game,' I added, hoping this might draw him out.

It didn't. Tom decided to take a gulp of beer while he thought this over. Then he said savagely, 'Get that thing out of here – *and* that woman.'

It was a weak rejoinder and he had lost the battle but I didn't feel I had won it. I'd careered round a dangerous corner, but still seemed to be playing a game of blind man's buff in which I was the masked victim in the centre of the circle vainly trying to find a way out that would lead to a murderer.

That was mentally. Physically I remained standing stock still at the centre of the party waiting for humble admirers to pay their respects to the Packard. The next person to approach me was Timothy Mild, although he showed few signs of paying respects or of being humble despite his name. Fair enough. He'd been with me at Staveley when Joan had dumped it on me. He seemed to be everywhere in the Moxton case, I reflected: he worked with Philip, he knew Joan, he knew Sam West and now it turned out he knew the Herricks. Fair enough. Networking must be second nature to him in his job. But did he also 'know' Geoffrey Green? Timothy strolled up to me, champagne flute in hand and with a rather conscious air of relaxation.

'See you've brought the Packard then,' was his conversational gambit.

'I have,' I dutifully replied.

'And Wendy Parks too,' he added in jocular fashion.

'Of course,' I agreed. 'You know her?' Timothy met Sam at the golf club but did he know Monksford and Wendy too?

His champagne seemed to interest him greatly. 'Slightly.'

'But not Geoffrey Green?'

He must have been waiting for that. 'No. I met Wendy at a concert at the Royal Festival Hall. She's in its Friends Association and so is my wife.'

'The circles around Philip Moxton seem to be ever decreasing,' I commented.

Timothy parried this without the slightest hesitation. 'It's like that in the country, isn't it? I know the Herricks, I've met Wendy, I play golf with Sam West – he said he'd met you – I've driven through Monksford, stopped for coffee there once on the way through, so I might have met her there before I knew who she was. I do assure you, however, that I never ran into Geoffrey Green.'

'This case is full of coincidences,' I said genially.

'Case, Jack?'

I remembered that to him I was a car dealer doing odd jobs for the police on that front only. My turn to parry. 'The case of the Packard and the missing Volkswagen.'

'Ah yes, the Packard.' He turned to admire its curvy charms. 'Great car, isn't it? Forget the Volkswagen, Jack, but never forget the Packard or the game.'

So he did know about the game. Was he hinting that the Herricks might be more involved in Philip's death than had so far emerged? Or was he pointing the finger firmly away from his own motivation for wanting Philip out of the way? I'd liked him on our first meeting, now I wasn't so sure. Being liked – up to a point – must go with the territory in his position.

At this point Wendy rejoined me, greeting Timothy rather more casually than as a mere acquaintance – or perhaps that was my imagination working overtime. This was a casual occasion after all.

Perhaps it wasn't my imagination, however, because Timothy took the opportunity to suggest they went to get another drink and I didn't seem to be included in the invitation. I seemed to be seeing plots and spies everywhere, so the Packard and I remained in our twosome to see who might turn up next.

It proved to be Joan Moxton. Somewhere along the line she had become disconnected from John Carson, for which I was truly grateful. At this stage of the evening I could only take on one heavyweight at a time.

'What are you going to do with this thing?' she demanded, glaring at the Packard. 'You're not leaving it here, are you?'

She seemed very concerned, which was odd. Did the game scare her so much that she feared just leaving the car on Herrick territory would open it up again?

'No. I have to get home.'

'Taking that woman with you, I hope. What are you going to do with the car then?'

Here we go again, I thought. 'It's on hold until I'm absolutely certain none of you wants it back.'

A heavy sigh, then amazingly she grinned at me. Wow, I thought. I'm climbing the popularity stakes at last. 'We won't,' she informed me.

'Is the "we" you and John Carson?'

She looked astonished. 'Good heavens no. You don't understand, do you?'

'No,' I agreed wholeheartedly.

'As far as the Packard is concerned, John and I don't come into it. We run the Staveley Gardens. That's all. As I told you, now Philip's gone we can turn it into the dream place we've always wanted.'

Two happy customers anyway. 'Did Philip leave you the house too?'

'The right to live there, but with Barney's blessing I'm going to convert it so that we can hold horticultural courses there.' A sly glance at me. 'John lives in the Lodge and I don't use much of the house, so it will be put to good use.'

I still wondered what their relationship was. 'Sounds interesting,' I said politely.

So that was the arrangement, or what she would like to believe it was. This was a new Joan Moxton, one alive and enthusiastic. I doubted whether this extended as far as my concerns, however, but it was worth a go.

'Who,' I added, 'are the "we" you referred to in respect of not wanting the Packard back?'

She fidgeted a bit, but she was disposed to be informative. It must have been the champagne. 'The four of us,' she said. 'Philip, myself, Gwen and Tom. I gather you already know that we agreed in our Oxford days that the game must end when our fathers were both gone. Now they have, the game's over and you have the Packard. It's as simple as that.'

She was avoiding eye contact. 'No,' I said. 'There's more to it, isn't there?'

She still didn't meet my eyes. 'Only an angle you wouldn't understand.'

'Do the police understand it?'

Now she glared straight at me, 'If you must know . . . No.' She switched tack. 'It's not important and not relevant now I've got Staveley Gardens . . .' Then, 'Well, we agreed at Oxford that – no, I *won't* tell you.'

I put on my bulldog look. 'Then you must talk to the police.'

This made her hum and haw again, but at last she obliged. 'There was money involved.'

Not rocket science to guess that. 'How?'

'My father wouldn't tell us much, just that there was a sum involved over the Packard because of a bet between himself and Gavin. At university the four of us agreed that after both had died not only would the game end, but the proceeds of the bet would be split between the four of us equally. Philip changed his mind when his father died in the nineties and he discovered the proceeds had been far greater than he could have imagined. He didn't want to share it out. He told us he wanted the whole lot to go to Barney and he could divide it between the rest of us as he chose. We trusted Barney – luckily. All of us. He doesn't set much store by money, so apart from just one bequest to that woman of yours who's walked off with a cool three million and provision for Staveley, Barney has inherited Philip's fortune and we'll work the division out between us. So that's that,' she concluded defiantly. 'The game is over. No one can challenge *that*.'

Poor Wendy. For a moment I was sorry I'd brought her here, but then I reconsidered. Wendy wasn't going to be poor any longer and her presence had brought a few pheasants flying out of cover. As that was the only bequest, if Sam West had also been looking forward to a little something from his chum Geoffrey Green he'd be disappointed, but he had already got his life sorted.

Wendy's lifestyle on the other hand could be dramatically improved by what Philip had left her.

Then John Carson arrived to join Joan with his standard polite greeting to me.

'Taking this thing to the scrapyard, are you?' he snarled, thumping the Packard on its bonnet.

Joan for once stepped in. 'Let it be, John.'

Why, I wondered, should John care about the Packard? There was room enough at Staveley to house a dozen Packards. Were there yet more pheasants waiting to fly out?

As the evening wore on, I tried to throw myself back into the heart of the party for the interminable wait before I saw Louise again. I talked to Gwen, I talked to Moira, I even talked to Tom again. I saw nothing but smiling faces in the lamplit darkness and suddenly everyone seemed my friend. Even the Packard looked more at home. Someone had kindly fixed a spotlight on it which gave it a magical golden glow. Gradually eating and drinking petered to an end, although the dancing was still in full throttle.

'Later', I decided, had now come, so I went in search of Louise. I couldn't find her at first, although I knew she would still be here somewhere. Louise wouldn't stand me up – she's not like that. I did begin to panic, however, wondering if she had indeed done a disappearing act in order to avoid a difficult situation.

'Looking for Louise?'

I turned at the voice and saw Emma Herrick, drink in hand and looking highly amused. 'I am,' I admitted.

'She's nipped over to the house with my mum. She'll be back any moment.' Emma looked me over rather as she had done at our first meeting. 'I'm glad I've met you, Jack. She's not an easy lady, you know. But I reckon you're not easy either. Don't take any stick from her, will you? You're on a winning ticket.'

Was I? I glowed. 'I take it you and Louise are friends?' That explained the link between her and the Herricks.

'Bosom, Jack, bosom.' She laughed. 'Good luck.'

She tactfully disappeared, and in any case she had already lost my attention, because I could see Louise coming through the gateway from the house. The silver dress she wore was shimmering in the lamplight, as I walked up to meet her.

'Dance?' I asked.

I held out my arms and she came into them. Neither of us said much, as we moved slowly round, with couples leaping, jumping and singing. They were just shapes of vivid colour around us, as our bodies met each other once again.

'Shall we walk?' she whispered. 'Shall we talk?'

'We should.'

We slipped back into the Herricks' garden, and found a secluded spot where we could be alone. I could feel my heart thumping. I could see and feel her with me. Who would speak first? She tried and failed, so I began.

'I tried to reach you,' I said.

'I know. I couldn't face it. I ran away.'

'Because you'd closed the door on us?'

'It seemed to close itself.' She wouldn't look at me. 'It still does, Jack. I have to be free to dash here, there and everywhere.'

'Following your wandering star?'

'I'm afraid so.'

So this was it. The iron door had clanged shut and the prisoner remained inside. I felt very cold. I'd assumed all was going to be well between us, that this meeting was meant for that purpose only. How wrong can one be? Now the clown had fallen flat on his face again, and this time no laughter.

'And you?' Louise asked.

I swallowed, trying to sound casual. 'Various adventures, nothing changed. Still the constant star, but under that star was I born.'

'That's a quotation from *Much Ado about Nothing*.' She put her hand over mine.

'I know. I saw you play Beatrice.' I had put myself through agony to go up to London to see it, but in a way it had helped. It had emphasized the distance between her world and mine. She had been brilliant in the part, which had helped me understand more fully why she had left me.

I could hear her breathing. I could feel her hand tighten in mine. And then she said: 'I could follow a fixed star that wanders off course and pops back to home base – if we could work such a thing out.'

Drive slowly, drive carefully. 'At Frogs Hill?'

'Yes. Perhaps if . . .' Her voice trailed off. She needed my help.

Take it easy, take it calmly, I told myself. This was tough for Louise as well as for me. I had to ease up on the accelerator, change gear to give her time. 'Barney talked to me of a come-and-go girlfriend of his. When I saw you together, I thought it was you.'

'It isn't.' She relaxed a little. 'Emma's my friend and Barney's her cousin, that's all.' She looked down at our joined hands. 'Come-and-go. Are you agreeing that might be possible?'

Jump, leap, *now.* 'Yes.'

'It wouldn't be easy. There may be months away, there *would* be weeks away, lots of days away. Could you take that?'

Another tricky corner? This one I shot round a top speed. Too fast? Perhaps, but I'd take it anyway. *Now.* 'Yes, Louise, I can.'

After this, I was in such turmoil that I almost forgot about taking Wendy home, especially after Louise and I parted (with reluctance to say the least). Then it was from the sublime to the tedious. Timothy turned up again just as I was making my way back to find Wendy and the Packard. 'Glad I caught you, Jack.'

I wasn't at all glad. I was eager to get going with the rest of my life.

'Joan tells me,' he continued, 'that she's told you about the financial aspect of the game and the will.'

'Some,' I said guardedly.

He looked at me sharply. 'She likes stirring up mischief. I wouldn't go there if I were you. It's up to them to sort it out with Barney, although I've agreed to referee it informally.'

'You and the Herricks must go back a long way then.'

'Some way,' he conceded. 'They've told you about the game, I presume,' and when I nodded, he added, 'I wasn't so much referee as mediator there. Good practice for my career, but I didn't bargain for quite the degree of mediation I'd let myself in for.'

This was getting more interesting. 'In respect of Philip's murder?'

'No. In general. Although that wasn't why I was present at Staveley House when you called.'

'I assumed you were here to support Joan.'

He grimaced. 'She doesn't need support. I was there for quite
another reason.'

I had a bad feeling it wasn't going to be as simple as sorting
out Barney's division of spoils.'

'It's about what didn't happen,' he continued.

'Something to do with the big merger your bank's involved in?'

A sharp look at me. 'No again. And I'm only telling you this
because you seem to be in the thick of things so far as the
police are concerned, for all you say it's only over the cars.
The police know it already. At the time he died, Philip was
in the process of dramatically changing his will. I was involved
because it meant discussing it with the bank's board and myself.
He was intending to tie up all his money in a foundation under
the bank's aegis. *All* of it, including bequests and the main
inheritance. Including the bequest to Wendy.'

For a moment, I couldn't speak. This was mind-boggling. It
changed the entire murder case, surely, which was beginning to
prompt more corners and high banks than Brooklands race track.
Oddly enough, instead of confusing the issue, this one clarified
my mind like butter in hot sun. It all began to make sense. Philip
Moxton was afraid of being murdered, presumably by someone
with eyes on his fortune. What better than to stick it all in a
foundation so that that temptation was removed, and furthermore
he would be doing good to his fellow man by, in effect, giving
it to charity? However, that did mean that those whom he
suspected of wanting him dead would have to know about his
plans.

'Had he told his family this?' I asked bluntly.

'I don't know. I imagine he did. I don't know what the arrangement for Joan would have been – if any. When I mentioned the
foundation at that meeting at Staveley House, she didn't seem
surprised, nor did she give any impression that she supported the
plan.'

'Was it known outside the family?'

'You mean to the Herricks and your friend Wendy? Again, I
don't know, but I would think it extremely likely.'

NINE

The night is seldom the best time for logical thinking and never was that truer for me than now. I wondered what on earth I was doing, driving Wendy back to Monksford with Louise snuggling into every corner of my mind. With Wendy beside me, I ought to be focusing on Philip Moxton and this shattering information about his plans for a foundation, but every time I did so Louise charmed her way back and took over my thoughts again. I could hear Wendy chatting, but I had no clue what about. Louise took care of that too.

I thought Monksford would never loom up on the road signs and when at last it did, I nearly cheered out loud. When we drew up outside her home on the outskirts of the village, Wendy thanked me very sweetly.

'Thanks for inviting me, Jack. I'd been worrying over what the other side of Geoffrey's life was like. Now I know and I feel part of the pack.' She gave me a peck on the cheek and was gone, leaving me to my guilt over having invited her in the first place – especially as she wasn't and would never be part of the pack. I couldn't tell her that though.

When I finally arrived home, it seemed a dozen times more cheery than it had recently. After all, I assured it, as I put my key in the lock, Louise would soon be here with me. Not tonight, probably not tomorrow, but she would be here.

I made straight for the Glory Boot. This contains the vast collection of odds and ends of automobilia collected by my father, which is envied by the entire classic car world. The Glory Boot is a place for calm reflection, being in an annex to the farmhouse, and all too often I go there to sort out troubles away from phones, computers, doorbells and other distractions. Tonight was different, however. Louise had cast a spell over me and the Glory Boot and I felt back on track as regards this weird case.

Both Dave Jennings and DCI Brandon seemed to have some faith that I would come up with pointers and information that were eluding them. Brandon's particular bugbear, the Met, put

him in a damned-if-you-do (i.e. come up with a solution and it
turns out to be wrong) and a damned-if-you-don't situation. As
I saw it, it was my job to make sure that he and Dave avoided
the latter even if I couldn't guarantee the former.

So, back to this foundation, Dad, I mentally told the Glory
Boot's founder. If Joan and Barney had known about the foundation then it was probable the entire Herrick family had also
known, plus John Carson – and, I had to face it, Wendy. Just as
they all thought they had their futures nicely sorted out, the
game had taken this unexpected turn. I perched on a trunk of
as yet unsorted photos of races dating back to the days of the
De Dion motorcycles and considered whether the foundation
had been another throw of the dice in the game for Philip. Was
it a desperate effort to end it, because it was tied in with his
current will? Had he bought the Packard back and displayed it
so prominently at that open day at Staveley as part of that
process? I couldn't see what that might be, though. Nevertheless
the Herricks' appearance there had been no coincidence. Philip
had to live long enough to sign the foundation paperwork and
he hadn't done so.

This didn't entirely satisfy me as a theory. Nor I think did it
satisfy Dad, who still seemed to be hovering in his beloved
Glory Boot which indicated he disapproved of it too. OK, Dad,
I agree with you, I told him. There were other factors involved
and Geoffrey Green was one of them, because that brought
Wendy into the picture as well as the still possible opportunist
thief-cum-murderer.

I suspected Dad wouldn't like the latter theory and nor did I.
Back to the drawing board. On it sat the Packard and the
Volkswagen. The former had only one avenue of progress open
at present – the missing logbook. I'd tackle that tomorrow. The
Volkswagen was a different matter. I now knew it had either
passed through Richie Carson's hands or he knew something
about it. I wasn't happy with the story of this Golf. Certainly it
looked as if it were at least one motive for the break-in, but for
Philip's murderer to carefully unlock the garage, find the car
keys and drive it out didn't strike the right bells for me. To pinch
it after Philip had been killed would have been one hell of a risk.

Eventually I gave up. Dad seemed to have gone to bed in
disgust and I couldn't blame him. I would, in his shoes. But,

I thought happily, if I were in his shoes, I wouldn't have Louise to dream about.

The next morning provided me with a clear head, which was a bonus. Monday morning was even better. Louise had telephoned to say she would be here before the day was over. I'd replied that I would lay the world before her feet in the form of the best dinner our local pub in Piper's Green could run to, but she had brushed this aside. A supermarket takeaway would be fine. I could do better than that, I protested. I can produce the best spaghetti outside Italy if I have enough incentive. And today I had all the incentive in the world.

It galvanized my work too. My priority was to ring Brandon. His tone of voice was not encouraging when he heard why I'd rung.

'Did I know about *what* foundation?' he barked at me.

So the Met hadn't passed this on. As I knew all too well from my oil trade years, cooperation can equal territory protection where careers are concerned. I explained more fully and was greeted by silence with a touch of heavy breathing. I could imagine the thoughts running through his mind.

'Thank you, Jack,' he eventually said politely. 'No, I *wasn't* told.' A pause. 'It could change things.'

'It gives a whole new meaning to the end of the game.' I ran through the possibilities, half expecting a withering put-down, but it didn't come.

'This foundation would have served them right,' Brandon observed. 'The end of a hopeful dream if they'd expected the son to shell out to his entire family.'

'You've met Barney,' I pointed out. 'Not so far-fetched.'

'I don't go with this game as a motive in itself, but when they found out about the foundation it would have given them one very big motive indeed. No wonder Moxton was afraid of being murdered. Nothing to do with that Packard of yours.'

'You might be wrong there,' I said ill-advisedly.

'And so might you,' he whipped back. 'How's the Volkswagen search?' he added meaningfully.

'Away with the fairies. Carson wouldn't talk to me in person, but I had a brief phone conversation with him. There's been a slip-up. He'll get the car back asap.'

'You might be wrong there too,' Brandon commented. When I asked him why, he got his own back on me. 'Dave wants to tell you.'

He clearly wanted me to press him, but I reasoned that if he had information I'd be playing *his* game by pushing for it. I had enough games on my plate not to need another one. It was clear that the Met was keeping quiet on the forensic evidence in the Moxton case, which meant that Brandon's concentration on the cars was still his only hope of coming out of this mess with a career plus. That Golf was a pathway to it and might still come up with trace evidence.

Nevertheless I rang Dave, since he showed no signs of ringing me. He listened to my spiel and then shot at me:

'Brandon's right. We have got a line we're following up and it does lead to Richie Carson. Can't tell you more as yet. Trust this villain, do you, Jack?'

Go careful here. 'Why should he lie? I've given him immunity in exchange for information. Let's milk it for all it's worth.'

'Make mine a pint,' he snarled. 'And not milk.'

He was so pleased with his joke that I smoothly slipped in the suggestion that his team might follow up the missing Packard logbook with Swansea. The logbook had probably vanished for ever, but finding out the car's history in terms of registered owners could be done with the DVLA's cooperation, although it would take time.

Dave was not amused. 'Do you know how many man-hours that will take?'

'I've a fair idea.'

'All that for a *game*?'

'And for Brandon.'

'Ah. Seen to be doing? Is that the idea? OK, you're on, but make it two pints and lunch.'

Next on my list of priorities was Pen Roxton. If the national press had heard rumours about the proposed foundation, it was highly probable that Pen had too and I wanted to know what she was doing about them. She was a night owl, so I might still catch her in, even though it was already gone nine thirty in the morning. No phone call this time. I needed her help and with Pen that's tricky on the phone.

She lives in a most unlikely place, given her lifestyle of constant movement and that, contrariwise, is probably why Pen chose it. It's in a hamlet buried in the countryside called St Thomas, near to the Mallings. It gets its name from the legend that St Thomas Becket blessed a well nearby, one of several in the vicinity. Pen lives in an eighteenth-century red-brick cottage, and it even has a rose or two round the door. It looks innocuous, whereas its owner presents a different image.

It was ten thirty by the time I erupted into her life again, but when she opened the door I could see an oat flake or two around her lips. Good. I'd caught her still at breakfast.

She admitted defeat right away. 'Fancy an instant?' she asked.

'Why not?' One coffee in any form is a spur to my day and at a pinch I can manage two.

She led me through to her kitchen, piled high with a mix of kitchen ware, storage jars, notepads, a telephone and a laptop. 'Heard Louise was around these parts again,' she began in true Pen style, as she poured the boiling water into a mug.

'Did you?' Pen had been a pain in the neck when I first met Louise and she wouldn't be any less painful now. Louise can't stand her.

'Not in touch with you?'

I avoided answering this by reaching for a half-full milk bottle on the table to pour into my 'instant', then I suggested politely: 'Business, Pen?'

'Louise is business. *My* business.'

'Philip Moxton,' I said firmly.

'Great.' I had her attention now. 'What can you give me?'

Typical. Always 'give *me*' from Pen. 'Nothing. That's our problem.'

'Your problem,' she snarled. 'Not mine.'

'Yours too if you want a story.'

She considered this for a moment. 'Murder or the will story?'

That's my Pen. Trust her to be one step ahead. She'd already winkled something out.

'Which do you prefer?' I asked.

'Murder – if the line about the Moxton foundation is connected to it.'

'Ah.' I put on my best expression of disappointment. 'It was that I came to tell you about. Are you following it?'

She snorted. 'Old hat, Jack. Pity the great freedom of the press has been muzzled by an injunction. The news must have upset a few apple carts for prospective legatees. That's why you're here. Want to know who did him in to stop him signing on the dotted line. Well, you tell me. Who did?'

'I've no idea.' My best look of being perplexed.

She eyed me suspiciously. 'When you do, remember I'm your best friend. Right?'

'Of course.' I more or less had to be if I was to keep her from snapping at Louise's footsteps. It was time to feed Cerberus a titbit or two. 'There might be a story for you in the Staveley House—'

She leapt straight in. 'Now?'

'Possibly. Philip Moxton's sister Joan talks openly about her reconstruction of the gardens with the help of the head gardener there.'

She wrinkled up that quivering nose. 'Gardens? Can't use that. Boring.'

'Not on your watch.'

She brightened up. 'You're telling me that the foundation could have scuppered their plans for a pretty little garden? Is that their motive for murdering the brother?'

Reign in the horses! 'Bear it in mind, but don't, *don't*, rush off to suggest that to them.'

She looked hurt. 'I tread delicately, Jack. You know that.'

'Like a sledgehammer on an anthill.'

There's no malice in Pen. 'It gets results. Is this woman screwing the gardener?' she demanded.

I tread delicately too. 'No idea.'

'Tell me, laddie. Tell me.'

'He lives in the Staveley House lodge. He's middle-aged, his name's John Carson, his son Richie runs a stolen car racket and you've never heard of me.'

'OK. I'll check them out.'

Things were moving nicely. Faced with me or Pen, Richie might prefer to give information on the Golf to me, and with Joan Moxton she'd have a formidable opponent on the other front. 'My turn, Pen. You once threw out a mention of a bank robbery in connection with the Packard you saw at Frogs Hill.'

She looked guarded. 'Did I? Have a biscuit.'

There weren't any biscuits and she wasn't going to throw me off. 'I can't find out what you were hinting at.'

She grinned. 'Straight up, Jack? Cards on the table.'

'Agreed.'

'I'd no idea. Hoped you had.'

I sighed. '*Tell* me, Pen.'

'Nothing, Jack. Honest. It was only that I heard the boss's wife talking to Emma Herrick at a fashion shoot. Emma multi-tasks as a model when she's skint.'

Fashion shoot? Pen? My turn for suspicious looks.

She noticed. 'Mrs Boss dragged me along to take the photos. Me! Anyway, Emma was talking about her parents getting rid of the Packard now that old Gavin had died. She couldn't understand why her dad was asking over the odds for it. When she asked him he just said he knew it was daylight robbery but so what? He thought it was very funny apparently. Weird. So I thought maybe there was something in its background.'

She looked so anxious for me to believe her that I almost did. 'You've seen *The Ladykillers*. It featured a black Packard getaway car.'

'Saw it, but I wouldn't recognize a Packard from a Fiesta. Don't know much about cars.'

Even more odd. Firstly, she does know quite a bit about classic cars, and secondly I've never heard Pen admit she doesn't know about *anything*. I've seen her bluff her way convincingly through the thorniest situations.

'Your knowledge of De Dions is pretty extensive.' This was mean of me, because that was the one time the tables were truly turned on Pen.[2]

She stared me in the eye. 'It's straight up, Jack. That's what I heard. A robbery with a Packard. Honest.'

Honest? A suspicious word in itself when someone uses it – especially if the someone is Pen. And I *still* had no luck in following it up. I'd tried the local papers and archives, a time-consuming process as I didn't know when or where this robbery had taken place – even if it had ever happened. It couldn't have made headlines or I'd have picked up something in the national

---

[2] See *Classic in the Clouds*

press archives that fitted. If it had involved Philip Moxton or
Tom Herrick such a robbery would probably be after the mid-
seventies. Or, given that it was a classic Packard used, did it go
back to Donald Moxton and Gavin Herrick, in which case it
could conceivably have taken place in the late forties, fifties or
sixties? Did it concern any of them at all, or did it only involve
the Packard?

I remembered Sam West, who'd spent a year or two in banking
and might remember any tales of robberies. If I drove over to
see him I could then pop in for lunch in Wendy's café. She'd
been on my conscience. I seemed to be behaving to her as part-
friend, part-suspect. When I arrived Sam wasn't in, but my luck
was, as I found him at Wendy's.

'Bank robberies?' he asked, taken aback.

'Yes. Any with which Donald or Philip Moxton or Moxton
banks could have been associated with.'

He looked blank. 'I only did a couple of years in the 1960s.
Donald Moxton was around then, but he ran the banks, he didn't
raid them. He wasn't Mr Big in the Great Train Robbery if that's
what you're thinking.'

I laughed. 'Any robberies that occurred on his watch?'

'Can't think of any. I'll ring round and let you know if I hear
anything.'

Wendy joined us at that point and talk once again turned –
even without my help – to Geoffrey Green.

'What would he have been ringing you for that evening,
Wendy?' I asked.

'I hope it was just because he fancied company, not that he
was in trouble. I'd feel even worse about being out. I was over
at a friend's house and he rang my landline.'

'Did he ring from his mobile?'

'I don't know. The police said he'd been in London that day.'

'His Volkswagen was at the station when I parked there
around midday,' Sam contributed. 'When I got back from
Ashford around ten, the car had gone of course.'

I knew that. The neighbours had said they thought they'd heard
it pull up about eight and then Philip would have put it in the
garage, having called Wendy in vain to see if she'd like to come
over or if he could go over to her home. Did I know it was in
vain? Presumably yes, because otherwise it would have been

picked up by Brandon's team or the Met. But even they could not rule out the possibility that the call wasn't answered because Wendy had been at his home waiting for him.

I returned to Frogs Hill none the wiser about bank robberies. Even so life looked good as the day ticked on towards the evening that lay ahead. Would Louise be staying overnight? I had no idea, but there's such a thing as hope. I'm not too brilliant at touches such as lavender-scented pillows and the like, but I did my best.

I heard the sound of her car from a long way off, coming closer and closer. Len and Zoe had already left the Pits, but I had told them, somewhat diffidently, about Louise's return – whether temporary or otherwise. Even Len had looked pleased. He had clapped me on the back to express this sentiment, and only then did he remember the Bristol needing his attention.

By six thirty I had already been a quivering wreck pacing the gravelled forecourt, the crunch of my shoes making me even tenser. Then I'd returned to the garden to inspect nothing in particular. After that I'd gone round the house to check nothing in particular there too. Stupid. Because when Louise did turn into the gates everything shifted back into gear. Glory be! Here we were, at Frogs Hill, for the rest of our lives.

She sprang out of her car, came straight to kiss me and we were away. It seemed as if she had never left me. As we went together into the kitchen to inspect the feast I had laid on and then into the living room with drinks, there were a thousand questions to ask and yet there were none. A thousand things to say and none. She was here. She was wearing a blue dress, just as she had when I saw her for the first time – or was it the last time – or any time? It didn't matter. She looked beautiful. Her hair was longer than I remembered. That didn't matter either. All I could see was her smile, her eyes and that it was Louise.

She drew a deep breath as we went into the farmhouse. 'It's as I remembered it. Nothing's changed.'

'Can't afford the paint,' I joked (although it wasn't so much of a joke as all that.)

It was a meaningless exchange, but it filled the gap. We kissed again and then we went for a short walk in the fading sunlight, postponing the feast until later. It was the walk we had often taken along the Greensand Ridge, looking down on the Weald of Kent below us. I wanted to ask what her plans were, but I couldn't. Subject not advisable. She would tell me when she was ready – if she even knew them. Instead, romantic soul that I am, I found myself blurting out:

'How did you meet Emma Herrick?'

'On a film set. She's on the production side, though she's a pretty good actor too. And you?'

'I only met her at the barbecue and once when I was the patsy between them and Philip Moxton over the Packard.'

'I heard about that.'

'Are her parents and Gwen close friends of yours?' I hoped and hoped they weren't. I knew about Barney but if Tom and Moira were bosom friends as well as Emma it was going to be difficult.

'No. I know Emma fairly well, her family much less.'

'It's an odd one. You know Gwen was married to Philip Moxton?'

'Yes. Barney told me. I do like him,' she said defensively, as if I were going to accuse him of being a murderer.

'So do I, but that doesn't mean he isn't mixed up in all this.' Too late I realized that Louise was hardly likely to know what 'all this' was.

A silence, then she ventured to my relief. 'You're involved in the terrible Philip Moxton murder, aren't you?'

'I'm afraid so. Chiefly on the car side, but that could have repercussions on the wider case.'

'The Herricks don't seem very fond of your friend Wendy.'

'Probably because of Philip's will.'

She looked bewildered. 'I don't understand.'

I'd put my foot in it, but told myself that Gwen had talked without any restrictions to me so why not go ahead? 'They all expected to gain from Philip's will, according to a private family agreement.'

'I didn't know that. Barney said something about the money being left to a foundation.'

'That plan never went through. So the old will stands.' They *did* know about the foundation. There could be no doubt about that.

'Oh.' She pulled a face. 'With all of them inheriting?' She looked appalled. 'That's what they must have been talking about

– quite freely though. I knew Gavin Herrick slightly and I had the impression that Tom and Moira had thought he was well off – or was going to be. Not sure which, but it turns out he died skint. It was something to do with a game. Is that connected to the Packard?'

I groaned. 'I'm afraid so.'

'If the will was supposed to settle this game, the creation of a foundation might presumably have scuttled that?' she ventured. 'Gwen seemed in a state about it, but Barney didn't seem to mind and he would be the main loser.' She hesitated. 'I suppose it gives them all a motive in the eyes of the police.'

'It does look that way,' I said gently.

'But your friend Wendy,' Louise ploughed on. 'The Herricks seem to really resent her, even Emma. Why?'

How to answer this? Just a little money left to her, Wendy had told me. But it wasn't just a little. Not by my standards, nor hers. At the very least, she could give up the café, if she wished. But to the Herricks even three million shouldn't be that material to their future if Philip was as well off as we presumed. I wondered again what Philip's new will would have done about Joan and Staveley? Would she have been dispossessed?

I came up with some sort of answer for Louise. 'I don't know. I suppose it's because it *is* a big sum and Wendy is the classic girlfriend (or so they believed rightly or wrongly) who appears out of the blue as a money-grabber. They might assume she knew who Geoffrey Green was.' Not a pleasant thought for me. Not tonight when the world looked such a happy place.

'You're probably right,' Louise agreed. 'So what are you planning to do with the Packard?'

'It's going to live with us for the moment.' I relished the word 'us'. 'It's in the barn with the Gordon-Keeble. Do the Herricks feel strongly about Joan Moxton giving it to me?'

'I'm not sure. From what Emma told me, it seems to have been more than just a car,' Louise said soberly. 'Much more. You must know that the four of them, Gwen and Tom, Philip and his sister Joan, were all up at Oxford at roughly the same time.'

'Yes, but I think this affair went back much further. It began with Gavin and Philip's father Donald. The car was a sort of symbol of who was top dog.'

Louise looked puzzled. 'That doesn't sound right,' she said. 'Not from what Emma told me.'

'What then?' I asked. Could it be that I was about to hear the full story?

'I'm not sure, but I think it could have been over a woman.'

My hopes rapidly deflated. 'That was Gwen. Gavin went berserk when Philip married his daughter.'

Louise shuddered. 'Then I feel even sorrier for Barney who's caught in the middle. No wonder he is as he is.'

But how, I wondered idly as I took her hand and we began the journey back to the farmhouse, did anyone know *how* Barney really was?

Louise stayed that night. We loved and then we talked on the lavender scented pillows I'd rustled up at the last moment from some lavender stalks in the garden. The upshot of that talk was my wandering star would have a fixed abode for the next few weeks while she was filming in Sevenoaks. Beyond that . . . but we didn't think beyond that. Not yet.

She left Frogs Hill at six o'clock the next morning. I couldn't let her leave alone so like a regular couple we ate breakfast together and she drove off as the dawn came. All a dream? No. This time my star would be shooting right back this evening. We'd be eating the great feast we'd somehow forgotten to eat the previous evening.

With so much to think of and so little sleep, I wandered round in a daze, forgetting about the Volkswagen, the game and Packards. When the phone rang, I couldn't for the moment think of who Sam West was.

'Timothy Mild told me you were still asking about bank robberies,' he said, sounding rather hurt.

I smartened up my act. 'I was.' It looked as if my luck was turning in this case as well as with Louise.

'I rang up an old chum of mine. There was nothing we could think of in the sixties that had any link at all to Donald or Philip Moxton,' he said, 'but there was one pre-war, in the late thirties. His father told him about it.'

'Tell me more.' I did some rapid calculation. Philip Moxton wasn't even born until the 1950s, and Donald Moxton would only have been in his mid-teens. It wasn't looking good.

'There was a hijack on the daily delivery of cash. The money was lost and no one ever charged for theft.'

'So what's the connection?'

'The theft was from the first Moxton bank, then called Randolphs, in Hatchwell. It took place long before Donald Moxton bought it in the late forties and changed its name, though. The owner and manager was Alfred Randolph. I don't know if this has any connection with what you're after?'

It must have. Donald Moxton's first bank. I thanked Sam wholeheartedly. Then it struck me. How had Timothy known I was interested in bank robberies? I didn't remember mentioning it to him. The answer duly came to me. Pen had been at work.

TEN

The date had been 13th May 1938, an unlucky Friday. The robbery had indeed been at Randolphs Bank which was in the village of Hatchwell and that – I realized with a quickening interest – was not that far from Biddenford where Gavin Herrick and Donald Moxton had grown up. The amount stolen was £30,000. That doesn't sound a lot by today's standards, but for the 1930s it must have been a substantial haul.

Even though I was now armed with the year and the place, it still proved difficult to track down information about the robbery in the local press, although eventually I got there. A very unlucky day indeed for Randolphs Bank. Nineteen thirty-eight was the year of Chamberlain's September visit to Hitler in Munich when he had brought back – or so he thought – the promise of 'peace for our time'. Those on the reserve list for military service relaxed. In May, however, when the robbery had taken place, the threat of war had been at its height, after the annexation of Austria and murmurings of Czech mobilization, and so even bank raids seemed to have escaped notice in the national press. The Hatchwell theft had nevertheless received full attention in the *Cantium Press*, a local paper long defunct, which was probably why it had escaped Pen Roxton's eagle eye. There it was in front of me in Kent Archives microfiche form:

Daring Raid on Bank

Randolphs Bank in Hatchwell suffered a severe loss on Friday after its owner Mr Alfred Randolph, accompanied by two clerks and an armed guard, had driven his motor car from Hatchwell Post Office back to the Bank, having collected the day's money delivery. He, one of the clerks and the guard were about to begin the removal of the blocks of notes from the boot of the car to the safe inside the building, when a masked man ran from nearby bushes to the motor car, and drove it off together with the other clerk, Mr Donald Moxton, still in the rear seating. Mr Moxton's shrieks of alarm were to no avail. He was pushed from the motor car into woodland outside the village bounds and the thief drove off with the blocks of Bank of England notes still in the boot of the motor car. Mr Moxton, aged 16, was unhurt but owing to the mask and the robber's cap he was unable to tell the investigating police officer much about him save that he was a man of middle age, of stocky build and with brown hair. He is believed to have escaped with more than £30,000. The motor car is understood to be a black Packard imported from the United States of America and has not yet been found.

I whooped with pleasure at this discovery – to the sympathetic grins of my fellow researchers in the Archives – and slumped back on my chair with great satisfaction. A later edition of the newspaper reported the discovery of the said motor car at Robertsbridge railway station a week after the robbery. Thus two birds with one stone, the Packard and Mr Donald Moxton were now linked. All I had to do was answer a question or two. First query: was the black Packard *the* Packard. Answer: it had had plenty of time to be recovered after the theft and in due course to be acquired by the Moxtons and repainted. Next: was there any link to the Herricks here? Answer: not yet. Next: why did the bank get its cash through a post office? Did the Bank of England not use the train and its own fleet of cars? No answer to that either as yet. Next: why was the bank manager driving his own car and for what must have been only a short distance? Next: what about this armed guard? Didn't he have an eye open for masked robbers? And last – a delightful one this – surely it must have been an inside job?

I really relished the thought of that one. All sorts of interesting theories occurred to me as Donald Moxton was present at the theft. Forcing myself to be objective, however, this masked robber could be anyone, if this method of business was the bank's regular policy and therefore this was a daily or weekly trip to the post office.

My first job would be to walk the ground. Even if this robbery had nothing to do with Philip Moxton or his death, I could not be sure of that until I could rule it out with certainty. I needed to visit Hatchwell and I needed a companion for the trip. A man and a woman poking round a village would draw less attention than a sole inquisitor. True I had no plans to repeat the bank robbery but I prefer any information I gather not to be guarded because the informant is speaking to a possibly suspicious stranger. Louise was filming and in any case her face is so well known that anonymity would be the last thing her companionship would achieve, so I asked Zoe to come with me. She agreed with such alacrity that it didn't take many of my car detective powers to deduce her current job, rebuilding the brakes on a Morris Oxford, was not to her taste. She takes the view that if you've had a Morris Minor through your hands[3], every other Morris is definitely second best.

Hatchwell is way off the beaten track, but it's smaller and unlike Monksford is not moving with the times. It's frozen into them. When I checked it out on the web I was amazed to find that it still had a bank at all, though it was no longer Randolphs but Moxtons. I wondered why such a prestigious bank was still catering for a village, but then realized that there must be plenty of wealthy people living nearby who could well be happy to have an inconspicuous bank on their doorstep.

Zoe and I decided to take my precious Lagonda for a spin to Hatchwell the next morning. The weather was drizzly so it wasn't an ideal choice but even if we didn't look anonymous in such a car we would still be put down as carefree tourists.

[3] See *Classic Mistake*

'Maybe we'll be taken for a honeymoon couple,' I remarked to Zoe.

She snorted. 'As if!'

I flattered myself it wasn't me she was dismissing so lightly from her list of theoretical spouses, but Rob Lane, who rises and falls in her preference ratings quicker than the Dow Jones.

We became absorbed in a fascinating discussion of Desmodromic valve trains as we headed for Hatchwell. The Lagonda had been the right choice for this trip, being splendidly stately, as we were driving through a lush green countryside full of stately homes. It was hardly surprising that Elizabethan and medieval grandees had settled in this part of the world. There are such magnificent houses as Knole Park and the medieval Ightham Mote, and not that far away Sir Philip Sidney's Penshurst, and Anne Boleyn's Hever. This was an area relatively near to London but far enough away to keep their stately heads down (and on, save for poor Queen Anne). Added to that, Sir Winston Churchill picked Chartwell as his home and that wasn't far away either. When we reached it, Hatchwell seemed to be glowing with pride at being Kentish too and had caught some of the same eternal confidence that they were here to stay.

'Are you going to tell me what we're doing here?' Zoe asked as we parked. I hadn't explained yet, as she might not have come. It sounded a pretty unbelievable scenario and she doesn't like her time wasted (even though I pay her for it).

'Reliving a nineteen-thirties' bank robbery,' I told her.

She was instantly suspicious. 'Sounds like something out of a caper movie. This has got something to do with Philip Moxton, hasn't it?' she said crossly. 'What?'

'As yet, nothing. Does that matter?'

'Yes. If I'm to play Hastings to your Poirot, I'd like a clue as to how this meander into social history is helping.'

'Philip's father Donald was caught up in the robbery.'

She threw a theatrical hand to her brow. 'Not the Packard?' she gasped.

'The very same,' I intoned gravely.

'If this crusade helps get rid of that monstrosity from my working space, I'm with you all the way. Tell me more.'

I proceeded to tell her how it had been carried out, with it sounding more and more unlikely.

'You're kidding me,' she said in disbelief. 'That really is like a caper movie.'

'Truly, it happened, caper or not.' I had to bear in mind it had taken place over forty years before Zoe was born.

She sighed. 'Let's get going, pal. The sooner it's over, the sooner I can get back to sanity.'

I said that Hatchwell was frozen in time. Outwardly this was so, as it was essentially all in one long street with a few side turnings and a row of shops. Unfortunately although it still had a bank somewhere, the post office that featured in the story was no longer there – at least I don't think that in the 1930s the post office would have consisted of a small counter at the rear of a convenience store.

Enquiries provided me with the information that the old post office used to be in Manor Street, a turning off the High Street that led down to what still was called the manor, but was now a retirement home. The post office had been an imposing red-brick building now a private house, which told me nothing save where it was in the crime scene. Looking at it now, it was hard to imagine my Packard – was it significant that I was beginning to think of it that way? – waiting here to be loaded with the bank's cash, perhaps observed by the dastardly villain who was planning his audacious theft.

Randolphs Bank was our next stop. Zoe and I were directed back along the main street and told to take the second lane on the left. I could see now that there were fewer service shops than had at first appeared. There was a butcher with a greengrocer attached, a bakery, a convenience store and unusually an old-fashioned ironmonger. The rest were craft shops. Zoe grew impatient at my careful examination of these stores.

'Is this part of the robbery or are you just window-shopping?'

'Are you bored?'

'Only admiring how a great detective works.'

I took the hint and we found the lane to the bank, after a false trip down what proved to be the entry to the houses' rubbish bins area. Rose Lane ran down the hill past a terrace of cottages for about a hundred yards or so, and then I could see several larger houses set slightly back from the road before open country. The bank must be somewhere along there. The lane seemed to wind its way into a wood in the distance and then probably made its way towards Edenbridge. Zoe was getting interested now, and we found the bank discreetly nestling beyond the first row of cottages. It was in a large, rambling, oak-beamed house with a paved forecourt and a discreet sign to confirm that one had reached Moxtons. A cash machine was set into a tasteful modern brick addition to the bank's far side.

I could see why parking in the front of the bank would have been logical for the Packard as it returned loaded with its loot from the post office. There was room on the near side of the building for a car to drive through to its rear, but it would be an awkward turn for a spacious saloon car such as the Packard. The natural stopping place would be in front, so that the cash could be taken more speedily through the front entrance. Beyond the bank and its modern addition, was a farm track, still shielded by shrubbery on both sides as it had been described in the press article. Easy enough for a masked villain who knew the bank's routine to rush out and jump in the car while the staff, the manager and the guard were gathering round the boot. The Packard would have been self-starting and the key still in it, so all the robber had to do was turn the key and drive off into those blue hills yonder. The plan only misfired in that Donald Moxton had not yet made it out of the car and so had to be forcibly ejected at the first opportunity.

It was *still* a strange story. I couldn't see how Donald would have been involved in planning the theft at his age. He could have provided inside knowledge but that was hardly necessary as the routine was plain to anyone who kept a careful watch. For Donald to have been the mastermind himself was unlikely given his age. I wondered whether there had *been* a masked man at all and this story had been a concoction of Donald's to cover himself if he were the one who had leapt into the driving seat and taken off. No. Wouldn't work. At least one, and probably all three, of the three people standing at the boot would have seen him. I came back to the theory of his being the inside man, but it still didn't work for me. If he was, he'd have made sure he was out of that car when it pulled up outside Randolphs in order to avoid suspicion.

'A thousand questions come to mind, Poirot,' my Hastings remarked, when I conveyed these theories to her.

'To mine too. I shall enter the scene of this ancient crime, Hastings, and enquire of the staff what they know of this dastardly affair.'

'Leave this one to me, Poirot,' said Zoe grandly. 'I'm good with bank managers.'

This was news to me, but I stood aside to let her have her way. She strode in with great aplomb, but emerged a minute or two later with the aplomb missing.

'No one knew a thing,' she told me grimly.

'Failed to charm the bank manager?'

'No bank manager. Two staff, both female, one my age, the other still in her teens. Both thought it hilarious that there had even been a robbery in prehistoric times such as the 1930s. It's a sub-branch so one of them did have the grace to ring up the next branch up in the pecking order, but they thought it hilarious too. Wanted to know if we were getting them mixed up with *The Ladykillers*.'

I wasn't surprised. Nineteen thirty-eight was not only long ago in time, but in era, as the Second World War marked a huge divide in attitudes and lifestyle. I seemed to be stuck with a newspaper report and a Packard car.

'There must be somebody in this village who was around then. They'd probably be in their mid-eighties upwards,' I said in frustration.

'Pub?' Zoe suggested.

We gave it a try but the White Horse looked distinctly gastro and empty. There was no café, and the convenience store had no idea who its customers were or where they lived. I was left with the butcher, the baker and the candlestick maker as in the nursery rhyme – the latter being the ironmonger in this case. It looked an old-fashioned sort of shop, so I might be lucky. As we entered, it had the smell of ironmongers that I remembered from my youth, a smell that sums up screws, plugs, paints, pots and paraffin just as the Pits exudes a smell of petrol and grease. I felt at home here. On the left there was a long counter for customers to be served and staff actually serving behind it. Excellent. What was less excellent was that the staff consisted of one lad about twenty and Zoe was already pulling a face indicating we'd get nowhere with him. I still had a go.

'We're doing some family history,' I told him, wondering if

he even knew what that was. 'Know anyone round here who would have been around in the nineteen thirties?'

'Eh?'

I made it simpler. 'Do you know someone in their eighties who might be able to help us?'

'He's over there.' The lad pointed to the other side of the shop, which was shrouded in gloom but which I could now see boasted another counter, behind which was a very elderly gentleman engaged in sorting screws into tiny wooden drawers and taking no interest in us at all.

'Bill,' yelled the lad. 'You over eighty, are you?'

Bill looked up crossly. 'No need to shout. I'm not deaf. Not very anyhow. What d'yer want?'

Zoe marched grimly across to him, out to charm. 'This is a wonderful village. Have you lived in Hatchwell for long?'

He looked pleased. 'I have, young lady. Long enough to know where the original hatch was, that was the gateway to the village, see. Up on the old track. Know what the old track is, do you?'

Zoe looked nonplussed, but this was where I could help out, thanks to a friend who knew all about ancient tracks.[4] 'Ley lines,' I said.

He nodded approvingly. 'Sighting points. Markers. That's where the churches lie. Now, old Alfred Watkins . . .'

We were off. Alfred had written *the* book on ancient tracks way back in the 1920s and to listen to a soliloquy on the subject from one of his fans would be time-consuming, but perhaps worth it. Zoe clearly thought I was bonkers, but we waited until eventually Bill ground to a halt.

'Well,' he said, 'I've enjoyed talking to you but I've got work to do.'

'Me too,' I said promptly. 'Just a minute or two more of your time though. There was a bank robbery here in Hatchwell in 1938. Were you living here then?'

His eyes lit up like a router when the power's switched on. 'Robbery at Randolphs. I was a boy then of course. Friday the thirteenth. Unlucky for them all right. Talked of nothing else for months, we did. Playing cops and robbers round the place, solving the crime for the police—'

---

[4] See *Classic Mistake*

This sounded hopeful. 'Did you solve it? Who was this masked man?'

'If I'd worked that out proper I'd be owning the blooming Ritz by now, not this ironmongery.'

I dutifully chuckled. 'Did you see it happen?'

'Some of it, I did. I was at school, see. The old school – pulled down now by those vandals that call themselves a council – was opposite Rose Lane. A few of us saw the hullabaloo going on through the window. Half past nine on the clock. Remember that as clear as day. Not that days are clear, all those petrol fumes people keep filling the air with. Can't breathe sometimes round here.'

I thought of Hatchwell's traffic and compared it to the M25's as it circles London but decided not to comment. 'How much of the robbery did you see?' I asked. Keep on track or we'd be into climate change in a jiffy.

'There was old Alfred Randolph, he were the manager, dancing around shaking his fist, and folks were shouting and yelling. Old Jimmy Buttons, him being the village constable, came running, a-swinging his rattle Not that that was much good – he was the only copper around for miles. He got there as fast as he could, which wasn't that fast, him carrying the fattest stomach since Humpty Dumpty. Armed Response they call it now.'

Zoe was open-mouthed. 'How did he get reinforcements with only a rattle?'

Bill had to think about this, then came up with 'There was a police phone box in the High Street and the bank had a telephone, I reckon. Anyway, old Randolph couldn't believe his eyes, seeing his dosh and car going off like that. He got the car back but not the cash. It was found a week later.'

'So you didn't see the robber himself?'

'Can't say I did,' Bill told us with regret, 'but he was there all right. Talk of the town for days. Folks had seen him here and seen him there, seen him hiding in the bushes, seen him in the woods, seen the mask, he was tall, he was short, he was fat, he was thin.'

'Didn't the armed guard with them take any action?' I was still bemused.

'Armed guard? That was Bert Pink.'

'What was he armed with?' Zoe asked.

'Truncheon of course. Old Bert was proud of his truncheon. Prize bit of wood that. Polished up a treat.'

Zoe stifled a giggle, but not efficiently enough, as she earned herself a glare from Bill. 'Very handy was Bert with his truncheon,' he told her. 'Jimmy Buttons was too.'

I hastily intervened. 'So the bank manager drove the car to the post office himself every day and then carried the bundles of cash into the bank?'

'No, maybe twice a week, but always Fridays, they were special being pay day, see, and there were a lot of businesses round these parts one way and another. And Mr Randolph, he never did the carrying himself. Far too grand. The two clerks did that. Blocks they called them, blocks. Big heavy things, about this long –' he indicated a foot or so – 'and this deep.' He indicated about nine inches.

'Packed with five pound notes?'

'No. One pound and ten bob notes. Few fivers but they were rarer. My dad told me all about it – his sister was old Alf's typist. Fivers? I never even saw a fiver till after the war and then not often. Great big things they were, not the skinny little things we have today. You knew you had money in your hand if you held a fiver then.'

I was fascinated. 'How many staff were there altogether?'

Bill had to think about this. 'My Auntie Mags, then there was the chief accountant and under him the chief cashier and a couple of clerks. That makes five, don't it? And another one at the till, maybe two.'

'Donald Moxton was one of the clerks. Did he stay on after the robbery?'

'Fancy you knowing that.' Alert eyes fixed themselves on me. 'Ancestor of yours, was he?'

I'd forgotten my role as family historian. 'Distant,' I said.

'Ah. Well, he stayed on till he was called up in the war, I reckon. I think he came back after, not sure when, but back he came and blow me a year or two later he bought the bloody bank. Poor old Alfred, eh? Never got over the robbery, money never found, insurance wouldn't cover much of it, if any, then his son died in the war, and that was a real blow. No one to take over, see. Mr Randolph, he gave up driving around in the Packard.

His pride and joy it was, even after the robbery, but he had to sell it.'

'To Donald Moxton?'

'Wouldn't know about that, but it went somewhere. Poor old Alfred, eh? I was a young man then and didn't know what it was like to be old. Now I do and I don't like it.'

'What about the other clerk, the one in the car with Donald?'

'Wasn't from round here. A posh lad, he was.'

'You wouldn't remember his name, would you?' Hope flared up.

'I was only nine, but like I said Dad talked about it and so did Auntie Mags. Gary something . . .'

'Not Gavin?' I said, leading the witness, hope racing ahead of caution.

'That's it. Gavin. Gavin Herrick. Saw him on the telly sometimes. Another relation of yours?'

'Can you trust that?' Zoe asked doubtfully as we left the ironmongery, after I had assured Bill that Gavin was not my ancestor, merely a friend.

'Probably, but we can build on it anyway.'

'For what?'

'I'll let you know,' I told her grandly. I hadn't a clue, only that wild hope still flaring away.

Gavin Herrick, the Packard, Donald Moxton. At last I had three pieces that would tentatively fit even if I didn't yet know what the jigsaw was all about. What did look certain was that the game must surely be one of the pieces, which confirmed it had stemmed back much further in time than the 1970s. The drawback was that if this bank robbery began it, how did 'the woman' Gwen and her marriage to Philip come into it? Gavin and Donald were only fifteen and sixteen respectively when the robbery took place and they were connected by their work. War had come about sixteen months later, but when they were called up for military service they were in different forces.

After the war ended, Donald had remained in banking and Gavin had gone on the stage. How did they get together? Donald had bought the bank in 1948 when he was in his mid-twenties, but where did he get the cash? Buying a bank is a mind-boggling concept looking back from the twenty-first century, but I supposed it was not so much out of the ordinary then. Unusual perhaps for a private buyer but for a run-down concern such as Randolphs seemed to have been it might have been unremarkable.

My heart bled for Alfred Randolph, still driving around in his status symbol, the black Packard. With his son a victim of war, he would have had no successor and might have been grooming Donald to take over. True, it would have required some cash even if it had been a step by step transaction as Alfred gradually withdrew from the business. That was the most likely explanation, otherwise I was faced with a theory that two young teenaged boys hired a masked man and then divided the profits three ways. Unlikely, I thought. Again I considered whether Donald Moxton could have driven the Packard off himself and then pinched the cash. No. Even putting aside the fact that he had gone on working at the bank, it was not likely that he would have been able to drive a car at sixteen – given the few there were around in the thirties.

And that meant there was still a factor missing from this story.

We drove back to Frogs Hill and Zoe rejoined her battle with the Morris Oxford. I wasn't even as lucky as that. I found a message on the landline from Pen to ring her. I am economical with the number of people I give my mobile number to and dear Pen is not one of them, resent it though she may. She didn't sound happy.

'That you, Jack?' she said, when I called her back.

'What's wrong?' I asked. Her voice sounded very odd, croaky and somewhat slurred. Pen doesn't do drink, so it couldn't be that.

'You owe me.'

'What for?' I didn't like the sound of this.

'Your chum John Carson beat me up.'

'*Carson* did?' I was appalled. Grumpy old man or not, I didn't put him down as a physical assailant by nature. What on earth had Pen done to deserve that?

'Maybe it was his son, then.'

'It doesn't sound like Richie Carson's style either.' I was getting even more alarmed.

'His mob then. Must have been.'

That was possible, with or without Richie's approval, though

Timothy Mild might also have access to a suitable mob. 'Tell me what happened, Pen.'

'When I got home last night. Waiting for me. Trashed the car and then went for me. Wham in the face. Told me there'd be more where that came from if I didn't stop pushing my nose in. They'd push it in permanently.'

This was way over the top and effectively I'd set her up for it. 'Are you sure it was the Moxton story set it off?'

'As sure as the date of Christmas. A story about a garden. That's what you said.'

Guilt flooded over me. 'So what happened?'

'Joan Moxton wasn't too bad. Rattled on endlessly about some antiquated pleasure garden, so I asked her how her brother's death contributed to the story and did she think anyone on the estate could be responsible?'

I groaned. Typically tactful of Pen. Start with the bulldozer, then steamroller it later if she felt in a kind mood.

'You knew there was more to this than a garden, Jack.'

'Not this, Pen, not this.'

'Who else could have done it?'

'It could stem from your harassing Timothy Mild, Pen.'

A pause. 'I hear what you say, Jack. But that old goat at the lodge – he wasn't in chatty mode, and I had a feeling there was someone tailing me home. Laddie, I was right.'

'Did you get checked out at the hospital?'

'Yeah. I'll live to make your life hell.'

I ignored this. 'Did you get a story?'

'I've got one all right. It's *me*, Jack. I'm the story. Vicious Assault on *Gazette* Journalist working on the Philip Moxton case.'

I wasn't too sure this was wise, but Pen wouldn't be stopped.

'So what I want from you, Jack,' she continued, 'is the *real* story. What's your line? What's the case against Carson?'

I had to put her off and quickly. I thought fast and perhaps too fast. 'There is none, Pen. Richie Carson wouldn't risk a GBH charge to protect himself from a Volkswagen theft.' He might for his father's sake, I thought, if the Moxton murder was the issue, but no way did I want Pen digging in that direction. Brandon would tear me to little pieces and jump on them.

'I hear a silence, Jack.'

'You hear correctly. You've been warned off the Carson line, if you're right about Richie's dad. That doesn't mean that either of the Carsons is the answer to Moxton's death, merely that they don't want you poking into their little racket. Give it up, Pen, *and* whatever other line you might be pursuing. I've news of the robbery you asked about. I know you're on to that. That's why you tackled Timothy Mild.'

She didn't bother to contradict me. Instead I heard a sigh of satisfaction, much to my relief. I therefore told her most of what I'd found out and she listened entranced. I couldn't see any harm in telling her. It was well in the past and if she made deductions from it they could be helpful to both of us.

'Bless you Jack. You're a good mate.' And with this doubtful compliment, she put the phone down.

ELEVEN

I gave myself six out of ten as regards Pen. I'd given her a new line to play with but I'd no great hopes it would keep her happy for long. She'd be back sniffing at the mental gates I'd closed on her as regards the Carsons and Mild. I was finding it hard to think straight over that, however – indeed over anything. Having Louise at Frogs Hill was in danger of clouding everything else from my mind. Instead of a threesome at Frogs Hill we were now, blissfully, a foursome.

I'd warned myself that a foursome here might not be easy, even though Len and Zoe were big fans of Louise, but we seemed to be slipping into gear quite naturally. We'd come a long way in the two or three days she had lived here. Sometimes she would be there, sometimes she wouldn't. We'd even evolved a household plan. Sometimes I would cook, sometimes we would eat out, sometimes she would cook. I had been surprised to find she didn't like seafood. She couldn't understand my addiction to pasta. Even so, she had had a go at cooking carbonara and when I produced my (and Elizabeth David's) method of cooking scallops she did her best to enjoy them (well, she ate the pieces of bacon and it's the thought that counts).

We both knew daily life would be a roller coaster, and I had to school myself never to assume she would be there, only to be glad when she was – especially on the rare occasions she had the day off when she wasn't needed on set. The current film, a weird (to me) modern thriller based loosely on Shakespeare's *The Tempest,* was scheduled to end by the end of October in about three weeks' time, and then there was a big question mark over what came next for Louise, apart from a booking for a Christmas run of *Twelfth Night.* But we didn't look that far. Rejoice unto the day, eat drink and be merry – and especially the latter.

I had to tread carefully over the Philip Moxton case too, where Louise was concerned. Emma Herrick was her friend and theoretically Emma and her family were involved in the case. Philip's foundation plans gave them all a motive for wishing him out of the way quickly. Furthermore if Pen was going to be poking around about the robbery, it wouldn't take her long to tie it in with the Moxtons at least. I needed to be ahead of her. Knowing Pen, once she'd recovered from the shock of the attack, she would be back on any trail she fancied.

It was time to tackle Barney Moxton before Pen reached him again, as he was a central player in this case. I was sure Timothy would have warned the Herricks that I was in the picture over the foundation plans and therefore ensured that Barney knew I was coming. The news would then spread and the family react.

I duly drove over on Friday morning, parked and walked up the hill into the busy Rye town centre. Forget the modern traffic and the posh restaurants of Rye, just look at the outlines of the roofs and the upper storeys of the buildings and the old Rye is still to be seen. As I turned corners and then into the lane where Barney's emporium lay, nothing seemed to have changed in five centuries save that there would have been a lot more smells then.

I was mighty pleased to find that the news of my arrival had indeed spread. Barney had a shopful of tourists – and his mother. Gwen was sitting at the till doing her best not to see me as she chatted with a customer. No way could that be the case. Those sharp eyes had registered my presence from the very moment I came in and I wasn't going to be welcomed.

When the customer had left, Gwen opened battle with a decidedly frosty reception coupled with an air of resignation indicating that she knew she couldn't keep me away. Or, correction, she could, but that wouldn't look good when I reported back to Brandon and Dave Jennings.

In fact, Dave seemed to have retreated into the background. There had been no news of the Packard's registration details or of anything else. Odd, because Dave likes to be in the foreground, and preferable in the saddle, of every case on his books.

Gwen spoke first, once the shop at last emptied. 'I heard you were thundering down the warpath, Jack, so I'm the reinforcements.'

In my opinion Barney could fight his own battles, and he must have agreed because he grinned at me. 'Do I need them, Mum?'

'Probably not,' Gwen shot back. 'But I'm here anyway if only to look after customers while Barney is being grilled. Or vice versa if I am. Though grilled on what escapes me.'

I doubted that. Gwen was a tough cookie, as perhaps when she'd been Philip's wife she had had to be.

'What brings you here this time, Jack?' Barney seemed mildly curious rather than defensive.

'Still your father's murder,' Gwen briskly answered for me. 'So the sooner we can persuade this indefatigable bloodhound that we had nothing to do with it the better.'

Barney looked surprised. 'I don't mind talking to Jack. We talk to the police, don't we?'

'The police sniff around the crime scene, darling, but Jack seems to think that digging up the past with all four paws and then examining the rubbish heap will produce some kind of bone for which the police will pat him on the head.'

'Many a skeleton gets buried with the rubbish,' I commented.

Gwen ignored this. 'Let's get down to business. This is about Philip and his double life again, I suppose, so let me be clear about this. Philip only had one life and that was banking – whatever he chose to call himself.'

I decided to steer this my way. 'Like his father, Donald?'

A pause. 'Not entirely. Donald was quite different in character.'

'Grandfather was fun,' Barney contributed.

'To you maybe, my pet,' Gwen conceded. 'His idea of fun wasn't mine.'

'What was that?' I asked. 'Gameplaying?'

Gwen's eyes narrowed. 'Donald too was a banker first and foremost. Like Philip, like his own father, he wanted to win and he was just as ruthless – for all his *fun*. The difference between them was that Philip inherited his mother's staid disposition. Though he was obsessed with getting to the top and staying there, he didn't make bold moves. It was Donald who had the ideas and then handed them over to Philip to be developed in the years that they worked together. Donald was the adventurous one, but both of them moved people in and out of their way like chess pieces. People didn't count except as pawns. Neither of them was malicious, but they thought anything went in business and, indeed, at home. I should know,' she said wryly. 'Donald was a role model for Philip because he bought banks like knocking over pawns on a chessboard, removing all human obstacles. Like me. His eyes were always on the crown.'

'But you were the queen,' I pointed out. 'Your marriage to Philip must surely have crowned his game?'

Bullseye. There was a long pause now. 'Well, well,' she finally replied. 'Checkmate, Jack. Well done.'

'I liked Grandfather,' Barney interrupted, ignoring this exchange. 'Everyone did. But I suppose even Caligula and Hitler could be good company if they chose.'

Gwen sighed. 'Your grandfather was hardly a mass murderer, Barney. In a way, Jack, Barney's a throwback to Donald though, aren't you, my dear? Luckily without Donald's ruthlessness.'

'I hope so.' Barney looked anxious. 'I don't employ anyone of course, except for Lisa, who runs the shop at weekends sometimes.'

Gwen changed direction. Perhaps she realized she had been playing *my* game. 'So Mr Detective, what do you really want of Barney – and me, come to that?'

'Information about the bank robbery in which Donald and Gavin Herrick were involved.'

Barney looked interested, but Gwen's face darkened. 'You've been listening to fairy tales, Jack.'

'No, he hasn't, Mum,' Barney said eagerly. 'Grandfather told me about it. It was terrible. He thought he was going to be killed by the robber, just like all those stories of Bonnie and Clyde and John Dillinger in the States.'

'So it was no fairy story, Gwen,' I said.

I remembered Philip's words. 'There is, however, every possibility that I shall shortly be murdered.' Could that early episode
in his father's life have left a lasting fear? Had he blurted out an
inner trauma that had no basis in the reality of today? If so, the
fact that he was indeed shortly murdered must have been mere
coincidence and yet I couldn't believe that.

Gwen did not comment. Wisely perhaps. She and the Herricks
had clearly known about the robbery, no matter whether from
Donald or Gavin.

She switched tack. 'You mentioned my father. How did he get
into the story?' She looked puzzled, but it was a last ditch attempt.

'He was beside the Packard when it was robbed.'

'Do you know that for a fact?'

'I've good evidence. And Gavin must have talked about it.'

'He said they met *after* the war,' she shot at me. 'When was
this robbery?'

'Before the war. But it had to have been the origin of the game.'

'Why?' She was sounding defensive now.

'What else could it have been? The Packard was the symbol
of the game, and it was that Packard that was used in the bank
robbery in which Donald Moxton and your father were involved.'

Barney was looking upset. 'Do you think both my grandfathers
were bank robbers?'

'I doubt it,' I said frankly. 'But they were together when the
robbery took place.' Unless proven otherwise I was sticking to
this line.

'And both of them carried off its profits?' Gwen asked drily.

'That too seems unlikely, given their ages and the fact that
Donald continued working at the bank.'

Barney was looking worried. 'Grandfather Moxton did buy
Randolphs after the war.'

'That doesn't necessarily mean it's linked to the robbery,' I
said, rather regretfully. 'Ten years had passed by then. Alfred
Randolph could have been retiring, the bank could well have
been making a thumping loss and so having lost heart, Randolph
let Donald take over the ownership.'

Barney looked doubtful. 'I suppose that's possible.'

I changed the subject. 'Your father must have been disappointed
that you didn't take to banking.'

Gwen briskly intervened. 'Irrelevant, Jack.'

Use the accelerator. 'It's relevant to Philip's intention to leave all his money to a foundation.'

Gwen gave a strangled gasp. 'That is *it*,' she shouted. 'Get out!'

'No,' Barney said quietly. 'Stay here, Jack. I want to ask you something.'

Gwen looked as surprised as I was but she impatiently waved him on as though disclaiming responsibility.

'I want to ask if you would come to my father's memorial service in London on Tuesday,' he said.

I was taken aback, to say the least. I would hardly have expected *another* request to attend a family event, but regardless of Gwen's horrified expression I promptly accepted. 'Thank you. I'd like to.'

'Good,' he replied. 'Now about this robbery: did it have anything to do with my father's death?'

'It could have done.' I was struggling to come to terms with this unexpectedly assertive Barney. 'It must have been the origin of the game and that's a big factor in the case.'

'My mother believes that Wendy Parks killed him.'

Gwen raised an eyebrow, but didn't deny it.

'Any evidence for believing that, Gwen?' I asked. 'Have you even met her, apart from at that barbecue?'

'No, but she made sure she could get as close to Philip as she could.'

'How could you know,' I asked, 'unless you knew about his life as Geoffrey Green? Did you?'

'No,' she told me coldly, 'but we saw your dear Wendy at the Staveley Open Day, and Joan said she had been there at other times. No mention was made of Geoffrey Green.'

I found that hard to believe. It was news to me that Wendy had been at the open day, but it was quite possible, even though I hadn't seen her. Indeed, even if I had I wouldn't have remembered her from the scores of other people there.

'What other times?' I asked.

Gwen sighed heavily and theatrically. 'Joan saw her talking to John Carson one day. She'd been making enquiries as to who lived in Staveley House. Joan promptly saw her off the grounds but then your Wendy had the nerve to turn up at the open day too.'

'And that makes her a murderer?' I asked.

'It could. She was obviously blackmailing Philip by threatening to reveal his secret life and name. I grant you it's possible she's too clever to have done it openly. She might have made a joke of it, suggesting he left her "something in his will". It seems to have paid dividends.'

'Unless all the money had gone to a foundation, which,' I pointed out, 'would have affected not just Wendy but all of you, given your private arrangements for the game.'

'I wouldn't have minded about the foundation,' Barney broke in. 'I told my father so.'

Gwen's face was a study. 'You *what*?'

Barney grinned. 'I told him to go ahead, Mum. I did point out you'd all be upset, but he said he didn't care about that.'

I tried hard not to laugh, but it was difficult. So much for the game and gamesmanship.

'But the new will didn't get signed,' Barney added.

'No, it didn't,' Gwen snapped. 'Someone wanted her pound of flesh out of poor Philip. Your Wendy, Jack.'

So, I thought as I drove away from Rye, did the Herricks decide on drastic steps before all that lovely dosh left the game for ever? Nevertheless, if Gwen was right and Wendy had known who Geoffrey Green was, it did put a different perspective on his murder. I couldn't ignore the fact that the use of the kitchen knife suggested that it had been an unpremeditated murder, which spoke for his having been killed as Geoffrey Green, not Philip Moxton. That meant Wendy would be in the frame, but she wasn't sitting in it alone. There was another central player who linked the Moxtons, the Herricks and probably Geoffrey Green: Timothy Mild had his own reasons for wanting Philip out of the picture.

Wendy's café was crowded when I reached it on Saturday morning, but this gave me time to take an objective look at both Wendy and Monksford life. It was an innocuous scene, full of pleasant-looking people, no doubt each with his or her own troubles hidden behind their public faces. Sam West had asked me to let him know the result of my Hatchwell researches, so I had decided to come here and see Wendy too. I managed to find a table for two by the window, however, and staked my claim to it in the hope that Wendy could join me in due course.

I watched her flying to and fro from the kitchen with plates of food, wearing the same pleasant, if harassed, expression she always had while serving customers. She too had a public face and a private one, and it was interesting to watch the public one in action. Her astonishment at seeing me was real enough and so I think was her pleasure, which made my reason for being here tricky.

She came right over to me. 'What can I get you, Jack?'

I ordered a Welsh rarebit and asked her to join me when she could. She hesitated over this, however. 'Is it going to take long? I could come over to Frogs Hill tomorrow.'

'I can't manage that,' I said. Sunday was the day Louise had off, and no way could I forgo my first whole day with her.

It was half an hour before the café cleared sufficiently for Wendy to join me, and she was reluctant even then. I attacked head on. 'Why did you tell me you had no idea that Geoffrey Green was Philip Moxton?'

For a brief moment I thought I saw another side to Wendy, the cornered rat. It was so brief, however, that I could have imagined it. This case, I realized, was getting to me in a big way. I'd grown quite fond of Wendy and my personal feelings were becoming mixed up with the professional ones. Not good.

'Care to explain?' she asked icily.

'You were seen at Staveley twice, on the open day and before.'

She took one look at me and shrugged. Well and truly caught. 'The truth is that I caught a glimpse of Geoffrey's passport on that Bayreuth trip I told you about. The name on it wasn't Geoffrey Green, but I didn't recognize it. That set me thinking that he might be a master criminal so I tackled him about it and he came clean. He asked me not to tell anyone else, and I didn't.'

'And that's why he left you all that money?'

Another withering look from her. 'I was his friend, and if he wanted to leave me a nest egg I don't see it's any business of yours.' She reconsidered this. 'Sorry. Of course it's your business and police business too. I didn't *know* he'd left me anything, though he said he might.'

Not off the hook yet. 'You heard that he planned to change his will and leave his estate to a foundation?'

A split second pause. 'Yes. Timothy told me at the barbecue.'

'Not before?'

'No. And if Geoffrey had signed another will I wouldn't have got another penny. Which is what I expected anyway.'

She was regaining ground inch by inch, but she still wasn't there yet. 'And the visit to Staveley?'

'Female curiosity. I wanted to see the place and I thought I might get in to see the grounds if I charmed the lodge keeper.'

'No hope of that.'

'So I discovered. He was at the barbecue, wasn't he? He didn't seem pleased to see me there either.'

'Didn't you think it odd that Philip said he might leave you a nest egg but then decided to give all his money to a foundation?'

'Yes,' she said defiantly, 'but I've only heard all about that *after* he died. And now I've met the Herricks and Geoffrey's daft son I can see why he did it. He was sick of the lot of them.'

Nice one, I thought. The trouble is that in my job I have to see the worst side of everybody; they could be guilty until proved innocent. I had to apply that to Wendy too and I was faced with the fact that she was still on the list of those who would benefit very nicely from Philip Moxton's speedy death. The fact that I liked most of them could not stand in my way. Even Wendy, and even though we parted on bad terms – her choice, not mine.

Sam West counted as light relief after Wendy. I found him busily employed in autumn pruning, but he broke off with great pleasure. 'My wife was the expert,' he told me. 'I'm just a hacker. So tell me about this robbery.'

He led me indoors to his small conservatory and listened intently. 'That was Donald Moxton for you. Half rascal and half brilliant financier.'

'Could he have had anything to do with the robbery itself and that's how those rumours in the City about the Moxtons began?'

He considered this. 'It's hard to tell. It would make a wonderful story, wouldn't it? A bank robber turns up ten years later and buys the bank he robbed. But you know how rumours develop out of control. That one's neat though. Any truth in it?'

'I'd like to think so, but I can't see how it would have worked. There were witnesses who saw someone leaping into the car, and some must have seen Donald Moxton plod back to town after he was thrown out of the car. He couldn't have carried any of the blocks of notes with him and the car wasn't found for a while. If the robber took all the cash with him, he's hardly likely to honour any agreement to pay hush money later to a mere boy like Donald even if he had provided inside information. Anything's possible, but it would be a sophisticated operation for either of those teenaged boys. I grant you it might have given Donald the idea about buying the bank later.'

'More likely he learned what it's like to play with money,' Sam agreed, 'and then taught his son.'

'Philip Moxton wasn't backing the big merger though.'

It was a casual remark, but Sam answered it seriously.

'No. Timothy went through a bad time, but Moxton's death has brought it to an end. Merging with the Europeans is going to give the group all it needs to broaden the private banking arm product into new markets. Tim's sitting pretty now. He'll be chair himself shortly and won't need to bother with the Herricks and the game.'

'He told you about that?' He was even more of a central player than I had thought.

'Yes. The revelation that Philip Moxton had been living here under an assumed name came as a great shock to him as it did to me. He knew him so much better, though, that he must have felt betrayed, as he had considered himself a personal friend of the Moxtons. He was on good terms with the sister, he told me. He also told me about this game when the news about Philip broke and I'm sure it was he or perhaps it was Wendy after she had attended that barbecue who talked about a Game Book which someone kept to record each step. Perhaps it was Philip himself.'

What had happened to that, I wondered? 'Financial moves?' I asked. 'Over the sale of the Packard?' Weird, but then so was the game.

'I wouldn't know. I doubt it. I had the impression that the game was more important to all of them as a personal rivalry, though I'm not saying money didn't come into it.'

What was now clear was that it drew Timothy closer into the Herrick-Moxton circle than I'd realized. When – if – Dave Jennings came up with the information on the Packard's previous ownership, that might cover some of the ground that this Game Book held. I toyed with the notion that it recorded the proceeds of the bank robbery, how they were split between Gavin and Donald and what happened thereafter, but then I came down to earth. No one in their right senses would leave a fortune in one pair of hands while the rival hands held nothing – or if they did, it most certainly wouldn't have been for seventy-odd years. I toyed with the idea that Gavin had shares in Moxtons – but if so the Met would have dug that information out long ago and so, I thought with some amusement, would the Herricks. Every detail of Gavin's estate would have been examined.

So where did that leave me? Answer: with a conviction that the chess game was far from over, but I was beginning to see my strategy. Queen Gwen had done her best but it wasn't checkmate yet. This game was still ongoing.

TWELVE

Even as I joined the London-bound train at Ashford on Tuesday I still had doubts about attending the memorial service for Philip Moxton. It had not escaped my attention that from the Herrick and Moxton families only Barney had suggested I might like to attend. I doubted whether Wendy would be there. For me, though, it would be another excellent opportunity to see the clans gathered and, anyway, I had had a genuine liking for Philip on the few occasions I had met him. Did that give me a moral right to attend? A barbecue yes, but a memorial service was in a different category. I thought back to my meetings with Philip, my liking for him and my horror at the way that someone had removed him from this world. He deserved at least that his murderer should be found and if by being present I stood the slightest chance of getting further forward on this front, I should go.

There was another element too. This was the second time that Barney had urged me to attend such a gathering. Did he, I wonder, hope that I would pick up that missing piece of the jigsaw, a piece that as a family member himself he would be unwilling to supply in more direct ways? It was a piece on which I was increasingly focusing but it hadn't yet taken enough form to even call it a theory. Alternatively, Barney could be deliberately pointing the finger away from himself with this invitation.

I was still basking in the glow of the day Louise and I had spent at the seaside – Eastbourne, which is stony but stylish even on a blowy October Sunday. I suspected she was glad not to be able to come with me today. She was still worried about the Herricks and attending the service would make that worse for her, especially if Emma were there.

The service was being held at St Clement Danes in the Strand and the church was full, whether by invitation or not. I had difficulty getting in, but the magic word 'police' and the flash of an ID card achieved wonders. I was allotted a place as deferentially as though I were the Chief Commissioner of the Met. It was strange seeing everyone gathered in such formal circumstances and moving like automata to the demands of the day. Timothy spoke eloquently of Philip Moxton's genius, Barney of him as a father. His speech showed a different side of Philip as well as betraying a sophistication of phrase and humour that I had not hitherto appreciated. I'd realized there must be hidden depths to Barney but to hear them revealed here was moving. I told him so after the service as we congregated outside the church. I had watched him greeting people as they came out of the church, admiring his technique, which consisted of a simple hello to all and sundry. The tone did not vary for anyone, whether wearing City attire or for those who were family or friends. Though friends of whom? I wondered. Geoffrey Green or Philip Moxton? I saw Joan emerge, though there was no sign of John Carson. Nor could I see Emma. I did spot Wendy but when she spotted *me* she walked off.

'Who invited her?' I asked Barney curiously.

'I did. My father liked her so she had to be here.'

A simple reasoning, although I doubted whether Joan or the Herricks saw it that way.

I could see a lot of press people around, although Pen wasn't amongst them. Perhaps she was deliberately lying low, pursuing a line of her own in order, she hoped, to blast the case wide open – no matter whether in the right or wrong direction.

Barney told me there was to be a reception afterwards in the Savoy, to which I was of course invited. I liked the 'of course' – and the venue. The Savoy isn't my usual stomping ground and I made my way there with pleasure.

There's usually an unspoken programme for gatherings

following funerals and memorial services; the welcome drink, the greetings and condolences, and then come the glad hellos to friends or colleagues as guests reaffirm their own place in the world. Then follows a gradual thinning out, first of colleagues and then friends, leaving the family alone to face a different future.

And so it went today. Timothy Mild was talking to Wendy, apparently civilly. Tom and Moira were with Joan, their backs stiffly towards Wendy. Timothy's conversation with her was short-lived as he noticed me, however, and came over so purposefully I could tell that he had a mission.

'What's going on, Jack?' he demanded. 'I can't get a word out of the Met or your chap Brandon?'

My chap Brandon – I liked that phrase. It was flattering and doubtless meant to be. The Timothys of this world have polished phrases in their armouries ready to suit every occasion.

'Not much from him,' I rejoined. In fact I had heard from Brandon only yesterday. Some depressingly unhelpful forensic results had at last filtered through. Wendy's fingerprints were found inside the house, the blood was only Philip's. Nothing on the garage doors, save Philip's own prints. Nothing had as yet gelled therefore, especially as there was still no trace of the Volkswagen. There had been only one glass on the table; this had revealed Philip's DNA, but four matching expensive glasses in the cupboard suggested the sixth could have been taken away by his murderer. That meant he must have taken it before pinching the Volkswagen, but that didn't seem to add up either.

Brandon had asked me hopefully whether the Packard line was leading anywhere, and so I had given him the details of the robbery to cheer him up and he was indeed pleased.

'Pursue it, Jack,' he had told me.

'What about Dave's side of things? I haven't heard from him.'

'You will.'

'Is that about the Volkswagen or the Packard?'

'You'll see.'

Thanks, I had thought. No forward movement in that direction, but there was another chance here. I could see Timothy was not happy with my reply so I pushed ahead on another front. 'Things on course at the bank?'

I received no more than I expected: the stock reply. Fair enough. I'd given him one. 'Philip's a great loss of course,' Timothy said, 'but we're pushing ahead.' A big smile indicated that subject was closed too. 'Unlike your investigation, it seems,' he then smoothly added.

'Early days,' I said dismissively. 'By the way, I looked into that bank robbery rumour.'

He lost some of his suavity. 'So I heard. A good joke, eh? The great Donald being hijacked. Amazing you dug that up.'

'Did he joke about it himself?'

'Donald? How old do you think I am?' A forced laugh. 'He was fading out of Moxtons when I was coming up. I met him of course. Nice chap. Nothing like Philip.'

'But you got on well with Philip?'

'Of course. Except over this merger business. Nothing secret about that. But that didn't affect our friendship.'

'Yes, I gather you know all about the game. Was it you who kept the Game Book?'

The big smile vanished. 'What on earth is that?'

'Some sort of record of it, possibly financial.'

He frowned, and the frown took a long time to manifest itself into speech. 'It's true I sometimes found myself piggy in the middle between the Herricks and Moxtons, but this Game Book is nothing to do with me. It couldn't have anything of significance in it anyway.'

'I thought it might have been part of your piggy in the middle role if it contains the results of polite blackmail over the robbery for example.'

The frown became a glare. 'Are you implying it could have impacted on Philip's death and that I was involved? Just because his death gave Moxtons the push it needs, doesn't mean that I helped the push in any way at all. How could it? Can you see me creeping over one dark evening to Monksford, breaking his back window, finding a kitchen knife and stabbing him, thus covering myself in blood, after which I drive home to my wife? No way, Jack. Doesn't stack up.' He looked rather pleased with himself now.

'It doesn't,' I agreed. 'Especially as you claim not to have known where he was living or anything about his pseudonym.'

'Precisely.' He glared even harder at me.

'Although you do know Monksford, Sam West and Wendy.'

He seemed not to hear me but, in Lewis Carroll's immortal words, softly and silently vanished away, leaving me to track down Moira Herrick. She was stylishly clad in a charcoal-coloured jacket and skirt, and still managing to convey the impression that she was the queen of the occasion.

'So pleased to hear about you and Louise, Jack.'

'Thanks,' I said cordially. 'We're happy too.'

This guarded exchange over, she got down to brass tacks and I reckoned it wouldn't be long before the game was mentioned and if she didn't bring it up I would. I'd been led around the maze too many times and I was fairly sure now that I knew the way to the centre.

'We were so relieved we Herricks were welcome here today,' Moira cooed at me. 'Joan was marvellous about it. It really does mean the end of that wretched game.'

To me it seemed there was still another set to play in division of the spoils from Barney's inheritance, but even as the thought crossed my mind, she raised it herself. 'And in case you're wondering, Jack, Tom and Gwen have agreed with Barney to have a cooling off period until probate is granted and the tax position sorted. So that really does mean it's over and thank heavens for it. It's been hanging over Tom and me all our married lives and for poor Tom and Gwen long before that.'

Promptly on cue, the man himself arrived. 'What's all this about poor Tom?' he joked.

'I was telling Jack about our agreement with Barney, darling.'

Tom looked uneasy. 'Oh. Yes . . . he's a good fellow, young Barney. Just as well it's sorted out, eh? Philip wouldn't have wanted this wrangling to go on.'

'No?' I tried not to sound too disbelieving. It seemed to me that Philip was ensuring it did go on by his plans for a foundation. Throwing down this gauntlet would mean the game's financial basis, whatever it was, would be well and truly scuppered, as well as removing any basis for the murder he had feared. Nice one, Philip, I thought. But it went wrong, seriously wrong.

Moira flushed. '*No*. That's why he bought the Packard back from us and Joan has given it to you.'

'God knows why,' Tom muttered.

Moira glared at him. 'The Packard isn't something any of us would want to keep, not with all its—'

'Moira!' Tom cut in warningly.

'All its what?' I queried.

'Family connotations,' she finished lamely.

She had opened up Pandora's box. Now I knew I was not only on the right track, I'd hit the centre. Gwen had not been the 'woman' in the case, nor the queen on the chessboard. Far from it. So here came checkmate.

'The game was nothing to do with one-upmanship or Packards. Your mother was the heart of the game, wasn't she, Tom?'

By the looks on their stricken faces, I knew I was right. They didn't have to say another word, or even concoct another story.

'How and why did she die, Tom?' I asked.

'It's not something we talk about,' he said stiffly.

'You must.'

Moira took one look at Tom's face. '*I'll* tell you, Jack. Nancy died in 1965. How and why we don't know. Gavin adored her and so we *guess* might Donald have done from afar. Whether that had anything to do with the game we don't know. I can't see what, because when the four offspring, Philip, Joan, Gwen and Tom, decided to end it after their fathers' deaths they told Gavin and Donald their decision. They didn't seem to mind very much. After all –' she delivered this with the air of playing a trump card – 'the game continued *after* the Oxford agreement so Nancy's death can't have been involved.'

Tom looked so relieved, it flashed up a question mark for me. 'So why,' I asked, '*did* it continue?'

'Because,' Tom immediately replied, 'four years later Philip married Gwen.'

Neat but not neat enough. 'Against her will?' I asked.

That silenced them both. Someone had to stand up for Philip Moxton and I'm glad it was me. Even if I was still stuck in the maze. No good being in the centre if you don't know your way back.

'You seem to have upset Tom.' Joan plodded over to me, seeming rather pleased about it. Wearing a hat and navy spotted dress, she looked the most feminine that I had ever seen her. It suited her but I made the mistake of telling her that. She dismissed the praise instantly.

'I'd no choice,' I said. 'You've all been doling me out snippets for too long. One way or another I need the truth.'

'What gives you the right to play Solomon?'

'Because you, Tom and Gwen are too close to the situation to judge whether the game is a major element in Philip's murder. The game including,' I added, 'the part about Nancy Herrick's role.'

Her face darkened. 'Take care, Jack. Take great care.'

'And you too. The game isn't over yet.'

She gave a sort of harrumph, a cross between laughter and annoyance. 'That's what John says.'

'Is he here?'

'Unlike your friend Wendy, he didn't think he should attend.'

'My non-friend Wendy at present.'

She almost grinned. 'Not difficult with that lady. John says she's like her cakes. All squidgy jam and cream outside and tough as nails inside.'

'How could he know that through one chat with her at the Staveley Park gates?'

A cool reply. 'He can always tell, John can. That's why he's handling the management of our pleasure gardens.' Then she was off on a dissertation about alcoves, Greek statues, ha-has and vistas, so it took quite a time to get back to Philip Moxton and the game.

'The Herricks told me that the discussion of the will is going peaceably,' I managed to break in at last. 'Are you OK with the situation?' I thought she might slap me down but she didn't. She just looked surprised. 'Of course. I get the house, the gardens and the upkeep costs.'

'And Barney? Is he happy too?'

She gave me a curious look. 'Barney's always OK. He just does what he thinks best.'

'For other people or himself?'

'He's not Solomon either. Not always.'

Which, I thought as she suddenly decided she needed another drink and bustled away, must be somewhat worrying for those expecting to live on Barney's prospective fortune. I was not alone for long. I was moodily inspecting a canapé that had disintegrated half on to my shirt and half on to the floor when Gwen arrived, almost spitting with rage. 'I hear you've managed to wheedle the story of my mother's death out of Tom,' she fumed.

Take this gently, I thought. 'Wrong. Not wheedle and not even the full story. Gwen, the police are going to have to know what bearing this has on the murder. Does it have any?'

She calmed down and became almost reasonable. 'I don't see how. Barney told me about that robbery in the 1930s where Donald and Gavin were witnesses. That seems more likely to have sparked it off than my mother's death.'

A good try, but not good enough. I braced myself. 'Was it a natural death?'

I could almost see the wheels turning in her mind: death certificates, inquest verdicts, all could be checked by the police.

'My mother killed herself,' Gwen said at last. 'My father never told me why. He was devoted to my mother. Tom and I can vouch for that, and he never married again. He threw himself into his stage career. He seldom stopped acting, even at home. One day we would wake up to Falstaff, the next to Prospero, the next to Jack Worthing. Actors are their roles.'

Was that true? I wondered. What about Louise? I couldn't believe that of her. She cast her roles off with her stage make-up. Or was her life with me yet another role? My stomach seemed to turn over at that thought.

'So now you know the story,' Gwen continued bitterly, 'you need not go on badgering us about the game. It can die in peace, along with that blasted Packard.'

There had to be more, I knew that, but it wouldn't come from her. Had Nancy played her part in the Packard story? Had Philip married Gwen because of the game? Had it been Gwen's idea to marry Philip? Was she the pusher or the pushed? The robbery must figure in the story, but how? The boys were in their mid-teens at that point so Nancy was unlikely to have been involved.

Wendy was now talking to Timothy again, and they seemed to be conversing with an urgency that spoke of more than a brief encounter in her café. It would achieve nothing to barge in, so I waited until Timothy had departed and made a beeline for

Wendy. She seemed to be studiously looking in the other direction, but finally deigned to speak to me.

'You're out of place, Jack.'

'We both are,' I said pleasantly.

'Not me. It was Geoffrey Green who died, not Philip Moxton.'

'You're right.' I'd put a foot wrong. 'It must be hard for you
today.'

No way was I going to soften her. 'I'll get through it, thanks.
Without your help, so if you don't mind, Jack . . .'

She pushed her way through the crowd and I saw her making
for Barney, the 'daft son' as she had termed him. Business with
him too? I wondered. I circulated for a while as the party sepa-
rated into groups of business colleagues, now rapidly thinning
out, and those of friends and relations. Wendy was right. I had
no place here now and it was time to leave, so I made my adieux
and fought my way through the rush hour crowds to Charing
Cross rail terminus and then on to the Pluckley train. I was glad
that sanity would be awaiting me at the other end of my journey.
My daily driver Alfa was awaiting a new gear box and I hadn't
fancied leaving the Lagonda or the Gordon-Keeble at the railway
station all day, so Len was picking me up there.

I had to stand for most of the journey, which is no problem
in itself, but today I had stood for several hours at the reception.
I'd walked to Charing Cross. I'd fought for standing room in the
train and now had pop music in one ear blaring through a youth's
headphones and the other ear assailed by a high-pitched mobile
phone conversation. I couldn't relax and was ready for normality
in the comfortable shape of Len and a lift home. With luck Louise
might already be back at Frogs Hill or at worst she would be
back in an hour or two. Home is a fantastic word. I hadn't thought
of Frogs Hill in that way for many a long year. Just a short trip
and the evening would begin with Louise.

Quite a few people left the train with me at Pluckley, and as
we all walked to our waiting cars, I scoured the car park. There
was no sign of Len or his new love, a clapped-out Ford Granada
estate, although he'd told me that as he would be working late
it would be no problem to nip over and pick me up. He must
have broken down on the way to the station or forgotten, I thought
uneasily. Neither was like Len, however. I rang Frogs Hill, no
Len, no Louise. I rang Len's home. No Len. Mrs Len was

somewhat indignant, although I would have thought that by now she would be used to her husband's erratic (but self-imposed) hours.

The last passenger's car drove out of the Pluckley car park and I was alone in the dusk with a few cars as yet unclaimed, the lights of the Dering Arms pub twinkling a little way off, but still no sign of Len. Really worried now I rang Zoe's home. Again, no reply. She must be out on the town with Rob Lane. Taxi? There was none around. I couldn't ring Louise's mobile as they're forbidden on set, so I tried the Frogs Hill number again. Answering service only. I'd have to walk. No problem on a fine summer evening, but in the dark of an October one, not good. Anyway, ten to one I would find Len's Granada broken down along the Pluckley road. Needless to say, Len doesn't believe in mobiles. The quickest way home for me would be two to three miles along part-road, part-footpath – the snag was that the footpath lies across open farmland and then rises steeply up the hillside, which is not an attractive prospect in the dark.

There was no help for it, so I set out, hoping the light would remain good enough for me not to fall flat on my face and that the welcome sign of Len fixing his Granada at the roadside would greet me.

My march along the lane leading to the Smarden to Pluckley road with the occasional street light wasn't too bad – except that I didn't find Len on it. It was definitely beginning to seem that something was wrong, but I'd no alternative but to push on. A couple of cars passed me once I had reached the Pluckley road, but not Len's. Walking was easier here until I reached the point where the footpath branched off. The dusk made the lines of trees dividing the farmland look mysterious, almost threatening. The evening was nearly over, the birds were tucking themselves up for the night and the hedgehogs, foxes and badgers would be preparing themselves for their night's hunting. I picked my way along the footpath, said hello to the only dog walker I passed and struck out – and up – for Frogs Hill.

When with great relief I finally reached the footpath's end and joined the narrow lane that led to Frogs Hill, I'd never seen anything quite as welcoming as the farmhouse lights twinkling at me from afar. Home at last. I quickened my step – until I walked through the gates and the security lights blazed out.

All of them, not just the one I had triggered. *All* of them. *Everywhere.* From the rear garages, the farmhouse itself, the Pits. I saw Len's Granada, I saw Zoe's old Fiesta. What the hell was going on? Something must be seriously wrong.

I rushed to the Pits, the doors of which stood wide open, but there were no lights on within to suggest a late-night working for Len and Zoe. As I took this in, stars flashed before my eyes as the blow landed on me from behind with a sickening thud. I must have blacked out for a few seconds for as I opened my eyes again I realized I was stretched out on the ground, there was gravel in my face and pain everywhere.

As I tried to turn over, I saw the boot coming towards me.

THIRTEEN

P ain is a world of its own. I lived within it as images of faces swirled around me, anxiously doing their best to help. (I exclude, I hope, the gentlemen who put me here.)

Louise came and went from my consciousness. I was vaguely aware of her voice and sometimes briefly her face peering down at me, intertwined with those of others. I think one told me I'd been lucky, although that seemed a strange observation with my constant companion Mr Pain jabbing away at me. As time passed I gathered that the luck element had been that when Louise returned to Frogs Hill that evening, the security lights had indicated the obstruction of my body just in time to stop her driving right over me. I remembered the swoosh of her dark hair over me and of managing to get the words 'Len' and 'Zoe' out before I passed out again. There had been a few more flashes of consciousness as the paramedics arrived. Plus more pain. And more. I heard a 'Don't move, my sweetheart', but nothing more until I woke up in hospital.

When I opened my eyes and felt more or less back in the world, I saw her sitting by the bed and had automatically reached out for her. Mistake. Mr Pain circled in furious waves around me, while he decided where to attack first. Then he dug deep, and I let her hand drop. All that mattered was that Louise was here *now*, and so, apparently, was I in some form or other. For how long I couldn't be sure, so I got to the point right away.

'Len and Zoe?' I croaked. I wasn't sure why I was asking about them because there was a blank in my mind but I knew it was important to hear the answer.

'Unhurt, my love. Tied up in the Pits. Immobilized.'

'Faulty starter?' I managed to gasp.

'If you can crack jokes, you're on the mend,' she said lovingly.

Joke? Was it? Not sure about that. Cracking seemed a suitable word, though. It took effort to crack anything but perhaps effort was what I should be making. Dim memories of howling my head off as a child floated by and my mother's instructions to 'Be a brave boy now'. I didn't want to be a brave boy, if it meant enduring this pain. On the other hand, I supposed I had to make some attempt at it, so I did my best.

'How . . .'

My effort petered out. I had meant to ask what happened to me, but the words failed to arrive. Before I could try again a nurse marched up and ordered Louise out, which threw me back into my pain world. This seemed fairly standard procedure for some days, although they were punctuated with visits from Louise, Len, Zoe and I think Dave. He came in with Brandon, although that might have been a hallucination – especially as both of them had cheery looks.

Meanwhile every single machine in the hospital (or so it seemed to me) established the fact that I wasn't on the critical list; in fact it seemed I wasn't on any list, save for serious bruising inside and out and a whole raft of cracked ribs. The general attitude seemed to be, however, not that I was a brave boy but that it had been pretty stupid of me to have got involved in a pub punch-up. When Dave arrived with Brandon for a second time flashing police ID cards, this only confirmed the hospital staff's dark suspicions. No doubt the nurses would shortly have an armed guard to protect them from this desperado they were nurturing in their bosoms.

Only Dave looked cheery this time. 'Don't get up,' he told me. 'We've only come to decide which of us pays your bill.'

I managed a suitable laugh.

Brandon was more sympathetic, even if not cheery. He sized me up and down, and then said, 'Bad do, Jack. Who was it?'

'You tell me,' I suggested. They were the coppers, not me. 'They must have come at me from behind.'

'That's what Len Vickers told us and his assistant too. Three of them, they said. Masks of course.'

'Who have you been upsetting most?' Dave enquired.

'Half the establishment and half the underworld.' I meant this sarcastically, but Brandon took it seriously.

'Underworld first,' he said briskly.

'Richie Carson's lot and his father, but I can't see why they should want to show me their appreciation of my services. I'd had a message from them that they had the car and would get it back to us. I'd given him a clear passage on it, so there'd be no reason for him to lie.'

Brandon looked sceptical. 'Optimistic, Jack.'

'Murder wouldn't be Richie's style,' I retorted. 'It would draw too much attention to his activities. Even this attack on me would be pushing it and anyway I hadn't been giving him any grief. It's off his books as an issue.'

'Not off ours,' Dave blithely informed me. 'It's back in the police pound.'

I jerked so much with this announcement that pain promptly hit me like a sledgehammer. 'That was quick. How?'

'Tip-off. Untraceable of course.'

'Where was it?'

'Monksford station car park.'

I must have momentarily passed out – which was hardly surprising, I suppose. I knew I had because both Dave and Brandon were now looking sympathetic. This case was getting away from me fast, so I made a mental grab at this new rocket that had been fired at me.

'Why there?'

'When you've stopped malingering you can tell us.' Another cheery comment from Dave.

So I made a stab at doing so. 'Carson?'

'Junior or senior?' Brandon asked.

'Junior,' Dave kindly replied for me. 'Senior's got his head too firmly in a plant pot.'

I tried again. 'Any prints? DNA?'

'Testing now.'

Brandon took over. 'While we're waiting, you can tell us why you think half the establishment is after your guts. I assume you meant establishment as involved in the Philip Moxton case.'

'Yes.' Saying yes was less painful than nodding.

'Would any of them be heavy hitters?'

I thought, or tried to. 'Only Timothy Mild and not personally.'

'Would he have access to Richie Carson's mob?'

'It's possible.' I ran it through my mind but it came out blank.

'John Carson's more likely,' Brandon said. 'He's reason enough to want you *and* Moxton out of the way.'

'Agreed,' Dave said.

'Agreed,' I echoed enthusiastically. News of Philip's proposed foundation couldn't have pleased John unless Joan Moxton had known Staveley was safe. And that was a question mark.

'Why should Carson pick on you?' Brandon asked.

'Maybe I was getting too close to the truth,' I offered them hopefully. I'd be glad of a hint as to what that was.

I must be getting better because Brandon's gimlet look was back.

'Am I up to date with you on Father Carson?'

'As far as I know.'

Brandon let me off lightly on this unhelpful contribution. 'That applies to all of us. Put some thought into it, Jack. The assault on you is logged as GBH. I take it you'll press charges?'

'Hard to press anything at the moment,' I rejoined. 'Too bloody painful.'

In between dozes I had plenty of time to brood on the Volkswagen's surprise reappearance. Medical visits had tailed off and it turned out that Brandon had arranged for me to stay in for another few days past the time that I would normally have been kicked out. Tests over, my bruises now had to heal by themselves. I wondered why Brandon was so concerned until Louise told me she would have to be away filming in Dorset for a couple of days and, unusually, Len too was away from Frogs Hill. Brandon didn't want me there alone with only Zoe to protect me. Nice of him, although I assured him that Zoe on the warpath could protect me from Attila the Hun. Brandon's reply had been that Attila the Hun wasn't in Carson's gang.

Louise was leaving on Sunday and that day marked another

great event: I managed to hobble along the corridor to a patients'
day room. That's where Wendy found me. My first reaction was
that I would have preferred Attila, but I softened my view when
I saw how anxious and ill she looked.

'But it's terrible, Jack,' she told me after the usual commisera-
tions. 'Was it through this murder case?'

Might as well tell the truth. 'Probably. I'm not handling
anything else at present except a Riley and an old Morris. I can't
see their proud owners leaping into hobnail boots to express
dissatisfaction with Frogs Hill's service.'

She tried to smile. 'I'm sorry I got so ratty with you. The
Herrick and Moxton clans believe I'm the enemy so it was tough
when you seemed to be joining them. I'm not the enemy, I'm
really not. They pretend they're eager to see me and keep coming
to the café pestering me about Geoffrey. They don't really want to
know anything, they just want to make sure that they're seen
to be concerned on his account, so they bring Timothy with them
or even worse a journalist. That Roxton woman is a pain in the
neck. She's as ruthless as they are.' Wendy shivered, despite the
warm cocoon of the hospital heating. 'They *are* ruthless, believe
me. That's why Geoffrey lived under a pseudonym. He was scared
of what they might do to him.'

'Pen—' I began.

'Fat lot of good that did,' Wendy swept on, ignoring my inter-
ruption. 'They tracked him down and murdered him.'

'His killer could have been anyone who knew who Geoffrey
was.'

'Precisely,' she snapped. 'Joan Moxton and that awful Carson
man. *And* Timothy. An outsider like him could have killed
Geoffrey. I've been a bit worried, in fact. I'll tell you when you're
better. Probably nothing.'

I was still thinking about outsiders. 'Do you think of Barney
as an outsider? He seems to choose that role.'

'*No* is the answer to that question. Barney's the son of Philip
Moxton and Gwen Herrick for heaven's sake. Outsider? No way.
He's not as simple as he seems. He just opts out, Jack. If he decided
to opt in, do you think he'd stop at murder? Again, no way.'

This was a new angle, but I couldn't get my head round it.
'He didn't know about Geoffrey Green, did he?' was the best I
could manage in reply.

'Of course he knew, but it suited him and all the rest of them to appear not to know. Don't you see, Jack? That's *why* he was killed as Geoffrey Green – to shift the balance of probability – and that's why they're now accusing me. As if I'd murder him, or murder anyone.'

As she left, a great wave of relief followed by extreme tiredness blanketed me. My body might be recovering but my mind felt at the mercy of anyone who came along to brainwash me. Then balm in Gilead arrived in the form of Louise. She looked wonderful in a red check jacket over black trousers, and a perky little cap over her dark tresses. This was an oasis indeed.

'Phew,' she said, planting a kiss on my forehead. 'I've just run the gauntlet of a host of your admirers at the entrance.'

The press admirers of course would be waiting for her, not me. From which I deduced that although Louise did her best to keep a low profile on her private life, the news that she was living with me must be at least semi-public knowledge. No doubt with Pen's help. I'd missed the latest issue of the *Graphic*. The fact that I seemed to be some kind of detective and had been beaten up must add a great deal of spice to their stories of Louise's private life – these are spun out of fictional cobwebs as she is very canny about keeping a low profile.

'I'll send down my autograph,' I assured her.

'I just nipped in to say I'm off this afternoon. Back Tuesday evening, and then we'll be home together. I hate leaving you.' She looked at me. 'Perhaps I could—'

'No,' I said firmly. 'I'll be like Morse. Remember he solved the murder of the Princes in the Tower when he was incarcerated in hospital.'

'Then stick to Richard III,' she instructed me. 'Leave Philip Moxton to the foot soldiers.'

'I've always fancied being Mycroft Holmes, solving things from my gentlemen's club armchair. I can do a lot of things from this armchair . . .'

I reached out for her and there followed a short interlude when I was (a) grateful that no other patients were present in the day room and (b) grateful that my arms weren't quite as painful as they had been and (c) grateful that my attacker hadn't been able to get a direct kick on various other parts of my anatomy which only had a couple of days to wait with luck.

As Louise left I decided to hobble back to bed. I was through, spent, exhausted and ready for a doze followed by a touch of evening TV. Unfortunately Pen Roxton had other plans for me. She must have been waiting for Louise to leave and I only hoped she hadn't been peering through the keyhole with a camera.

'Got a pic of her,' she told me smugly as she marched in and planted herself at my side.

'Use it and that's the last help you get from me. Ever.'

She snorted. 'Help? Your help doesn't amount to a row of beans. You and your game, mate.'

'Glad I'm still your mate.'

'I tell you, Jack, that game's vicious. You know that now. First me, now you.'

'You're backing out?'

'No way. I'm in with a chance and not one I'll be sharing with you, my darling.'

I groaned. 'Don't, Pen, don't do it.'

'They won't get me a second time. Sorry they got you,' she added belatedly. 'Those folk play rough.'

'Who do you mean by they?'

'Those Herricks, especially that bruiser Gwen. And that fellow Barney is an odd one. I'm on to them, and they don't like it one little bit, so that's why I dog their footsteps.'

'You've stirred them up again?'

'Of course. Said I was printing the story of this robbery and their so-called game.'

'What happened next?'

'Warned off by my boss. I told you his wife was a mate of the darling Herricks.'

'So you've dropped it.'

'No way. Just taking the robbery angle to see what falls out of the trees.'

'Take care, Pen.'

'Sure. Taking care to get the story, that's me. That robbery's tied up with the banking world somehow which could have had a lot to do with Moxton's death. Someone's sitting pretty now.'

I was getting seriously alarmed, and I opened my mouth to voice even stronger objections but she forestalled me.

'He's in this merger, right?'

'If by he you mean Timothy Mild, the answer's yes.'

'It's his big chance. Right? Then along comes a little piglet like me who threatens to blow it to smithereens with the story of how the first Moxtons bank was bought with dirty money.'

'Could you prove it, Pen?' I asked wearily. 'All we know is that Donald Moxton and Gavin Herrick were in the car. It was another ten years before Donald bought the bank and there was no hint of a story in that.'

'I'll publish it, Jack. I will – right or wrong,' she added.

At least she was straightforward and I thought – hoped – she was merely winding me up. I had another go at reason.

'So now the theory runs that a sixteen-year-old boy steals a fortune, invests it cleverly and buys the bank ten years later. Sixteen, Pen, *sixteen*. Is that likely? Did no one at the bank suspect? Where did he hide the loot so that it was untraceable? How would he know how to invest it? Did he stuff it in his wardrobe for years and his mother never noticed?'

Pen's eyes gleamed. 'Don't forget his accomplice, Jack.'

'Don't tell me.' We were back on this false track. 'Gavin Herrick. That makes two ingenuous teenagers.'

'They could have fixed it between them,' she said obstinately. 'That's why the Herricks are so cagey. They know the truth all right.'

'Sorry, but I don't buy the story, Pen.'

'Don't remember telling you it was for sale. Besides,' she added in dulcet tones, 'even if it wasn't true it could still blow Timothy Mild's carefully timed merger to bits. There have always been rumours going round the banking world about the Moxtons. They upset a lot of folks with their hire 'em fire 'em ways. A lot of people didn't like Donald one little bit, so all Gavin Herrick had to do was blackmail him.'

'Go away, Pen.' My head was spinning and I couldn't reason with her any more.

She looked hurt. 'You're not yourself, Jack.'

'And nor are you, Pen. You're tackling too broad a canvas.'

'But I'll paint a pretty picture,' she chortled, as she waved me goodbye.

Please, no more, I groaned to myself as I staggered back to my bed. I should have known I wasn't going to get away that easily, however. Sam West arrived, rather uncertainly and bearing

a basket of fruit – plus for good measure a travelling chessboard.
I looked at it blankly. Was he inviting me to a game?

'I thought it might help pass the time if I left it with you,' he
said apologetically, perhaps reading my expression correctly. 'It
can be fun playing against yourself.'

'Thank you,' I said weakly. I wasn't up to playing noughts
and crosses let alone chess.

'Even if you don't play,' he said brightly, 'you could think of
Philip Moxton's murder in terms of pawns, bishops and knights.'

I gazed at him speechlessly, feeling like Alice in Wonderland
landing in the midst of a set of crazy people.

'My feeling is that you should think of the pawns in the Moxton
case, Jack.'

My only feeling was that I was a pawn myself temporarily
battered off the board. 'Who are they?' I asked to be polite.

'I'm not sure,' he replied seriously, 'but I think Wendy is one
and she's at risk.' He was pink-cheeked at the effort of telling
me this, so I concentrated hard. 'That's why I came,' he continued.
'Oh,' he added belatedly, 'and to see how you were of course.'

'Wendy at risk? Why?' I couldn't see it.

'Banks and powerful people can strike anywhere and at anyone
they choose.'

'But why Wendy? Because she knew Geoffrey? So did you.'

'That's true, but not as she did. Geoffrey could have told her
things that other people wouldn't have liked. She could have
information.'

'Have you talked to her about it?'

'Yes. She says she hasn't any but I don't believe her. You ask
her, Jack. She said there was something you hadn't asked.' He
glanced at my immobile self in bed. 'When you're better.'

With a faint recollection of Wendy having referred to something
she wanted to tell me, I was doing my best to ponder this one
after Sam departed, only to be presented by a worse situation.
To my horror I saw Gwen Moxton bearing down on me. I wasn't
up to fighting back at anyone either physically or mentally. I
don't know how James Bond copes with such situations but
I was flesh and blood and both of them were currently quailing
at what was before me. Hospital patients should be issued with
Do Not Disturb placards.

'Sorry to hear what you've been through, Jack.'

Gwen didn't look at all sorry. She looked more as if she was sizing me up for a second round.

'Who did it?' she continued.

I longed to say that her family was high on the list but restrained myself. 'No idea,' I replied.

'How about John Carson?'

Right. I could cope with this. 'There were three of them.'

'His son's gang. Isn't he a mobster of some type?'

So she knew about Richie. 'I don't know who they were working for.'

'You're not suspecting Joan was behind this, are you?'

'I'm not up to suspecting anything much at present.'

Gwen was relentless. 'Or me, or Tom or my poor Barney?' she continued. 'I can tell you that none of us attacked you.'

'It's a police case,' I told her in a desperate attempt to close the subject. 'They aren't paying me to investigate my own GBH.'

She stared at me, unamused. 'It could have been your girlfriend had you beaten up. Not Louise of course.'

'Thank you for that.'

Gwen didn't notice the sarcasm. 'I meant Wendy Parks.'

'Three burly blokes beat me up.'

'A woman like her could have strange companions.'

'Such as?' I hoped this would squash her but it didn't.

'John Carson for one. I never liked him.'

I began to wonder if Gwen had been commissioned to put the Herrick and Moxton case for innocence on behalf of them all, for she waxed eloquent for some time on the subject of John Carson. She even had me wondering whether Wendy's prowling at Staveley Park had been quite as innocent as she made it sound. Finally I had had enough of this Wendy-baiting. I was quite capable of pursuing that line myself – even if not right now.

'Wendy told me you've all been over to see her, including Timothy,' I said, fighting back. 'Why?'

She glared. 'Why not? Barney wants to know her better. He feels it's time to build bridges.'

'She didn't get that impression.'

'More fool her. But then she is either a fool or a murderess. Take your pick.'

FOURTEEN

By the time I was signed off on the Wednesday morning I had had a great many strategic dozes. By that time I was able to function with some degree of normality, especially as Louise was at the hospital to drive me home. She had a silver blue Ford Focus into which I was just able to manoeuvre my aching body. She'd come back to Frogs Hill too late the previous evening for the hospital to risk my precious self in sending me home alone, but Louise had wangled a rescheduling so that she could pick me up today. Len, now back at his post, and Zoe too, had offered to do so, but Louise had been adamant about coming herself. I was aware that her film would shortly be wrapped up and that as yet she had said nothing about what came next. Perhaps she didn't know. Perhaps she didn't want to tell me.

I decided not to be pessimistic. I don't think either of us doubted that we were off to a flying start in our relationship, but neither of us wanted to push the other into saying so. Or so I was presuming. Every now and then the word 'next . . .' came up or even worse, the word Christmas but both of us shied away from tackling that issue. Louise had a father and brother whom I'd never met plus a mother who was doing her own thing with a new husband somewhere or other. So far there had not been time to go deeply into family involvement but there was plenty of time ahead – I hoped.

After Louise had to leave me at Frogs Hill for the rest of the day, frustration set in. Although I was back home I had strict medical instructions not to drive, and immediately became the passive recipient of more phone calls and callers than I could have wished. I couldn't complain of neglect.

'You OK, Jack?' Zoe would put her head round the door at frequent intervals and in between her visits Len's gruff voice would ask the same thing. In between these enquiries tea, coffee, sandwiches and soup would appear. Finally I became so used to my standard answer 'Doing fine, thanks' that when I actually *wasn't* fine I couldn't bring myself to say so.

On Friday afternoon, however, there was a phone call I couldn't ignore or fob off. It was Sam and it wasn't a 'how are you?' call. It required prompt action.

'Any chance of you getting over here, Jack?' It sounded serious.

'When? What for?' I asked cautiously.

'Now. I'm anxious about Wendy. I told you she had said something rather odd. That there was a question Jack hadn't asked. Then yesterday she said she was worried about what to do. Do you know what she's talking about? I can't get hold of her by phone and I've been ringing all day now. The café's been closed all day too without explanation.'

'I can't drive.' I felt a first-class chump, and options skidded through my mind. Len? Zoe? Even so, did I feel up to the trip? 'Could Timothy drive over and go with you? Is he around?' I asked hopefully.

'No, and I don't want to go alone. Could you come over with your lady friend if she's around? I wouldn't ask if I wasn't getting desperately concerned.'

My heart sank. 'What about the police?' It was a last-ditch attempt as I'd seen Louise drive into the yard. She was back early and I had to wrestle with my conscience.

'Wendy's probably only out for the day, so I doubt if they'd come,' Sam replied. 'Look, don't worry. I *will* go alone.'

We left it at that, but I wasn't happy about it. Louise picked that up right away when I explained. She grimaced too. 'Must we?'

'No must, but I suppose I should. We'll just set our minds at rest and have dinner in the pub on the way back.'

'Done.'

Dining out at pretentious restaurants has to be the norm for Louise in her working capacity, but it's not her personal choice. What pleases her best are the quiet tucked-away pubs and restaurants where we can either be alone or if that's not possible those not dogged by her peers in the film world or the press. The Piper's Green local suits us splendidly in this respect – provided that Pen isn't hiding under the table.

I rang Sam back to say we'd be over shortly and he was almost hysterical with gratitude. 'What with Geoffrey's murder and everything else, I tend to get overwrought,' he apologized.

'No problem. We'll pick you up on the way,' I told him.

As we drove to Monksford, Louise listened without saying much as I explained as best I could why Sam might justifiably be worried. She was as glum as I was – so I suppose it was a good test of our relationship, even if it was one I could do without.

'The woman's probably celebrating with her next sugar daddy – or whatever you call them when you're as old as Wendy,' Louise said crossly.

I didn't reply. I bore in mind that Louise was no great admirer of Wendy's but even so her set face began to grate on me. She was usually so calm and understanding. Not now. Or was it me? Or both of us?

Sam was ready and waiting for us at his door. He slid into the Focus's back seat with more expressions of gratitude to which both Louise and I tried to reply politely. It was hard though.

'Did you try Wendy's number again?' I asked him as we set off.

'Yes. No reply.'

The drive to her home was a short one from where Sam lived but there were few lights along the way. Wendy's barn conversion was close to the road but the farmhouse was set some way back, so it was unlikely that her neighbours would be aware of her every movement. I didn't get the impression they were great chums. As Louise turned off the road to approach the house I could see no car standing outside Wendy's home nor any lights although a security light flashed on as we turned in.

'She always puts her car in the garage,' Sam said when I pointed out that her Astra was missing. 'It might be in there, but it's more likely that she is out or away. You'd think that she would have made alternative arrangements for the café, wouldn't you? That's what worries me.'

Me too, I thought, as I climbed slowly and painfully out of the car after Sam. Louise elected to stay in the car which was a relief. The house curtains were drawn across from what I could see and there were no lights on inside. Nor was there any reply to the bell. My initial reluctance to come here was giving way to concern and perhaps this was mutual because Louise decided to join us after all. She had brought a torch from the car so we picked our way round to the rear of the house, where another light flashed on. No sign of life there either. Sam then volunteered to climb up to peer in the high rear window of the garage.

'Her car's in there,' he cried out. 'Shall I call the police?'
'No. I will,' I told him. At least I knew who to speak to, which
is often vital. I hoped and hoped it wasn't in this case.

At first I received a cool reception from Uniform, but my
mention of Brandon and that Wendy was a major witness in the
Philip Moxton case provided the hook for instant action. Shortly,
not one car but two drew up. The first contained an inspector
and a constable, the second held Brandon and a detective sergeant.
We were briskly questioned and Louise's face and name caused
a short furore. Brandon shot me a puzzled look – or so I inter-
preted it. What was a clown like me doing with Louise Shaw?

We watched as they went through the obvious procedure and
then conferred, while Sam grew more and more jittery. I could
understand why. Wendy could have gone out with a friend who
had picked her up in her own car – but why leave the curtains
drawn? She could have gone away for some days. She could
have done this or that – but perhaps she hadn't. Perhaps she was
inside.

Since there was no woman PC present, some bright spark
suggested that Louise should go into the house first as being the
least likely to cause alarm if Wendy was merely in a deep sleep.
I vetoed this immediately, even before seeing Louise's horrified
expression. I insisted that she should return to the car and I would
go into the house myself, as Wendy knew me. Either Brandon
or his sergeant could follow on. Both did so and Louise stayed
with Sam. Full marks to her.

I led the way after the door was forced, a position I didn't
care for despite the stalwart company. Each room I looked into
on the ground floor was empty of Wendy, so I gritted my teeth
for what I feared I would find upstairs. Stairs were hard enough
to climb for me at the moment without added torture.

There was no one in the first bedroom when I pushed the door
open calling out her name and the thump of my heart died down
a little. The second was a different matter. I'd prepared for the
worst, but when I saw it I couldn't take it. I could see Wendy
apparently deeply asleep, but I knew she couldn't be. No way.
Perhaps I was still weak from my hospitalization but I felt close
to tears, unable to move.

'Wendy,' I called in a voice I didn't recognize as my own.
Then again: 'Wendy!'

It was Brandon who had to push me gently aside when there was no reply. He went up to her, touched her, turned round and nodded to his sergeant. It was obvious that no Wendy now lay there. The body was cold.

The chill communicated itself to my own body as I retreated to the doorway and Brandon and his sergeant went into action. There was nothing I could do at this scene. I was a double intruder both on a woman's private life and on her death. I had to leave it to the police and very shortly afterwards to the forensic management team to go about their business.

It was one o'clock in the morning by the time Louise and I reached home. Sam had been released much earlier. Neither Louise nor I were hungry by that time but I heated up some soup for us. It was difficult even to take that. Our earlier discord had vanished, both of us too tired and shocked by what had happened to want to stake out our own emotional boundaries.

'You've got to work tomorrow,' I said to her, appalled at what I'd put her through. Her schedule takes no note of weekends.

'I'm not due in until ten,' she told me. 'Anyway –' she tried to look cheerful – 'it's good practice for us.'

'Practice for what?'

'Our future, on the presumption that your life is always like this.'

Her words 'our future' were an instant cement. The chill disappeared, warmth spread through me and we clung to each other as though this were a parting not a beginning. We *were* beginning, with a new 'us' based not on fairy-tale reunions but on something far more tangible.

'My life isn't always like this,' I assured her. 'Sometimes it's a whole lot better.'

It took some time before she stirred in my arms. 'Did Wendy mean a lot to you, Jack?'

'There was no time even to call her a friend. I misjudged her though, so I feel bad about that and for not seeing things clearly.'

'You thought she killed Philip Moxton?'

'It was one scenario, but that's now discounted.'

'Is it?'

I stared at her, not understanding at first. 'Someone murdered her, sweetheart.' Then belatedly I saw her point and wondered how on earth it could have eluded me. 'You mean it could have been suicide. I haven't been thinking straight. You're right, she could have killed herself. I've been too focused on Philip's murder to see that angle. Theoretically Wendy could have killed him, seen the pace was hotting up and taken her own way out.'

'Theoretically? So don't you believe that's what happened?'

I had to be honest. 'No.'

'So you think that poor woman was murdered.' Louise began to shake. 'And I was so horrible about her.'

I saw tears running down her face. I'd never seen her cry before and it frightened me. I had a lot to learn. Perhaps we both did. I held her in my arms until the sobs subsided. 'I'll never let that happen again,' I vowed.

'Never let me cry?' She managed to laugh.

'No. Go through another ordeal like that.'

'Perhaps it's good for me. I read too many scripts, Jack. I need to deal with real life.'

Brandon was on the case with a vengeance, which wasn't surprising. Even though there was no proof yet as to the cause of Wendy's death or to its possible connection to Philip Moxton's death, he would have a clear field with no Met involvement. *Yet*. He made it clear to me that I was hired as part of his team and sick leave was cancelled. Full stop. So that meant I was back at Monksford on Saturday morning, thanks to Zoe at the wheel of my Alfa. She and Len had come in specially having heard the news. I had been bent on driving myself to Monksford, but Zoe had other ideas. Officially I still had a few days to go. Some car detective, I growled to myself. I can't even drive.

At least Wendy's body was no longer there, which meant I could try to convince myself that this was simply an objective crime scene with no personal connection. It did help – a little. Zoe said she would hang out in Monksford village while I was doing my duty, and I braced myself for what lay ahead.

'Still think she stuck a knife into Geoffrey Green?' Brandon asked me, when I was duly logged in and kitted out.

'No, but I think she suspected who did.'

'And that was who?'

'I can't be certain because she didn't name names, but Timothy Mild fits the bill.'

Brandon tried this one out for size. 'That would make the Met scream,' he said with pleasure. 'Did she have any evidence?' 'Not that she told me.' Then I forced myself to ask, 'What killed her?'

'The usual. A hefty dose of sleeping pills.'

'Self-administered?'

'Could be. There was nothing by the bedside or anywhere else though. No suicide notes, no signs of preparation, so it doesn't look likely. The lab is going through the remains of a nice cup of comforting cocoa left downstairs.'

'Any evidence of a companion over the cocoa?'

'None so far. Her nearest neighbours in the farmhouse heard a car or two pass that night, but whether they stopped or came here or drove on is a moot point. Is there any reason she would have killed herself apart from this Moxton case?'

'None that I know of. On the contrary, the legacy he was leaving her would have enabled her to lead an entirely different way of life.'

'She seems to have stirred up a hornets' nest with the Moxtons and Herricks. Enough to cause this result?'

I hesitated over this one. My inclination was to say no. It would be easy to say no. Annoyance over the will could hardly have led to this – if 'this' was murder. But there were elements of the game as well as Philip Moxton's murder that were still missing. If I threw in the attack on me for good measure I couldn't answer 'no'. So that's what I told Brandon.

He nodded. 'My reasoning too.'

I came home to a barrage of messages. I'd switched my mobile off deliberately, so now I had two lots to deal with, both on that and my landline. Bad news spreads. What was happening? Timothy wished to know the situation from my own lips. Gwen wanted to know more than the radio had provided. Joan insisted on hearing all about it. Len, who'd hung on in the Pits until Zoe and I returned, was more easily dealt with – certainly more easily than Pen who had turned up at the scene of the crime just as Zoe and I drove away from it. One glimpse of her outraged face told me I'd be hearing more shortly. She wasn't here, thank heavens. Probably still terrorizing Monksford. There was also a message from Dave Jennings to say Brandon was emailing me the Packard logbook info to give me the registered ownership details at last. With Wendy's death the Packard had slipped to the back of my mind, so I went straight to the computer. I was still working out the implications of what I read when the doorbell rang.

Moira was standing on the doorstep with a very grumpy Len, who couldn't wait to offload her and stalk right back to the Pits. She'd been ringing the bell for 'ages' she told me in a pained voice and this nice gentleman (Len) had assured her I was in.

'I heard the terrible news,' she explained. 'You weren't answering calls, so here I am. I want to know what's going on. Did Wendy kill herself?'

'The jury's out on whether or not she was helped to do it,' I replied truthfully.

Her eyes glistened like halogen headlights. 'Murder? Nonsense. She was as guilty as hell of killing Philip and couldn't face the consequences.'

'As I said, the jury's out,' I repeated, disliking this woman more and more. 'Anything else?'

'Yes, but I'll come in. You look rather shaky.' She peered closely at me.

'I am.' *Go away, go away, go away!* I silently begged.

I thought she'd catch the implication of the 'I am', but no. She still came in, following me through to the living room. 'She killed herself. That's obvious,' she repeated. She looked more agitated than I had ever seen her.

'Why should she?' I asked wearily. 'She's due to inherit a wad of money, and there's no evidence that she was guilty of anything at all.'

'I suppose her family will inherit now,' Moira continued crossly, with no sign that she'd heard me. 'Although perhaps not if the police can prove that she killed Philip. It makes no difference to us of course,' she added hastily.

Charming of you, I thought. Time for pointing out a few home truths.

'Quite. It means they'll be on your doorstep again.'

She sat down rather suddenly. 'Why? We've told them what little we know, and we'd no reason to kill Philip or Wendy.'

'Monetary reasons,' I pointed out less than gently, 'make for powerful motivation.'

'That was the game,' she said uneasily. 'And that's over. We're entitled to our share.'

I pounced. 'The quarter share you all agreed at university?'

She leapt too eagerly at this. 'Yes.'

'You told me Nancy Herrick wasn't involved in the game, so this quarter share stems from what Gavin had demanded from Philip.' I was blazing a trail into unknown territory, but with interesting results.

'What on earth do you mean?'

Somewhere I had hit a nerve. The trouble was that I didn't *know* what I meant, so I plunged further.

'Somehow Donald and Gavin fixed that 1938 robbery on Randolphs Bank between them.'

Her relief was obvious, but she made a good stab at hiding it. 'Are you implying that they were thieves? I can't speak for Donald Moxton, but Gavin had nothing whatsoever to do with the theft, other than being present.'

'But Donald did.'

'Perhaps.' She was very flushed now. I had her on the run.

'Tell me, Moira, or tell the police. Whichever.'

'It has nothing to do with Wendy's death. Besides, Timothy would kill me if—'

'Timothy?' I repeated when she broke off 'Or Tom?'

'If the truth got out,' she finished sullenly, ignoring my question.

'Which of them?'

'Timothy,' she yelled at me. 'And it had nothing to do with Gavin. It was Donald. Gavin realized he was involved in it, so Donald eventually had to cut him in.'

'Gavin blackmailed Donald?'

'Not for money.' Moira looked shocked.

'Then what for?'

'I don't know. I think it was just the Packard.' She burst into tears, but they moved me not.

Here we go again, I thought. 'Forget the Packard,' I said patiently. 'First, it was Donald who carried out the theft?'

'Well, yes, in a way—'

'What way? Tell me, Moira.' Silence, so I continued, 'Donald had an accomplice, didn't he? And that had to be Gavin.'

'No.'

'Then who?' If there really was a villainous masked man and
Gavin was standing outside by the boot with the bank owner,
then the villain couldn't have been him. Nor Donald. If Donald
was involved in any way with the theft, however, the villain had
to have been someone he knew. My mind produced from its
archives an interesting fact. Gavin and Donald had both been
brought up in Biddenford which was very close to Hatchwell.
Donald's father had a shop there, a greengrocery. Donald had
stayed at Randolphs until the war and returned to the bank after
it. So if Donald wasn't the villain himself, it could have been—

'His father,' I said. '*He* was the masked robber.' One look at
Moira and I knew I'd scored a bullseye. She was white in the
face, either with terror or fury.

'It was his plan, not Donald's,' Moira burst out. 'Donald
admitted it to Gavin. His father had always wanted to better
himself, because he had little formal education, and thought up
this scheme. He was very clever over the disguise, and Donald
knew what was going to happen of course. His father invested
the money and after the war it had increased so much that by
ten years later he was able to buy the bank in stages and put it
in Donald's name, so that they could play bankers together.'

At last! Something which made some sort of sense and threw
a whole new light on investing in one's child's future. 'Why
didn't you tell us earlier for heaven's sake?'

'Timothy said if these rumours were substantiated, it would
ruin the merger because it smeared the Moxton name. Philip
always ignored them because he was a good chess player. Eyes
on the target and how best to get there. Besides, Donald's father
was a *greengrocer*. That wouldn't have looked good in the City,
not in those days anyway. Moxtons would have been a laughing
stock and now it probably will,' she ended despairingly. 'Timothy
will never forgive me.'

I ignored her social comment. 'So Gavin blackmailed the
Moxtons for a share of the loot?'

'*No*! I already said that he didn't,' she shouted.

'Then why did you all think you were entitled to split Barney's
fortune for him?'

She glared at me. I thought at first she was going to ignore
the question, but unwillingly she gave way. 'It's a long story.
Gavin had bought the Packard from old Randolph and said

jokingly that he'd only sell it to Donald for a share of the loot – which at that time was invested in the bank and would be worth very little. Donald took umbrage and said stuffily that he would leave a few shares in the bank to Gavin in his will. Gavin hadn't been serious about it, but he was pretty annoyed at Donald's snootiness so he said he'd keep the car and Donald could do what he liked over the shares. Donald must have realized that if Gavin kept the car it would be a permanent reminder that Gavin had the whiphand over the robbery issue. Donald didn't like that idea and told Gavin he was still going to leave the shares to him in his will as payment for his share of the loot. Gavin agreed, more to get rid of Donald from his life than anything else, but said he was going to keep the Packard. There,' she said, with relief, 'does that satisfy you?'

'Getting there. He didn't get rid of Donald, did he?'

'No. It went on which is why, as we told you, their children agreed at university that when both Gavin and Donald died, they would split the money equally, sell the Packard and call it quits. Unfortunately when Donald died in 1994 Philip told them he wouldn't honour that. Instead he would leave it all to Barney and he could do what he liked with it. Tom and Gwen were furious but what could they do? Nothing except have an understanding with Barney. Then we heard about this stupid foundation from Timothy and it all got worse. That was the last straw. We'd been counting on that money.'

The last straw? 'Did one of you take drastic steps to ensure the will wouldn't be signed?'

'Not by murder,' she yelled at me. 'We just tried to persuade him.'

I tried a new bait. 'Presumably Philip would still have left the house and gardens to Joan in the new will, so she wouldn't have been affected?'

'She didn't know that until after he was dead,' Moira said sullenly. 'Philip was entirely unreasonable.'

'Perhaps not from his point of view,' I said drily. 'Unless there *was* a blackmail element why did the four involved in that university agreement think that any money should come to them at all?'

'The game,' she said dejectedly. 'They had all suffered, and so have I.'

'In other words, the Packard. But why did that go on being an issue? That meant the game wasn't over.'

'Don't you believe me?' she asked, past fury now.

'Not yet. You tell me that Nancy played no part in the game and the Packard was merely a symbol of it. So how did a few shares evolve into a legacy of a multimillion fortune?'

'It just did. It grew.'

I wouldn't get further on that – yet. So now for my joker card, in my hand courtesy of Brandon's email. 'You told me Gavin bought the Packard from Alfred Randolph in 1948. Can you tell me then why the Packard's official registration details show that it was Donald, not Gavin, who bought it from him?'

'I don't know,' she yelled at me.

'The Game Book might reveal that,' I said reflectively. 'The one Philip must have held.'

'I don't know about that either. I only know what I've told you.'

Plus, I thought, what she *hadn't* told me. Wendy had referred to a question I should ask. I had assumed that she had meant asked of her, but perhaps I was wrong.

FIFTEEN

'What are you prowling around for, Jack?' Zoe demanded, as I hobbled round the Pits on Monday morning. 'You're supposed to be resting.'

I knew I was driving both Len and Zoe mad. They wanted to be alone with their new assignment, a 1960 Fairthorpe Zeta.

'Only until tomorrow,' I retorted. 'I can get behind the wheel again then. Meanwhile, you might take a look at the Packard because—'

'Don't,' she said dangerously, 'even think of keeping that monster around.'

'What have you got against it?' I demanded. The Packard needed some tender loving care before I could even consider what I would do with it. The wheel bearings needed greasing, upholstery cleaning and the exhaust clamps tightening. That was just for starters, although there was no way I was going to paint it its original black. I noted uneasily that I was thinking in terms of what I *was* going to do rather than what I *might* do if . . . Scary!

'It's more what that car's got against you,' Zoe retorted. 'I love Packards, but since this one entered your life you've had nothing but trouble. It's caused trouble for seventy-odd years, but you're wandering around as deferentially as though it were a 1930s' Bugatti.'

'It's history,' I said mulishly.

'I wish it was,' Zoe whipped back. 'At present it's a cross between an albatross and a dinosaur.'

'Look at its styling.'

'Look at its steering,' she countered.

'What do you suggest I do with it? Sell it now? That would be treason.'

'Treason to who?' She stood there, hands on hips, an aggressive and unmovable figure. I had to come up with some kind of answer.

'The game, I suppose.'

I can't have been in my right mind because Zoe fell about laughing. 'The *game*, Jack?' she spluttered. 'You're playing it all right. Fallen for it hook, line and sinker.'

'Laugh away,' I said, irritated. 'Anyway, I can't sell it yet. Not till the story's over.'

She didn't give up 'What *story*? This game or the murders?'

'Both. They're linked.'

'Not yet from what you've deigned to tell us about it. So give me one other reason that Len and I should spend our valuable time on this when I could be working on something constructive.' Her eyes strayed longingly to the Fairthorpe.

I tried hard to sound confident. 'With the Packard here, I feel I'm on the same wavelength as the Moxton case.'

Zoe gave me a look of pity and told me she had something better to do than play games with a nitwit. I retaliated by asking her what was so special about putting a stud in a Zeta.

She replied, 'Because the stud is the nail in the horseshoe that carries the rider who saves the kingdom. Weren't you taught that nursery rhyme as a kid?'

She won. She acknowledged this by condescending to say

she'd take another look at my beautiful dinosaur later. I retreated to the barn where the Packard at least seemed glad to see me. The more I stared at it, however, the more its relevance in the case defied me. Seventy-odd years ago when that robbery had taken place the world had not yet plunged into another war, bank managers like Alfred Randolph were pillars of the community and two junior clerks could accompany the bank's owner in his personal car round to the local post office to pick up bundles of cash accompanied by one man armed with a wooden truncheon. Judging by today's standards the robbery in Hatchwell had been more like a civilized, if illegal, change of cash ownership.

Had any robbery really been as simple as history appeared? Even if violence-free, the Hatchwell robbery had resulted in the ruin of Randolph's life and business, and had had lasting effects on both the Moxton and Herrick families. For me at least and surely for them the Packard symbolized that event, and while the game and its players still awaited that final link to one, probably two, murders, the Packard was here to stay. Whatever Len and Zoe thought!

That at least was a decision made, so partially satisfied I wandered back towards the Pits.

'Morning, Jack.'

A red Fiesta drew up in a swoosh of gravel and Emma yelled over to me as she exited gracefully from it. From the passenger side, so – to my amazement – did Louise.

Louise? I was indeed losing my grip. 'I thought you were on set,' I called out as I walked over to them.

'Not today. Tomorrow and then the day after it is the wrap. We hope.'

I decided not to think about what would happen then. Today was already difficult enough.

'We thought you'd like a day out with the girls,' Emma informed me, somewhat smugly.

I was instantly suspicious. 'Why the honour?'

'We like your company,' Louise said demurely.

They were both looking at me expectantly, so there was more to this than their merely taking pity on a man who couldn't drive and hobbled like a Victorian chimney sweep. Why this ambush? More thugs on the way? Pen Roxton hiding round the corner of the lane?

'Get in,' Louise ordered me, holding the rear door open. So I did, after ensuring that Zoe and Len could do without my company. They said they thought they'd be able to cope.

So I climbed aboard. 'Where are we going?' I asked, still suspicious.

'You'll see,' Emma told me blithely.

'This is something to do with the game, isn't it?' I persisted.

'Dear Jack,' Louise said soothingly. 'It's not just something. It's the end of the game.'

'I wish I had a tenner for every time I've heard that,' I muttered crossly. 'Is this yet another version?'

'We've packed a picnic,' Louise continued as if I hadn't spoken.

'A *picnic*? It's mid-October,' I pointed out.

'Don't be such a softie. It's warm enough.'

'For October, maybe. Are we going to the seaside?' This sarcasm wasn't ideal because it made me think of Wendy and her beach hut which she and Geoffrey would never visit again.

'No.'

I took the hint and thereafter left them to it. It was clear I wasn't going to be told anything until such time as they chose. In fact the signposts indicated we were heading for Sevenoaks and the word picnic therefore suggested the ancestral home of the Sackville family, Knole Park. It has a huge estate, ideal for picnics and watching its flocks of deer stroll by.

I was right. 'Very nice,' I said cautiously after we had driven in stately fashion along the long approach to the car park and lugged baskets and rugs to a suitable grassy patch from which we could observe nature. Curiously, we bypassed a great many suitable grassy patches before my companions appeared satisfied, and I grew impatient.

'Don't be a crosspatch,' Louise scolded me, as I helped lay down rugs and unpack baskets. I hoped we'd be making this picnic a short one, as clouds were gathering, it was only warm while we were on the move and here we were stranded in the middle of nature's best with no shelter. Usually I'd have thought it fun; today I was still too full of aches and pains to do so. Nevertheless I made a supreme effort, once the banquet was laid out in splendour and I had been ignominiously assisted to ground level to collapse on to the rug.

'OK,' I said. 'Tell me.'

Emma glanced at Louise. 'Work first?' she queried.

'Go ahead,' my true love replied.

'This,' Emma declared grandly, 'is where the game began.'

Somewhat of an anticlimax. 'I thought it began with a bank robbery,' I said.

'In one respect, yes,' Emma replied. 'In another, no. I've been deputed to tell you about it because I wasn't involved. This is what *really* happened. And don't think I'm enjoying this,' she added warningly.

In other words, don't make waves, however much I felt like splashing around and even if it was the umpteenth *real* story that I been fed.

'The game itself began here,' Emma continued, 'on a day in 1948 when Donald Moxton and Gavin Herrick met by chance for the first time since Donald had been called up for military service in the Second World War.'

'Fascinating,' I murmured, trying to sound amiable, but failing dismally. How could this be leading anywhere except round the mulberry bush one more time?

Louise scowled at me as Emma took a deep breath which suggested that I wouldn't be sharing this picnic lunch if I didn't behave myself. 'Donald was having a picnic here with his girl-friend when Gavin suddenly popped up. He was a struggling actor at that time, and was here to do some research for a role. He recognized the Packard in the car park, and tracked Donald down.'

First stumbling block: 'Your mother said Gavin bought it from Randolph. The registration details show that Donald did. Which is right?'

Emma looked uncertain. 'I don't know.'

'My money's on Donald,' I told her firmly. 'It must have appealed to his father's warped sense of humour when he bought the bank for Donald.'

'Perhaps you're right,' she said uneasily.

'Whichever of them it was, pinching his car too was a bit tough on old man Randolph, wasn't it?'

'You say it was Donald.' Emma regained her confidence. 'The Moxtons *are* tough.'

'Tell me what happened at this picnic,' I asked.

'After the bank raid, Gavin had gradually worked out what

might have happened. He said it was something about the way
Donald had behaved afterwards, although he had no proof. So
having bumped into him by chance at the picnic he joined them
and started teasing Donald about it when Donald's girlfriend
went to the loo.'

'Foolish of Gavin perhaps.' So far this more-or-less tallied
with Moira's version.

'No perhaps about it. Donald went bananas and wanted to
know how much cash Gavin wanted not to spread the story
around. Then it was Gavin's turn to go bananas. He said he
wasn't a blackmailer, however much he disapproved of how
they'd treated Randolph. Donald couldn't believe this, so Gavin
made a half-jokey, half-serious offer to get out of the situation.
His price was the Packard.'

Groan from me, reproving look from Louise. This was not
Moira's story. Whichever of the two versions was the truth, they
both had weak points. The element of blackmail and the relatively
unimportant switch of ownership of the Packard. I looked at
Louise imagining that day in 1948 when Donald had set out for
a picnic with *his* girlfriend. Then I thought of Wendy and the
question she said I hadn't asked. I knew now what that question
should have been.

The price of silence had been far above Packards, far above
rubies.

'Gavin's price was more than the Packard,' I said. 'He wanted
the Packard *and* Donald's girlfriend.'

'Yes,' Emma continued resolutely, '*if* Gavin succeeded in
wooing her for himself. Donald, being the gentleman he wasn't,
agreed albeit with reluctance, perhaps arrogantly assuming she
would prefer to stay with him and Gavin's bid would come to
nothing.'

'And the girlfriend was Nancy, later Nancy Herrick.' Of course
it was, *of course.*

'It was. My grandmother.'

'A high price.'

'I think it must have been,' Emma said seriously. 'Especially
for Donald because Gavin did win her and then—'

'Then?' I picked up gently when she broke off.

'There was something more,' Emma added awkwardly. 'Donald
refused to hand over the Packard. Gavin saw red and said he'd

take the shares in the bank instead. They weren't worth much then, you see. Donald refused and said he'd leave him their worth in his will. I doubt if he meant it and Gavin didn't believe him anyway. He didn't much care about it at the time because he was set on having the Packard. Which Donald still refused.'

I began to see light in these murky waters. 'That developed into the argy bargy over Philip's will? Pretty tough on Philip, having to deal with his dad's misdeeds.'

Emma reddened, and Louise leapt furiously to her defence. 'Jack, don't take sides.'

I apologized, genuinely. I think it was a sign of how much the game was getting to me that I was finding this hard to take. However much I sympathized with Philip Moxton, it was too soon to make judgements.

'Gavin did marry Nancy,' Emma continued. 'Donald married not long afterwards, and as you know both couples duly produced four offspring between them. But then something awful happened . . .' Emma looked at Louise in appeal.

'I'll tell him,' Louise said awkwardly.

I felt a real heel – perhaps somewhat unreasonably since this picnic had been their idea, but nevertheless my churlishness hadn't helped.

'In the late fifties,' Louise said steadily, 'Donald Moxton began an affair with Nancy. Gavin can't have been an easy person to live with; I gather he played around even though he adored Nancy.' Louise was clearly finding the going tough too for she glanced at Emma, who bravely nodded.

'Then Gavin found out,' Louise continued, 'and there was an almighty bust up. Nancy and Donald called it off and Nancy devoted herself to her family. Gavin demanded the Packard and Donald had no choice. He had to hand it over or run the risk of rumours circulating round the City about the bank being purchased with dirty money. The game – though Emma doesn't think it hadn't acquired that name by then – was over, or so Gavin thought and he put the Packard up for sale. Donald promptly bought it anonymously and then displayed it with great ostentation outside his home.'

Just as Philip did when he bought it through me, I thought. 'What happened next?'

'Gavin demanded it back. Or else.'

'The "or else" being?' I enquired.

'He'd spill the beans about the bank robbery.' Emma had got her second wind. 'This was about 1960, and Donald was on the brink of taking over a London bank and turning his chain of private banks in the south-east into an unlimited company.'

'So he gave the car back to Gavin?'

'Sold it actually.' Emma grimaced. 'A fair price though, so my grandfather accepted. Only for Nancy's sake though, and that also meant Donald had to honour his pledge to leave those shares in Moxtons in his will.'

'And that was the end of the game until recently?' I asked as neither woman seemed to be meeting my eyes.

'Far from it.' Emma bit the bullet. 'A year or two later Donald and Nancy started their affair again.'

I tried not to sound too grim. 'We seem to be lacking a few emotions in this story. Was this true love or mutual point-scoring?'

'I don't know,' Emma confessed. 'My grandmother was an amazing woman according to my father and I suppose both men must have had something that drew her to them. She wouldn't just have been a cushion being tossed between the two of them. Perhaps they were all three devil-may-care adventurers in their own way. After all, I didn't know them,' she added desperately, 'and nor really could my father and Gwen have *known* them. Who does know their parents except in how they relate as parents?'

I thought of all the things I could reply to that, the chief one being that after their death one has time to reflect. What reflections did Tom and Gwen have about their parents? The lives of the Herricks and Moxtons had collided, however, and whatever the effects on their families nothing could now be changed. 'So the game continued?' I asked.

'No. Donald and Nancy broke up again two years later.'

'With Gavin's help?'

'Yes,' Emma replied stiffly. 'Very much so, I'm told.'

'And what then?'

'My grandmother killed herself.'

I was appalled, blaming myself for forcing the issue. 'I'm so sorry, Emma.'

She shrugged. 'Well, I've told you now. You can see why everyone was so diffident about it.'

'And that was in nineteen sixty-five?'

'Yes. As a result of that, my grandfather gave the Packard to Donald and told him he never wanted to see him or the car again and he expected him to honour the shares in the will for the benefit of Nancy's children, if not Gavin himself. That was supposed to be the end of the game.'

'But it wasn't?'

'No. Gavin couldn't leave it at that. He decided to nick the car back.'

I groaned. 'How on earth did he do that?'

'One day Donald was visiting the original Randolphs Bank, by then Moxtons, and couldn't resist taking the Packard. Gavin had found out about the trip and couldn't resist temptation. He wanted to show Donald he still remembered the robbery and that he still held the whip hand over making his information public. My grandfather was a wonderful man,' she added, 'but he'd lost Nancy and he bore the grievance with him to his death. Donald felt pretty bitter too over Nancy, but he had a mean streak in him which Gavin lacked. Gavin had a weakness though – he hated losing a game. So he pinched the Packard while Donald was inside and left a note to boast about it. He knew Donald couldn't report the theft for fear of Gavin speaking out about the robbery, so Gavin kept the car on display in front of his home. The upshot of that was that Donald arranged to have it pinched back. Gavin couldn't object because the car was still registered, albeit in Donald's name.'

'Like two teenage kids again,' I commented.

'I agree. My parents and even Philip and Gwen thought it crazy, especially when Gavin pinched it back yet again at a particularly tough time for Donald. Donald decided he'd had enough. He couldn't do anything very drastic because 1970 was the time he was making his bid for a seat on the London Clearing House. So he played a waiting game.'

'What happened next?' I have to admit I was now hooked.

'He encouraged Philip to get to know Tom and particularly Gwen, while they were up at Oxford, ostensibly to end the game. Just before the younger ones went up, Joan and Gwen, in the autumn of 1972, Donald pinched the car again, but this time hid it so carefully that Gavin couldn't whip it back. Gavin was furious and it was open warfare but they couldn't go too far for fear of damaging their children's prospects.

'So,' Emma continued, 'that was when the four offspring got together and decided the game had to come to an end for good. They all knew about the robbery and agreed that when Donald and Gavin had both died, any money that could be said to have resulted from that robbery, which would now be invested in shares, would be split four ways. Donald wasn't happy about the plan, but Philip was, so Donald kept brooding about it, keeping the car under lock and key. Then he played his trump card. Donald's son Philip married Nancy's daughter Gwen in the late seventies and the balloon went up. This time Donald stood firm. The car stayed where it was – with him.'

I was beginning to dislike Donald Moxton, charmer or not.

'Donald's career,' Emma continued, 'was going from strength to strength and so was Philip's after he joined Donald at Moxtons. Gavin was prospering too, so the row went quiet for a while. When Gwen gave birth to Barney everyone apparently agreed this was wonderful and it really did mark the end of the game. Unity at last, tra-la-la. Donald even gave Gavin the car to celebrate the occasion.

'That lasted for another few years. Then Gwen divorced Philip or vice versa – I don't know which. All I do know is that the settlement was a measly one either because Philip himself wasn't earning that much or because he was successfully hiding his assets. Donald therefore agreed to contribute a little more to it provided the Packard was returned to him. Gavin refused so Donald refused the top-up. Gwen brought Barney up to appreciate economy while Philip resumed his meteoric rise in his career. On it went until Donald died in 1994.'

'And?' I asked, when Emma stopped.

'Gavin played fair,' she continued. 'He gave the car to Philip as a reconciliation gesture.'

'What was Philip's response?' I was ready to disbelieve anything now.

'When Donald died, Philip announced he was going back on the 1970s' agreement to split Donald's share of the money four ways after Gavin too had died. There was no reason why he should, as special arrangements would have been made for Joan to have Staveley House and the gardens. Instead, Philip said he'd draw up his own will to leave all the cash from Donald to Barney who is half Herrick and half Moxton; Barney could then do what he liked with it. That worried Barney because he felt that the scales were tipped against the Herricks because of the arrangement Philip had made for Staveley, so he persuaded his father to give the Packard to Gavin Herrick straightaway.'

'And did he?'

'Yes, but now Gavin has died and you've come into the picture, Jack, by buying the car back for Philip. Cunning move.'

'Thanks. Is there by any chance £30,000 in old banknotes hidden somewhere in the Packard?'

'There is not,' Emma assured me. 'We've looked.'

'So the car could be sold for charity once the case is over?'

Emma looked aghast. 'Philip's murder? What's that to do with the game? Or Wendy's come to that. You can't still think they're connected?'

'I do.'

'My parents thought we'd get rid of the game issue by telling you all this,' Emma moaned. 'I don't see how they could possibly be connected.'

I had to answer this. 'Two reasons,' I said sadly. 'The first is that what you have told me is what *you've* been told and what your parents believe. The Game Book that Philip kept might tell a different story.'

'My mother mentioned that. But what if it doesn't, even if you do find it?'

'It doesn't alter the fact that Philip was about to leave all his cash to a foundation which was one more stage in the game. Therefore . . .' No, I didn't have to spell it out. Their stricken expressions told me I'd got the message over.

To say I was in the doghouse was an understatement. Louise was struggling to be fair to both sides. I sympathized. I'd nothing against the Herricks (well, not much), but though Emma's account of the game made sense I still had to find that link and the Packard would remain here at Frogs Hill in all its majesty to remind me of that. I felt sorry for it in fact. It was drizzling with rain when we arrived home and it was parked outside the Pits looking very forlorn. I offered it a silent

apology as I drove it round to its barn garage. Zoe had done
a good job on the wheel bearings so perhaps she was growing
fond of it too.

Dave Jennings had been trying to reach me while I'd been out,
which jolted me back instantly to the Volkswagen and why it had
been returned to Monksford? And why the railway station? It
could be that it was a more neutral dumping ground than Geoffrey
Green's home, but it ran the risk of being noticed on its arrival,
even though being a village there wasn't CCTV coverage.

So far so good, Sherlock, I reproached myself, but any Sherlock
worth his salt would ask why go to so much trouble when the
Golf was of so comparatively little value? And after that Sherlock
would enquire why it wasn't abandoned in the middle of the
countryside?

Time to tackle Richie, I decided. Dave first, though. I managed
to catch him just before he left for the day by which time he had
already solved what he had called me for. It was clear I was not
in his good books either.

'Any good forensic on the Golf?' I asked.

'Go through Brandon,' he growled.

'Haven't time.'

'OK, if I must. But this didn't come from me. In fact, it didn't
come at all. There were prints and DNA.'

'Carson's?'

'No.'

Of course not. It couldn't be so simple. 'Whose then?'

'A match with a villain called Mike Parker. Thought to be one
of Carson's men.'

'Thanks, Dave. I'll ring him.'

'If you must, but before you barge off on some crazy mission,
hear this. Parker's no longer with Carson.'

'Where then?'

'Last spotted on a mortuary slab in Calais ten days ago.'

Great. Some days the winds don't blow in the right direction.
'How long had that Golf been in the station car park?' I tried
on him.

'Reported seven days ago. Been there 48 hours.'

After Parker's death, though. 'Well, well. Carson's work?' I
asked.

'The French are handling it. No link to Carson so far.'

Time to update that, I thought, as I rang off. Carson wasn't pleased to hear from me. Tough. 'Meet you same place, same time tomorrow morning,' he snapped. 'But I heard you were incapacitated, Jack.'

'I shall be capacitated again tomorrow morning. But I'm not waiting. It's now, Richie.'

'OK.' Audible yawn. 'Now.'

I took his surrender gracefully. 'I appreciate that, Richie. Volkswagen Golf. Geoffrey Green's. I gave you the ID.'

'I told you I'd deal with it. I did. It's back with you.'

'I know. Your chap's prints were on it, when it was found in Monksford Station Yard.'

'What chap would that be?'

'An ex-one. Mike Parker. Very ex. Found dead. *Before* the car was back in Monksford. So, Richie, the theft of the car won't be pursued. Two corpses in connection with theft are a different matter. Who pinched it and who drove it back, the latter so carefully as to avoid prints?'

Richie sounded upset. 'No prints, no pack drill, Jack. Do some thinking. Take warning when warning's given. That Golf is nothing to do with me or my dad. Family's family.'

That was interesting. Why was John Carson still involved with this? 'Why—' I began, but Rickie forestalled me.

'That car's back where it came from. Nothing to do with any murder, see?'

'No,' I said honestly.

'Got to go, Jack.' The line went silent.

I did think, but to no purpose, and as a result Louise was silent too. At last she asked, 'Are you sorry we arranged that picnic? I thought it would be fun and clear the air.'

I looked at her in amazement. I'd assumed she would realize what was bugging me, but she seemed just as uncertain of the ground under her feet as I was. We weren't yet dovetailing our interpretations of each other's moods. It was early days.

'Just bringing the office home with me,' I assured her.

She cheered up. 'That's all right then.'

'I'll just pack up the office with this: what do the words "back where it came from" imply to you?'

An eyebrow was raised. 'In connection with what?'

'That Volkswagen stolen from Philip Moxton and now found in Monksford station car park.'

'Then it means it came from the car park,' she answered patiently.

I kissed her. 'Bless you. We all thought it was pinched from Geoffrey Green's home.'

'Why?'

'It was gone, but it wasn't.'

She giggled at this fatuous analysis. 'That,' she said gravely, as she departed to prepare supper, 'is not the standard of detection I expect from you.'

I could see why. I'd assumed that Brandon and Dave *knew* it had been in the garage. The keys had gone, and no car keys were found in the house. But if the Golf had been stolen at the station *before* Philip had arrived home that day, a whole different picture of his murder might emerge. True, he might have driven the Golf home and left it in the drive, but my money was on Richie's gang pinching it from the station and Richie returning it there.

Where did that lead me? Simple. How did Philip get home that evening? Did he ring the police and report the theft? No, I'd have heard if he had. He couldn't report it because it would have opened up a can of worms over his identity to have the spotlight on Geoffrey Green's car.

That answered that. Next, what would Philip have done? It was so blindingly obvious now. He had rung Wendy, but she wasn't there.

Or was she? The horrible scenario played itself out for me. She had been there. She had driven up to the station to drive him home, they had quarrelled and she had killed him. Proof? Thankfully none. I had time to sleep on it.

'Shall I start cooking supper?' Louise called.

I had heard her banging a few dishes around as an unsubtle hint that I should join her.

'Yes, we should. Sorry to be so work-bound.'

'Did I put my foot in it over the picnic, Jack? I thought it might help.'

'I know, and no you didn't. Your lovely feet are welcome anywhere.'

'*Did* it help?'

I considered this. When is the truth not the truth? Bigger brains than mine have battled with this problem over the centuries, from Greek philosophers and Pontius Pilate, progressing onwards to Francis Bacon. I seemed to recall he had excelled in Machiavellian politics in Good Queen Bess's time and so it was an especially important quandary for him.

I was no philosopher, but Louise needed reassurance. 'I'm further along the road, much further.'

She wasn't fooled. 'Which road, Jack? Are you stuck because the game isn't taking you the way you hoped?'

'It is, but I still have this nagging feeling that this missing Game Book may produce an entirely different picture than we've got already.'

'So where is it?'

I could see she was doing her best to be patient. She wanted supper and who could blame her? 'If the Herricks don't have it, and Timothy Mild says that he doesn't, then Philip must have kept it. But where? He was a secretive man so it wouldn't be at Staveley, we know it's not at Monksford, so where?'

'His safe? Bank vaults?'

'It would have been found.'

'Left with Wendy?'

I stared at her, my new scenario very clear in my mind. 'It could just be. Especially if she were putting pressure on Philip; that could have been part of it.' The fact that she had probably been killed herself didn't necessary rule this theory out; indeed it strengthened it, because the knowledge that she kept it could have led to her death. Then I realized it wouldn't work. Brandon's team would have found it. No, it was somewhere else. Somewhere accessible, but not too obvious.

A howl from Louise. 'You've defrosted prawns for supper. You know I don't like seafood.'

The love of my life looked as though she was about to throw the entire bowlful right over me. And then she did, in one swift moment.

I carefully wiped the icy cold pink objects off my hair, and shoulders before kissing her. 'Seafood,' I said. '*Seafood*. That's where Philip hid it. Wendy's beach hut. Which he loved to visit.'

There was only one snag. I didn't know where it was.

SIXTEEN

I was free. I was a man again. I could *drive*. Sam West had gone into action right away when I had called him about the beach hut. He had no idea where it was either, but he had caught Wendy's number 2 at the café and had been told the hut was at Highchurch Sands near Hythe, not far from Folkestone, and that there was a key kept at the café. Sam had arranged to pick it up and I could pick him up. So far so good and I was raring to go. So, I was told, was Timothy Mild who, when Sam rang him, demanded his right to be present if this Game Book was there. He was the game's unofficial umpire. Forget the City, he too wanted a day at the seaside and he'd meet us there. Forget the City? He could afford to now that he had benefited from Philip Moxton's death.

Highchurch Sands has a fine stretch of coastline and, from my dim memories of it as a child, it is a paradise for youngsters. To my grown-up self, however, the church no longer looked as high up on the Downs as I recalled, and the sands were no longer sands. The beach was splendid but pebbly. As I drove through the village I could see it was now reduced to one or two shops and cafés. The promenade was lined with a row of villas in splendid Edwardian seaside style, noble white stone edifices with little balconies. It was off-season but these empty buildings still stared defiantly out at the sea before them. No wonder Napoleon and Hitler had quailed at the idea of invading along this coast. The message the row of villas conveyed was 'don't mess with us, however dismal we look today'.

As Sam and I reached the beach, the huts looked like a small edition of the row of villas, although the huts were gaily painted in pinks, greens and yellows. The first one was even more striking in ostentatious red, white and blue, but that Sam assured me was not Wendy's. Hers was number 24 according to the key tag. I couldn't have envisaged Philip Moxton enjoying a restful day in that wooden Union Jack.

Sam had been on the glum side as we drove here, and now

that we had arrived and the cold breeze whipped at us, he grew even glummer. I told him to stay in the car but he refused. 'It's my fault,' he said, clutching a bag containing what he described as 'the essentials', a Thermos and biscuits. 'I should have thought of this long ago.'

'Did Wendy talk about the hut to you?'

'Yes she did, but she never mentioned Geoffrey coming here with her, or if she did I'd forgotten.' A pause. 'Was her death suicide or murder? Do you know?'

'Not yet.'

I did know but it was classified. Brandon was treating it as murder. I could see Timothy waiting for us outside a hut, and his body language suggested he was equally depressed for all he'd been so keen to come. It was hardly surprising given the circumstances and the reason we were here, but it wasn't helped by the fact that the sky was overcast and the general venue uninviting. In such conditions beaches such as Highchurch Sands can look weirdly beautiful to those of an artistic bent, but for most people it takes sun to make them attractive.

Timothy barely stopped to nod in welcome as we reached him. Wearing a heavy raincoat over a suit, he of all of us looked the best equipped for inclement weather, but he certainly didn't want to prolong the greetings. 'Let's get this over with,' he grunted.

That suited me, and Sam too from the look of him. Back in the village there would be life. Here there was only a bleak reminder that both Wendy and Philip Moxton were now dead, and that their murderer – or perhaps two murderers – remained at large.

The beach was still desolate with not even a dog walker in sight, and one look inside the hut as Sam unlocked the door and pulled it open made me as eager as Timothy to get away as soon as possible. My earlier euphoria at being able to drive again had evaporated, and I thought longingly of Frogs Hill, of the Pits where Len and Zoe would be happily working away and of the evening ahead with Louise.

The hut was as dismal as the beach inside. No mod cons here. A couple of deckchairs, a small cupboard surmounted by cups and plates, a few paperbacks, a portable table, and – more hopefully – a large plastic storage box. Sam busied himself with the

Thermos flask and cups, while Timothy without a word made a beeline for the box. I remained in the doorway as between them my two companions took up most of the room available, so I watched while Timothy rooted through piles of magazines and from what I could see not much else.

'Nothing here,' he said in disgust.

'Are you sure?' Sam looked even more worried. 'I agree with Jack. It does seem the obvious place, if Geoffrey didn't keep the Game Book at home.'

I agreed. To say this was a let-down was understating my gloom. 'Are you certain neither Wendy nor Philip mentioned it to either of you?' I asked. I'd been crazy to pin my hopes on this – and yet it had seemed an obvious way forward. Timothy just shook his head.

'Have some coffee,' was Sam's answer, as he handed us each a cup.

Perhaps he hadn't heard me. I repeated the question.

'No book,' he replied this time.

'And you're positive you never saw it, Timothy?'

'Quite sure,' he barked at me. 'Nor did I ever hear Philip or Gavin talk of it.'

The coffee didn't seem to taste of anything, or was it my mouth that was suddenly sour? Timothy was lying unless . . . Sometimes situations turn upside down quicker than logic can follow. This one did so *now*—

I saw Timothy's sudden look of wariness, I saw Sam's fanatical expression.

'There isn't a Game Book,' Sam said tranquilly. 'As far as I know, that is.'

'Then what—' Timothy broke off. He had realized as I had that there was something very wrong here.

'It's your fault, Jack,' Sam accused me. 'And the police's. You were all taking too long to sort it out. I had to step in for Wendy's sake, but I was too late so Timothy has to answer for it, don't you, Timothy? I hope you realize that, Jack.'

The scene registered itself on my mind like a camera shot. Image retained, recorded for ever. The normality of the scene. The cups of coffee, the beach hut, the scattered magazines, the waves breaking on the shingle. I could smell the sea air.

But the gun in Sam's hand wasn't normal, nor the look of

disbelief on Timothy's face as Sam shot him and the face disappeared in a mass of blood and matter.

Sam's expression didn't change at all, not even as the blood spattered on the walls, the floor and on Sam himself mingling horrifically with the spilt coffee. The blood even reached me in the doorway where I stood paralysed with shock, my ears echoing and numb with the explosion.

Then blessedly my mind went into overdrive. Turn and run along the beach? No way. I'd have a bullet in my back in seconds. Make a dash for the rear of the hut and the sea wall? Same result. Throw the coffee at him? Same result. He'd be ready for that one. In front of me was a man past desperation, past caring, past reason.

'Don't worry, Jack.' Sam chuckled, a chilling noise in this nightmare scene. 'I had to do it. You must understand that.'

I struggled to school my voice to 'normal'. 'Shall I call the police?'

He considered this, with the gun still in his hand. 'Not yet, Jack. I need to explain why you have to die as well. It was your fault, the whole thing. Wendy was a nice woman and I liked her. But she was a blackmailer. There was no Game Book, although she told me there was. It was a weapon for her.'

'Who did she blackmail?' I tried to sound *normal* but I was staring at that gun. Was this my voice speaking? Was that gun going to bring my death any moment now?

'Shall we sit down and I'll tell you about it?' he offered. 'It will be more comfortable that way.'

Comfort? With Timothy's body right there in front of us? With the walls and our clothes covered in blood.

'Let's take the chairs on to the beach,' I said brightly. Someone *must* come along at some point.

'No. It's much better here. I can concentrate and we won't be disturbed. Pull that door closed though.'

For a moment I considered making a run for it with all its risks. I decided against it. He was very conscious of that gun and ready for any move from me. He wanted his pound of flesh and watched me closely as I pulled the door shut. My last look at the world?

'Tell me all about it then,' I told him, as I carefully took my place where indicated in one of the chairs and watched him take the other. 'Then one of us can ring the police,' I added, to keep the idea in his mind. Some hopes.

He really did want to talk, it seemed. 'She blackmailed Timothy and Geoffrey. Poor Geoffrey. He was in such a state about it. She wanted him to change his will.'

Codswallop. Immediate questions sprang to mind, but I nodded benignly. Knowing the true answers would be no use if the information died with me.

'Just Timothy and Geoffrey? Anyone else?'

'Oh yes. Barney. I think that's his name. She talked about the barbecue you took her to. She was so pleased about that. That's where she dreamed up the idea of the Game Book. She liked that, she said it made her feel part of the game.'

'But why did Timothy kill her? He wasn't part of the game.'

Sam looked puzzled. 'I suppose it was because Timothy had killed Geoffrey Green and Wendy blackmailed him over that. I didn't know. I thought it was that madman John Carson. I met him once in Wendy's café. Not a nice man. He was asking questions about Geoffrey. She'd seen him at Staveley House too.'

'But why did Timothy kill Geoffrey? And how?' I persisted. I didn't dare look at the ghastly sight at my side. It was getting harder and harder to think of anything other than my own security system which was whirling away inside me.

These questions displeased Sam. 'You're playing for time, Jack. You know very well why and how he did it. Timothy and Philip came down on the train together from London that night and drove to Geoffrey's house in his Volkswagen. They left the car on the drive, so Timothy took it to drive away to his own home after he'd killed him. As for why, it was for his career over that merger. You know that.'

Sam was looking at me like a pleased puppy. I couldn't work out his game plan. All that was important was he believed I was swallowing this fantasy.

I knew now that it hadn't been Wendy or Timothy who drove Philip Moxton home that last evening. Wendy had indeed been out when he called and Timothy had not been with him. It had been Sam who had returned to Monksford from Ashford and found Geoffrey stranded after the Volkswagen had been stolen. No doubt a bit of private enterprise by Richie Carson's ex-chum Mike Parker. So Sam had given Geoffrey a lift home and they had talked afterwards. Whatever they discussed had led to Sam killing him. Then he left in his own car, which would not have been tested for forensic evidence because he was never a suspect. He'd no motive – or none that I could think of right now – and only, I had thought, a slight acquaintance with Geoffrey Green. Could Wendy have been a blackmailer? I didn't care. Let it be, let it rest. I had to get out of this place if I was ever to see Louise again. Which was highly improbable. Sam had not forgotten that gun in his hand. I had one slim chance.

So I chattered on, thanking my lucky stars that I had brought my Blackberry today with its button keyboard, and not a touch screen. Sam was so busy talking, listening, and keeping an eye on my nearest hand – the left one – that my right was able to creep further into my side pocket and touch that wonderful Blackberry, button by button. Slowly, slowly I found my way to the right keys to press those all important digits. Then I left the line open and slowly, slowly withdrew my hand, praying that whoever answered would keep on listening. Meanwhile, talk, talk, *talk loudly*. Talk about how Geoffrey and Wendy must have loved this beach hut, beach hut, *beach hut*, painted *pink*. Mention Highchurch not being that far to drive from Monksford . . . Then panic threatened to overwhelm me. The nearest Blackberry cell might not be precise enough in location to bring help in time, and I could tell Sam was growing bored with my chat. I had to calm myself and get back to what interested him.

'Why was Wendy's death my fault, Sam?'

Again I displeased him. 'I told you. You were taking too long.'

'Too long for what? Did you want the police to find out that you were Geoffrey's killer?'

I thought I'd gone too far – much too far – but he did reply. 'Perhaps I did, Jack. Perhaps it was time.'

A gamble but it might, just might work. 'So shall we call the police now?' Keep my voice *loud*.

'If you like, but by the time they get here you'll be dead. We both will.'

I fought panic again, little by little, breath by breath. Keep calm and carry on. Carry on . . .

'Why kill me though? That's not fair, Sam.'

'It is. If it wasn't for you Wendy would still be alive. I didn't want to kill Wendy, but she was talking too much to you. She actually suspected *me* so I had to explain to her that Timothy was the killer of Philip Moxton and then kill her that evening, very gently though. You do understand?'

I hadn't understood enough. Wendy's 'I suspect . . .' and that unanswered question had not been directed at the Herricks, but at Sam. 'Did she blackmail you?'

'No. I don't think she blackmailed anyone. But she wouldn't have liked it if she'd known I killed Geoffrey.'

I was getting desperate, and had to force myself on. 'Why did you kill Timothy though?'

'That's easy. He was a banker, as bad as Donald Moxton. He and some journalist friend of yours had been doing some investigation into the past and he had no right to do that. So that was your fault too. He told me you began it.'

Steer clear of my involvement. 'Is that why you killed Geoffrey? You'd found out he was a banker and his real name was Philip Moxton?' This might be a rich vein to keep him talking. And talk I had to. Even though it was next to a dead body that might shortly be joined by mine. 'Why kill him though? There are plenty of banks and bankers.'

'Not like the Moxtons.' Sam leaned back in his chair as though we were just relaxing over another coffee, but the pistol remained in his hand. 'Philip Moxton ruined my life.'

'How?' I tried to sound eager to know.

'He ruined my career.'

I scrabbled in my mind to remember what he'd told me. 'You were in banking just for a year or two in the sixties. Philip Moxton could only have been a child then or a teenager at most.'

'Did I say Philip? I meant Donald. Same thing. I was a deputy manager at a bank and doing well until he bought it. 1963 that was. He sacked us all, just like that. A week's wages. Closed the branch and took the business to the next village. There were no million pound pay offs in those days, no redundancy payments at all and so he could sack people just as he liked. I didn't even get a reference as a deputy manager. It was a tough time.'

'But a long time ago. Donald died in 1994.'

'In the late seventies Philip Moxton came into the picture.'

'You worked for him?'

'My wife Alice did. She was Donald's private secretary for over fifteen years and went on working for him when he had officially retired. He still ran an office at Moxtons' headquarters.

Then when he died in 1994 Philip took her over for a year or two but then told her flatly she wasn't smart enough and was too old to adapt to modern technology, so he sacked her.'

'I'm very sorry.'

He ignored this. 'People like the Moxtons never realize we have feelings. They don't care. It was a large part of my wife's life and he took it away from her. It broke her heart and that broke mine. She died only a few years after he sacked her. We moved here because I thought the garden might take her mind off it, but it didn't, so I knew that if ever I had the chance I'd pay the Moxtons back. I knew Donald by sight, but not Philip – Moxtons Bank doesn't go in for socializing with their so-called inferiors. So I didn't recognize Geoffrey Green. When Wendy told me who he was I realized my chance had come. So I took it. I'm sorry Wendy had to die though. I wouldn't have done it if it hadn't been for you. That means I now have to kill you and then myself.'

There's always a tendency to grin when staring at tragedy, perhaps in a vain effort to counterbalance it and I found myself oddly light-hearted. 'Why not the other way round?' I joked.

I'd meant it as a silent thought, but I must have spoken aloud, as I struggled to keep myself alive as the seconds ticked by.

'That's funny,' Sam said eventually. 'I liked you, Jack – at first, anyway. So I'm very sorry to have to do this.' The pistol was raised and quivered.

Reflex action.

I threw myself from my chair straight at the door which hadn't completely closed, bending as low as I could for extra impact. The door burst open, I half stumbled, half fell horizontally through it as the gun went off. My ear drums reverberated, everything went blank and then the gun went off again.

I opened my eyes. I wasn't in heaven, I wasn't in hell. I lay sprawled full length on the pebbles, there was blood around me and I was staring at a pair of black shoes.

'Louise?' I choked. That was how I'd first met her, sprawled at her feet. Was she here already? Was this heaven after all?

The boots crunched, someone squatted down at my side and cautiously turned me over. It wasn't Louise. It was Brandon.

'Been in another punch-up?' enquired the orderly as I was wheeled into A and E. 'Not long since we got rid of you last time.'

They must have given me something to put me out because in due course I was aware of being wheeled out again and deposited into an ambulance with Louise at my side. So that was all right, provided she didn't turn into Brandon again. The blood, she explained gently when we reached Frogs Hill, was from a superficial wound. Other than that, I only had – guess what? – severe bruising.

When I woke up with a comparatively clear head the next day, the curtains were blowing in the breeze, the autumn sun beamed at me and the smell of toast floated up from below. The only problem was that it wasn't Louise at my side. Unless I was still dozy from the knockout, it was Liz Potter, my former lover and now friend. I was petrified.

'Louise?' I croaked.

My friend glared at me. 'Thanks, Jack. I'm Liz, remember?'

'But Louise is all right?'

She was immediately contrite. 'Yes, she is. She asked me to sit by your side as she couldn't. Sorry, Jack, but I've all you've got for the next hour or two. Colin loved the idea of my baby-sitting you.'

I'd have laughed if I'd felt up to it. Her nerdish husband dislikes me intensely (and with little reason).

'Sounds good to me,' I said.

The next thing I knew Richie Carson was sitting there and Liz had vanished. I promptly closed my eyes. It must be a hallucination. It wasn't. He leaned forward and peered at me.

'Sorry, Jack. Got on the wrong track. Thought you were after my dad.'

I gazed at him. 'What for?'

'Murder one,' he said, obviously surprised I had to ask. 'Dad gave me what for when he found out about your mishap that evening.' He then proceeded to bend down and inspect the underside of my bed.

'Thought you might have a bug under there,' he explained, when he re-emerged. I wondered vaguely what kind of bug he had in mind, before I focused on the fact he wanted an off-record chat. 'Dad got curious about where this Moxton bloke was living when he wasn't at Staveley House and so was his boss, Miss Moxton. So he followed him back one day, and thereafter used to keep a bit of a check on him like. Who he was seeing and that. I got the idea you were pinning Moxton's murder on him, so I had to show you the error of your ways before you went too far. The boys duffed you up a little, and then I put the Golf back there to show it wasn't Dad who nicked it at the house. Actually it wasn't down to me in the first place. One of my boys thought he'd go in for a spot of freelance work on his own account. Took me a while to sort that out and get the Golf back for you. Knew you'd be grateful.'

'Oh, I was, once I'd got over the duffing up.'

'I made up for it, didn't I? Took the car back. Station seemed to be the best place for it, where it was pinched from. A hint to you, Jack. See?' He put his face close to mine to show his sincerity.

'Yes,' I murmured shutting my eyes again.

'Good to know you, Jack.'

'Likewise,' I murmured.

When I cautiously opened my eyes again, Liz was back and all was well. As well as could be expected, that is. Late in the afternoon, Brandon paid me a call. I was downstairs by that time, which made interviews rather more dignified. 'Feel like talking?' he asked.

'Never better.'

'Right. So there's you, a gun or two, a few books and magazines and two dead bodies. We heard the last two shots, which was the third? Two of you, I know. The third man I didn't know.'

'We none of us did,' I said obliquely. 'Chesterton's invisible postman. Always there, but we didn't think Sam was a player.'

'In this game of yours?'

I considered this. All along I'd been sure the game and the death of Geoffrey Green aka Philip Moxton were linked, and in an unexpected way I had been right. Sam West, like Alfred Randolph, had been one of the many forgotten casualties of the Moxton banks, which had sprung from the Hatchwell robbery that began the game. Had it been Sam whom Philip Moxton suspected of wanting to kill him? I'd never know the answer to that.

'In a way,' I replied to Brandon's question, and he listened intently as I told him the story of that day on the beach and of the deaths of two men.

I'd have to make a formal statement asap, he told me, and then asked me if I had any hard evidence.

'The gun?' I came up with. It wasn't much, but his would be the only prints on it. It wasn't much and I was sure they and the Met would dig out far more at Sam West's home, in his car and through unidentified prints and DNA at Wendy's home.

Brandon actually clapped me on the back. 'Thanks, Jack.'

'What for?' I asked, as I flinched with pain.

'Through you, I'll have solved the Met's case for them.'

I didn't need a nursemaid after that, other than Zoe. I didn't mind the Herricks coming either, together with Joan and Gwen. They had come to express sympathy, but with an air of self-righteousness at being innocent all along. And then came Barney.

'Hello, Jack,' he said.

'Hi,' I said cautiously. He was clearly here with a mission, but what was it?

'I've been deputed to tell you.'

'Don't let it be that the game's over, please.'

'But it is.'

'Can't be. I've still got the Packard. Does your family want it back?'

'No. But the game's over because we've found a permanent solution.'

'Which is?'

'I'm putting all my father's money into a foundation.'

My mouth, as they say, dropped wide open. 'You mean your family won't get a penny?' Was that funny? It was to me, but—

'That doesn't seem altogether fair,' I ventured.

'They've all agreed,' he said cheerfully. 'The money is tainted in a way, and perhaps that's why my father had intended to set up a charitable foundation.'

'Yes, but—'

'My mother and Moira are going to run it – paid of course and pensioned. It's a wrap, Jack.'

'Which leaves you and me,' I said to Louise when she returned that day from her own wrap.

It was still just about light enough to stroll out into the garden. The sun was already sinking but the garden was just as colourful with its autumnal tints. Still blooming. Still here, just as we were. Or were we? We were both silent, perhaps both realizing that something had to be said and not knowing what. So we stayed silent until we made our way back past the barn-cum-garage where my classics live. And outside stood the Packard, its buttery yellow paint still gleaming out at us.

'There it is,' I said. 'It's just you, me – and the Packard. Your very own getaway car.' There was the hint of a question in my voice.

'I won't be needing one, Jack.'

I put my arm round her. 'Nor me. The Packard game is over. Ours is just revving up.'

The Car's the Star
James Myers

The Starring Car

1935 Packard Series 120 Sedan (Saloon)
The Packard One-Twenty (or '120') was produced by the Packard Motor Car Company, of Detroit, from 1935 to 1941. The 120 model designation was replaced by the 'Packard Eight' model name during model years 1938 to 1942. The 120 was an important car in Packard's history because it signified that Packard had for the first time entered into the competitive mid-priced eight-cylinder car market.

It is probable that the 120 saved Packard's bacon back in the mid-thirties (Great Depression) years. Otherwise, as this theory goes, Packard would most likely have been defunct by 1940, as were Duesenberg, Cord, Marmon, Peerless and Pierce-Arrow.

Jack Colby's own classic cars

Jack's 1965 Gordon-Keeble
One hundred of these fabulous supercars were built between 1963 and 1966 with over 90 units surviving around the globe, mostly in the UK. Designed by John Gordon and Jim Keeble using then current racing car principles with the bodyshell designed by 21-year-old Giorgetto Giugiaro at Bertone, the cars were an instant success but the company was ruined by supply-side industrial action with ultimately only 99 units completed even after the company was relaunched in May 1965, as Keeble Cars Ltd.

Final closure came in February 1966 when the factory at Sholing closed and Jim Keeble moved to Keewest. The 100th car was completed in 1971 with left-over components. The Gordon-Keeble's emblem is a yellow and green tortoise.

Jack's 1938 Lagonda V-12 Drophead

The Lagonda company won its attractive name from a creek near the home of the American-born founder Wilbur Gunn in Springfield, Ohio. The name given to it by the American Indians was Ough Ohonda. The V-12 drophead was a car to compete with the very best in the world, with a sporting 12-cylinder engine which would power the two 1939 Le Mans cars. Its designer was the famous W.O. Bentley. Sadly many fine prewar saloons have been cut down to look like Le Mans replicas. The V12 cars are very similar externally to the earlier 6-cylinder versions; both types were available with open or closed bodywork in a number of different styles. The V-12 Drophead also featured in Jack's earlier case, *Classic in the Barn.*